ONLY ANGELS FORGET

Rosamund Clay

VIRAGO

Published by VIRAGO PRESS Limited 1990
20–23 Mandela Street, Camden Town, London NW1 OHQ

*A CIP catalogue record for this title is available
from the British Library*

Typeset by Centracet Cambridge

Printed in Great Britain
by Bookcraft (Bath) Ltd.

For P. D. R.

1

Sometime in the first six or seven years of my life I was walking down a country lane in Devon on a pale half-summer sunshine afternoon with my father, hand-in-hand between the thick green hedgerows, listening to sheep and lambs calling to each other across the fields, and cuckoos throating echoes from one side of the village to the other and a blackbird singing from the top of an old yew tree, and I remember feeling so safe between those green walls with the thin road pulling us on, and my father took me into the cold grey stone church, and I peeked behind the blue curtains and saw the choirboys' sandwiches, and behind another curtain at the other end there was a blackboard with numbers chalked on it for the bellringers to read, so they would get the order of sounds right, 5 3 4 2 1, or whatever, like any musical score; the score of *Chu Chin Chow*, for example, that translated into choruses carrying young men in uniforms away from the sweat of the trenches into caves of jewels where people dined off oysters and honey instead of the spectre of death: but death comes all the same, to them, to me, to every living thing; they had a real camel in *Chu Chin Chow*, I used to go to the stage door with eyes as big as the camel's and see it turned out of its box every night to troop shaggily protesting across the set of the navy banqueting hall stuck with friezes of peacocks, which made me think I wanted to be an actress myself and swagger across the stage pretending to be an object of glory, with everyone's eyes on me, the eyes of women and sometimes of little children and of men who would line up at the stage door waiting to see me make my own entrance as important as the camel, as Robert did when he first took my hand and put his face next to mine, and then standing beside it when we looked down into the still water of the pond by his house in Cape Cod that summer of 1948; and he said this is forever Molly, and we walked in the forest until the sun striped the ground at right angles to the treetrunks like the tracery on a bakewell tart; and he flashed an opal ring at me as bright as Ali Baba's crown, under the stars, it was always under the stars; and Isobel the child was born one night when London was bombed and I looked up into the sky afraid the stars might fall out of it, and stumbled around in the gloom and the doctor said she'd die if I didn't let her have the injection and I did and she cried and I lay there thinking what have I done, I shouldn't have been a mother at all; if Mother had stayed alive I probably wouldn't have been, but I was young and flighty when she died, I only wanted to get away from those endlessly polished linoleum floors, the clock ticking to the smell of haddock, the pewter brooch bloodlessly gripping the stiff white collar, I wanted my own life; and Isobel's father Evan who gave her those eyes, who went off to Africa, I can't recall his face now, I haven't seen it for almost fifty years, I see other faces instead floating past me like white round shiny candles: Tony's, eager and funny in Manchester when we did that Shaw season together, Elaine telling me her life story on the top of a bus with the rain streaming down the windows and that young lad listening all ears, Neil, devious, enchanting Neil, who died of blood cancer, we all have cancer in our blood he said, it just gets some of us more than others, Piers my boy-lover, making tunes on an old piano, dreaming of crotchets and a thousand golden trumpets: and Maurice, making me look at his apple orchards in the Dordogne and telling me what an old fool I was: which I am, an old shrunken frame of a woman, trapped in a body no-one designed, nothing more than a question mark really; but the mind doesn't alter, the heart and the passions beat on, and the soul floats somewhere around trying to get a look in: you've had it, Molly Kargar, you know you have, and you've had more than most — more of the peaks and the valleys, more of the applause and the laughter and the tears, more of the sordid times, tripping with baby Isobel over bodies in the underground in the war, smelling the stench of the shit buckets, boiling babymilk in a Yorkshire attic, rescued from death by a doctor who didn't understand the first thing about life or death, that one always leads to the other, but you can never be sure which way round it is; more of the good times, the conjugations in musty bedsits and five star hotels, sunlight in California, a small white boat steaming across the South China Sea, water everywhere, it's the same water everywhere, at my birth and at hers and then Rebecca coming forth in a gush of limegreen fluid blinking quietly with a wisdom her mother never had; poor old Isobel, my child Isobel, how did she come out of me so closed and tight, no dancing light in her eyes, the magic all locked up inside her, just like Mother really, though what difference it makes in this world I'm sure I don't know, I'm glad to be leaving it really, all the people I love have gone and I'm silly enough sometimes to imagine them up there grinning and holding their blood-red wineglasses out ready to toast me when I manage to detach myself from this place and fetch my memories together jumbled like a bad tapestry of colour and sound and scent and motion and drape it round me or perhaps get on it like a magic carpet, so I sit crosslegged as it passes over landscapes I know too well or not well enough, Isobel is down there somewhere, busy complaining about something, her hands in the sink, watching the tap drip onto the dishes, oh Isobel, where are you Isobel, you belong to me, you're the only thing that ever did really, but my eyes are tired, I don't want to see anything more now, I want to go back to those clear white images in the Cape Cod pond, to the old safety of the embrace of water and a man, or down the thin gravelly road edged with meadowsweet again, where I heard the cuckoos and the wood pigeons and saw the pastel lambs with my father when it was spring and the green world was at its beginning.

2

The gardens of the Villa Cellini are splendid, every bit as good as the brochure promised. One always worries about that, especially when you hear so many stories about unreliable travel agents who tell you about swimming pools that aren't there and not about railway lines and discos that are.

On my first morning at the villa, I walk down to the lake. It's a thick smoky blue, holding in it pictures of the frothy clouds that hang like a frown over everything – the pink and white villages round the lake's edge, the tourist boats resting after a hard summer, the bright seagulls screaming on the glassy water. If I turn to my right just a little, there's a pale gold sun trying to illuminate the atmosphere, though all it succeeds in doing is casting a glimmer over the surface of the lake. Water hits the old stone wall beneath me with a series of slaps like tired women beating carpets. Nature and housework: tides of routine, repetition. If I touch the cold stone with my hand, it isn't at all friendly. Further down still, I look into the water, it's surprisingly clear – I can see the contours of every stones at the bottom of it. I put my hand in, and make the stones change places, disturbing the elements without anyone to criticize me. I'm away from everything, even away from memories of Mother, who made it all possible – though God knows how many times she changed her will, it must have been a dozen times before she finally decided she couldn't avoid making me her inheritor.

Back in my room in the villa, I open the windows wide so as not to waste the wonderful air, and lie down on the big white bed for a short rest. I'm tired, what with the journey and all the organization beforehand, and now the change of air. But although I try to make myself comfortable, the pillows seem to be stuffed with foam, and the whole white glare of the room makes me feel as though I'm inside some piece of inhospitable equipment, like a refrigerator.

There are two windows in my room. One holds a view of the water with a foreground of grass and tall Lombardy pines. A road curls round them down to the village. Humps of mountains sling themselves across the lake. In front of the other window there's a horse-chestnut tree heavy with clusters of brown balls. Its crispy leaves contrast in their reds and yellows and browns with the dark silhouetted blue of the mountain behind. I watch the leaves, the wind moving them, but not all in the same rhythm. One in the middle dances like a fibrillated heart. Its image looks for others in my brain, finds one that's alike, invites me to come and look.

I'm sixteen. My hair's curled under in the fashion of the late fifties; I'm wearing a stiff white blouse tightly pulled round my waist into a blue leather belt, my skirt billows out, encouraged by layers of hooped petticoats. The taste of new lipstick sits thickly on my lips. I'm on a seat in a park in Chiswick next to a young man called Peter, it's a late August evening, and the lamplight's shining through the leaves above our heads down onto Peter's black polished shoes. I can't breathe – because of my belt and Peter, who is about to kiss me. I've never been kissed before. The scent of Peter's aftershave rests in the air between us, his hand moves sideways, crablike, from his own navy blue knee to lie like a nesting pigeon on my fluffy skirt.

'Isobel?'

'Yes, Peter?'

'Can I kiss you?'

But I went to a girls' school, where the rules of English syntax were very properly taught, and I knew the request ought to have been, '*May* I kiss you?' The magic of the moment was eaten up by grammatical considerations. Thirty years later, here in Italy, the only romantic aspect left is that image of leaves shining and dancing in the light.

I've wondered since if this was the beginning of my disappointment with life. Peter was too old for me, in any case, he wore too much aftershave, Mother liked him too much. Years later, she told me he'd married a social worker, and got a job teaching mathematics in a polytechnic. That was one of Mother's quirks, she always made it her business to keep track of other people's destinies; she had a head full of intimate details about all kinds of people whose paths had barely crossed with hers. She wasn't nearly as good at world events: most of these passed her by. She marked time by what happened to her, not by what happened out there, or to the rest of us.

It's difficult for me to think of my mother with fondness. But this, I realize, was almost a fond thought, it slipped sideways like Peter's hand into my consciousness when I'd forgotten for a moment to keep guard over it.

'I wonder if anyone here can explain this one for me?' says the American Professor Goldman, with a fervent look on his polished face. 'Why is the lion in his cage, while the tiger's allowed out?'

Riddles aren't my speciality, and I haven't been following Professor Goldman's conversation. But I can see he's looking at the tapestry which hangs on the wall behind the large dining table. About three metres square, with a background of dull gold, it carries exquisite capering figures of animals, mixed with flowers and vegetation embroidered in dark greens and reds. A caged lion stands on the right.

'It's historic, you know,' Goldman goes on, 'the Countess Vittoria Lenno owned it. It came here as part of her dowry in 1748. She was something of a handful, that young woman. Married a much older man, it always causes trouble. The Pope took an interest in it all when she had an affair openly, while still married to the Count.'

'That was accepted practice in eighteenth-century Italy.' This is Carla Dichter, the stern Italian wife of a German poet, both of whom are also guests at the Villa Cellini. 'So it was in much of Southern Europe. Here it was known as "cicisbeismo".'

Goldman stares at Carla Dichter trying to work out how she knows more than him. 'Of course Mrs Dichter, you come from these parts originally yourself, don't you?'

'It was the subject of my doctoral dissertation, actually — concepts of morality in relation to the institution of marriage, an historical perspective.'

Some of us are still looking at the tapestry, which, as well as the lion and the tiger, boasts squirrels, cockerels, peacocks, a wolf and a lamb. It's one of the many beautiful and valuable objects decorating the Villa Cellini. The villa isn't an ordinary hotel, it's a private home, in which people pay a lot of money to be treated as house guests. I think Gina and Tomaso Lucca, the couple who manage the place on behalf of some company (which has several such places across Europe and North America) must regard themselves as missionaries in the promotion of international understanding. They're certainly very careful to introduce their 'guests' to one another, and make sure we sit next to the right people at dinner. (Or in the case of Professor Goldman, as we're all quickly realizing, the wrong people.) You can see how much Gina Lucca cares for the villa when you watch her walk round in the mornings inspecting things, her spectacles strung on a gold chain round her neck, noting the bulbs which need replacing in the chandeliers, overlooked dust on the marble ornaments, newspapers untidily folded, the Bechstein's open lid, a dead chrysanthemum.

The Villa Cellini, a sixteenth-century building, stands at the point where the lake divides into separate arms. It is surrounded by twenty acres of private gardens, and the ornamental iron gates at the end of the driveway are guarded by an intercom and two Dobermanns. The brochure even says a guard patrols the grounds at night, which is something I appreciate. It's rare to feel safe.

Mr Jefferson, my boss, was the one who first told me about the Villa Cellini. I've had the same job for the last fifteen years, as secretary to a Harley Street gynaecologist. I know it's boring, but there never seemed any reason to change. After Mother died, and I went back to work, Mr Jefferson said to me: 'Isobel, you need a holiday'. I probably looked pale, and had lost weight, so when Mr Jefferson said: 'I think you should go somewhere where you'll really be looked after,' the mere thought made me tremble. It was a grey day in October, the London sky was a sieve full of grey English cabbage water, people hurried by with grey depressed faces. I remember standing there, shiny brochure in hand, seeing this Italian villa poised on a hill in a landscape of the kind one only sees in Renaissance paintings, lit with a precise, heavenly light. I could hear Mother laughing at me, at the incongruous thought of her daughter – plain, sensible, old Isobel – going to such a place. So I thought, okay Mother, you win, I *will* go! You never know, perhaps something wonderful will happen to me there. Something wonderful at last, the kind of thing that only happens to other people.

Caroline Goldman is shouting at me across the table. She's predominantly orange; orange skin, orange lips, orange hair; an orange bangle clanks against the table as she moves her orange hands amongst her food. 'Do you have children, Mrs Lennox?'

'One, a daughter, Rebecca. She's eighteen.'

'So she lives with you still? Or is she away in school?'

'She's still with me.'

Mrs Goldman looks at me curiously, but I'm used to such looks. 'My husband and I separated when Rebecca was three.'

'I'm sorry to hear that.' I doubted her sorrow, actually.

'So you live on your own?'

'With Rebecca, yes.'

'How will she manage without you, while you're away?'

'Very well, I expect. Excuse me, I have to make a telephone call.' I don't actually, but Mrs Goldman's interrogations are making me feel trapped. In the ladies' room, I wash my face with cold water and comb my hair. Forty-eight. My hair's beginning to go grey, and when I smile my face sorts itself into historical curves. But my skin's clear, and people have said the bone structure inherited from Mother — high cheekbones, a clearly cut chin — can make me look younger than I am. There are shadows under my eyes, though. I can't smooth them away with my fingers. I don't mind them really, I certainly wouldn't ever do anything to disguise them, not like Caroline Goldman.

After-dinner drinks in the villa are served by a waiter with a trolley, a kind of upmarket icecream salesman. I ask for an Italian liqueur, a grappa (Mr Jefferson told me about it). The fire in the drawing room's been lit, we're all attracted towards it: Hugo Dichter, the stooped, silent poet, with the learned Carla; Mr Moore, a painter with a monkish way of watching everything, and his wife Susie, who seems remarkably tall. Then there are the Krauses, another American couple; Thomas, an athletic silver-headed businessman, and Martha, a little pink and white thing, with whom Thomas is much occupied. I feel sorry for Martha somehow, though I don't know her, and shouldn't presume to say so. I don't know any of these people, we're all strangers to one another. I feel uneasy with them — I'm less used to this sort of company than they are. So I'm quiet, timid like a cat sitting looking at a saucer of cream. I hope they'll think it's British reserve.

'May I introduce myself? We haven't met.' A smartly dressed balding man extends his hand towards me. 'Isaac Simons.'

'Isobel Lennox.'

'Pleased to meet you. I've just arrived. Have you been here long?'

'Two days.'

'It's a wonderful place, isn't it?'

'It is. Are you here simply for pleasure, Mr Simons?'

'Well, I've come here to write. Is that pleasure?' He laughs gently. 'I suppose it might be.'

Mr Simons is apparently writing a book about conflict in interpersonal relationships. He's a psychoanalyst by training. He needs time away from his patients in order to understand what they're telling him. He looks as though he comes from a wealthy background – his clothes weren't bought from any run-of-the-mill high street store, the waistcoat beneath his suit and sprightly blue bow tie is as smooth as cashmere. I don't have any personal experience of psychoanalysts, though there are some in the building where I work. I used to warn them when the traffic wardens came round, but, although they thanked me nicely, they asked me to feed the meters for them, which is illegal, so I just let them get tickets now.

Mr Simons and I sit down together on one of the white sofas by the fire. 'Are you here on vacation, Mrs Lennox?'

'In a way.' The warmth of the fire – which is more psychological than physical, as it hasn't been lit for long – combines with the grappa to make me relax a little. The setting of the place helps too. Despite myself, I start to talk to Mr Simons a little about Mother's death. In the process I remember a lot of things, some of which I think are better forgotten. I'm glad he can't see into my head.

She wasn't ill, not really. That was the problem, she'd been complaining about it for years. She wanted to die because she couldn't enjoy life any more. Her eyesight had gone – for the last two years, she wasn't able to read, even with a magnifying glass. And her hips, both of them, had been broken and put together with metal joints. She could hear only with one ear, and then only when she wanted to. Her spine was very bent, which gave her indigestion and all sorts of problems. She could hardly walk. It wasn't much of a life, I could see that. She said her body had given up, but not her mind. And what was the point of a mind without a body? Her mind was agile, she didn't miss a thing. Until the last few months, that is. Then she did start to repeat herself and forget things. She said sometimes she heard words but she couldn't make sense of them. It was disturbing to watch her deterioration, but it was far more disturbing for her than for me. It was her life, after all.

She lived on her own until the last year. She was impossible, really. Her house was full of ornaments from the past, absolutely crammed with them. She'd bought it to contain the objects, not for any other reason. She insisted on staying in it by herself. But she couldn't look after herself properly. She broke things all the time, she fell over and hurt herself, she even set fire to herself once. Pretended nothing had happened, but the whole sitting room went up in smoke and the fire brigade had to come in. I kept trying to persuade her to move into sheltered accommodation, but she wouldn't. She said she wanted to stay in her house, and if she couldn't do that, she'd rather be dead.

It was a nasty house, I hated it. It wasn't where I grew up – I grew up in a whole series of flats, and then a house, and then another larger house full of lodgers, in London. Mother was always on the move. Until her mid seventies when she said she'd decided to settle down at last, and she picked on this place in Kent, this red-brick house down a lane with little square rooms and a garden with a stream in it, and overgrown plants: such a mess! She gathered all her possessions from all her different lives – she'd been an actress and a kind of dilettante artist and writer – and put them all in there and moved herself into the middle of them and sat there thinking about the past for the next twenty years.

When she was eighty-eight, she fainted one day. Her eighty-year-old friend from the village found her. After that we hired a series of people to live with her, rent free, they didn't even have to pay their share of the bills. In return for a small wage, they kept an eye on her. It was a thankless task. She hated them all. As soon as they arrived, she tried to turn them against her, so they'd go, and they all did.

The one who stayed the longest was a dedicated Quaker, a man in his twenties, a most unusual person, quite gifted, I thought. He'd trained as a nurse, but was now working for a church organization of some kind. It suited him to live rent free and care for someone like Mother. I can't say I haven't wondered sometimes about Steven. What is a man in his twenties doing looking after an old lady? She didn't leave him any money, but I'm going to give him some. She left the oddest will. But Steven: is he what they call gay? He's got a face like an El Greco Christ. My daughter Rebecca said, 'Don't be silly, Mother, of course he's gay. It stands out a mile!' It didn't to me. But the great thing about Steven was that he recognized instantly what Mother was trying to do, and for a long time he didn't let her upset him. He saw through her manipulations. He wouldn't let her play games with him. When she was rude to him, he was rude back to her. She used to get quite offended; she would ring me up and say, 'Steven's going mad, do you know what he said? He told me there isn't any food in the fridge because he expects me to die soon. Can you imagine that, Isobel?'

Steven rang me up one day and he said, 'Mrs Lennox, I think you should come down and see your mother. She won't get out of bed, and we're going to have to do something about her. I can't take responsibility for her any more. Perhaps she needs to be in hospital?'

So I went down. This was August. It was incredibly hot. In the lane there were clouds of butterflies. Mother lay in bed in the sitting room – Steven had moved her bed in there – with the gas fire on. The atmosphere was stifling. She looked at me with watery eyes, and she said, 'Isobel, I'm going to die. I've decided I'm going to die. I can't keep going any more. There isn't any point in it. Everything hurts. Everything is too difficult. I should have died years ago.' It sounded awfully rational. 'I've even been thinking of Mother lately, how lucky she was to die in middle age without knowing what it's like to be old and unwanted. I talk to her sometimes, it's a comfort, you know.'

Then she said, 'There are some things I want you to do for me. You are my daughter, after all.' She always gave me a kind of accusing look when she said that, as though she were intimating some actual crime. The first thing she wanted me to do was to cut her hair. She had the most lovely long silver hair, really thick, just as thick and silky as it had been when she was a girl. She'd worn it long all her life, she'd never had it cut. It was her best asset, she said. And here she was, asking me to cut it. 'I can't manage it any more, Isobel,' she said. 'I can't lift my hands to plait it. You'll have to cut it off.'

I took the scissors out of the drawer and put a towel from the bathroom round her shoulders and I cut it. Clip, clip, clip! The scissors made a grating sound, as if the hair itself were in pain. The silver fell to the carpet and lay there in great curls. I picked it up afterwards, and put it in the dustbin.

When I was cutting her hair, I saw how thin her skin had become. Like yellow paper. It had become too big for her body. All its elasticity had gone.

The second thing she asked me to do was to burn some letters. 'They're in the chest in my bedroom, Isobel. There are three large brown envelopes tied in red ribbon; I want you to take them out and put them in the incinerator and burn them. But you mustn't read them. Just burn them.'

They were just where she said. Three bulky envelopes bulging with God knows what. I don't know, but I can guess.

She had a little incinerator in the garden. She never took any notice when that part of Kent became a smokeless zone in 1964. 'The smell of wood in the chimney, the scent of bonfires, how can they deprive us of that? I don't care about pollution. We're polluted enough: why worry about a bit of smoke?'

I went back to the house. 'I've done that, Mother. Now, what else would you like me to do?'

'Come and sit down, Isobel.' She indicated the chair beside her bed. 'Have you heard of euthanasia, Isobel?'

I knew what was coming then. I thought I'd better say straight away how I felt, it wouldn't have been fair to have let her hope I'd do what she wanted. 'I've read about it, Mother. I know what the arguments are, but I'm afraid I'm not prepared to help you. I simply couldn't do that.'

She didn't seem to have heard. 'There's an organization, Isobel, I joined it years ago. It's not legal, but then lots of things aren't legal when they ought to be. I've got a bottle of pills – don't ask me where I got them because I won't tell you – but I've got them, they're in my handbag, in the drawer over there.'

I was angry. She spent her life assuming I'd do what she

wanted. No doubt, when she joined this thing years ago, she had assumed she could rely on me. But I really don't approve of it. I think there are some things we shouldn't try to control. The moment of death is one of them. We aren't gods. We shouldn't pretend to be. Mother did – had already. When I was a child, she tried to kill herself over some stupid business with a man. Oh she didn't tell me that was what she'd done: but I worked it out. Children know a lot of things adults think they don't. I don't like abortion, either, for the same reason, it's taking the law too much into our own hands.

'I told you, Isobel, it's time for me to die. I can't do anything any more. All the people I loved are dead. Why should I stay alive?'

I wanted to say – for me. You might want to stay alive for me, Mother. Or for your granddaughter, Rebecca. To see what happens to us. Don't you want to know what happens to us, Mother? I would, in your place.

'All the people I love are dead.' Exactly. You're not talking about me or about Rebecca, are you, you're talking about your friends, about your men, about the exotic figures who wandered in and out of your life while we, your family, had to struggle for the odd moment of your attention. No, Mother, I won't help you to die. 'Why do you need help, anyway?'

'Because I'm afraid I won't do it right. I won't swallow the pills properly. Or I'll be sick, or something. You must help me, Isobel. Don't you love me? I'm your mother. This is the last thing I'll ever ask you to do.' She looked at me, and her eyes were great grey places full of pleading.

She turned her head away from me. 'Go away, Isobel. I never want to see you again.'

So there she was, all on her own, having got rid of Steven, telling me to go. I was tempted to call her bluff and say, alright, Mother, if that's what you want, have it your way. That's what nobody ever did, you see, they never stood up to her. What she really wanted was limits; she needed someone to say, look here, Molly, you simply can't do that! She needed a few feet stamped in anger, and out of that anger would come respect, and because of that respect she wouldn't be able to dissemble and manipulate any more.

But of course I couldn't walk out. Being an only child is a

terrible burden. I was born when Mother was forty two. She wasn't a very maternal person. She had two brothers, but one's dead and the other's an invalid – no help there. They talk about community care a lot these days, but what they mean is women like me, struggling to keep a home together, fighting to earn the money and pay the bills, looking after our children – we're the ones that have to care for the old people too. It's an impossible situation. Even when Mother was able to cope on her own, I had to organize her life, as well as mine and Becky's. Ever since my daughter was six or seven I've had to run round after Mother; I've had to sort out her telephone and electricity and grocery bills, I've had to go and see her when she's ill, I've had to help her fill in forms, I've had to chase round the shops to find shoes to fit her, I've had to listen to her lies and abuse – yes, abuse, Mother was an angry woman, very bitter. She felt she never got what she wanted out of life, and I had to bear the brunt of that as well.

Before I left I hired an agency nurse. I explained that Mother was difficult, but this nurse seemed to know all about it. Or else she was being paid enough not to care. I didn't like leaving her like that, but I couldn't do anything else, could I?

I went to see her again a week later. She hadn't meant it when she said she never wanted to see me again: well, she'd meant it, but she wasn't going to stick to it. I knew Mother, you see. We never referred to that conversation again, either of us. I felt it was important for me to take a stand.

The nurse met me at the door. 'I'm afraid I won't be able to stay here, Mrs Lennox. Your mother's quite the most difficult case I've ever had.'

I sighed. 'Why, what has she done now?'

'She pretends, Mrs Lennox. She pretends all the time that she can't do things when she can. She won't go to the toilet now. But she could perfectly well, if she wanted to. She pretends she can't even pick up the telephone. It's by her bed. But she says she hasn't got enough strength in her wrist to pick up the receiver. So she rings the bell by her bed for me all the time. Several times a night as well. Treats me like dirt. Never apologizes.'

I wanted to say, but you're being paid £9 an hour. She

shouldn't have to apologize. I pay you to look after her, however troublesome she is.

The money was another problem. Mother had some money invested – enough to pay the bills, buy food, pay to have the house cleaned. It wasn't enough to pay for these expensive nurses. So I'd had to get her stockbroker to sell some of her shares. Eating into your capital, it's called. 'What do you need your capital for, Mother?' I'd asked her, because she was continually objecting. I don't know how she thought I could pay for her nurses out of what I earned.

It wasn't worth getting angry about this nurse. I would have to take matters into my own hands. I telephoned her doctor. 'What do you want me to do?' he asked crossly, when he came.

'I want you to have her admitted to hospital,' I said.

'I thought she didn't want that.'

'She doesn't. But there's nothing else to be done, now.'

'You're not able to get over to see her much yourself, then, Mrs Lennox?'

'Dr Willard, I have a job to do. I can't just take time off. I have to keep myself and my daughter. We live in a very small house, just enough room for the two of us. I couldn't possibly look after Mother, even if I wanted to.'

It hurt me to say it, but it was true. I couldn't desert Becky now, could I?

Dr Willard wasn't pleased, but he did have Mother admitted to hospital, and he did tell her she needed to go. He stood by her bed and took her spindly hand in his. She opened her eyes and looked at him with some veneration. 'Hallo, John, it's nice of you to come and see me.' She called him John, treated him like a friend, or as something in between a friend and servant – which is the way she treated most people.

'Molly, my dear, I think the time has come to make a decision about you. You can't go on like this, can you?' She was watching him like a hawk. 'I think we should arrange a bed for you at the Royal.'

She waited before giving him her considered response to this. She could still be amazingly lucid when she wanted to be. 'Well, I'm sure that's very thoughtful of you, but I don't think I'll go, thank you John. I'm quite all right here.' It was very politely put. 'So long as Isobel gets rid of that awful woman. Isobel!' She summoned me from behind Dr Willard. 'Isobel, have you got rid of that woman? I told you I didn't want her here.'

'She got rid of herself, Mother,' I said, as quietly as I could.

'Thank God for that. She was awful, you know. She stole my newspapers.'

'I thought you couldn't read the newspaper any more, Mother?'

'I order them, I pay for them, it's not her business to steal them, is it?'

'Come on Molly,' said Dr Willard attempting to be jovial. 'How old are you now, eighty-eight, eighty-nine?'

'You know perfectly well how old I am, John. I'm ninety. That's fifteen years too old for anybody.'

'Well, how old you are doesn't really matter. What matters is that you can't look after yourself any more. We can't just leave you here on your own, can we?'

'Isobel could do it,' said Mother, then, 'if she wanted to. But she doesn't, do you Isobel?'

'I've explained my situation to Dr Willard, Mother,' I told her firmly. 'I don't want to discuss it again, now.'

'You never want to discuss anything difficult, do you Isobel? It's all avoidance with you. Why, I believe you'd avoid life, if you could.'

'Now, now Molly. Think about what I've said, please.'

'It's my tea time,' she said.

I went to make the tea. She always had Earl Grey. She abhorred tea bags, but she didn't know that she now had her Earl Grey in tea bags, I'd found them in my local supermarket.

Dr Willard followed me into the kitchen. 'We can't take her by force,' he said. He looked as though he'd rather not be involved in any of this. It was distasteful to him, like the washing up, or burning smelly dressings. 'There's nothing wrong with her mind, is there?'

'No, not today. There is sometimes.'

'Mrs Lennox . . .'

'No, it's all right, I'm not going to have an argument with you.' He was a pretentious little man in an overcrisp dark suit, an ordinary country doctor trying to be something else. 'I'll talk to her when she's had her tea.'

I had to sit her up before she could drink her tea. That took quite a lot of arranging – she had to have her pillows a certain way, she wanted her pink shawl round her shoulders. And then she began to talk as though none of this were going on. The brother of one of her friends had just died: 'I remember Gordon scrumping apples from the orchard next door, he was caught one day, but we got away!' She giggled raucously. The people next door were blocking her driveway with their rubbish, she'd never liked them, she thought they were trying to force her into an old people's home. The new vicar – such a fetching young man – had been over to talk to her. She was going to leave the church some money so they could have the inside repainted. She'd never been a believer, but she knew there was a power greater than any of us somewhere. . . .

'Mother,' I tried to interrupt the flow, 'Do you remember Dr Willard was here earlier on?'

'Who?'

'Dr Willard.'

'Who's that?'

I couldn't tell if she'd genuinely misplaced the memory, or was being devious. 'Dr Willard. John. Your doctor.'

'Oh, him. Don't have much faith in him. You know what he's trying to make me do? He's trying to make me stop taking my valium. I've been taking valium for forty years. I don't see the point in stopping now.'

'He thinks you ought to go into hospital, Mother!'

'If I go into hospital, I shall never come out again.' This sentence was uttered like a series of gunshots; there could be no mistaking their nature, or their intended target. I felt full of small smoking holes.

Mother was right about some things. She didn't ever come out of hospital. That was August 13. She died in hospital a month later, on September 15.

Of course I went to see her whenever I could. It was difficult from the part of London where I live, Shepherd's Bush. The whole journey took two hours.

As I said, Mother never referred to the conversation we had about euthanasia again. Except indirectly.

One evening, she said, 'Isobel, you haven't been a bad girl, you know. Just rather boring. And too conventional. That's why you won't do what I want, isn't it? You're frightened. I don't know why you're so frightened. I didn't bring you up to be like that. I don't know why you're still a secretary. Don't you have any ambition, Isobel? I can't stand people without ambition.'

I was used to these accusations. I'd heard them many times before.

'Something went wrong between us, didn't it, Isobel, a long time ago. I don't know what it was. When you married Gerald I gave you up for lost. My daughter! Sometimes I looked at you, and I couldn't understand where you'd come from. You certainly didn't seem to have much to do with me!'

I wanted to say, do you really expect me to sit here and listen to this, Mother? I've got better things to do than listen to your insults.

It was as if she knew I was thinking this, because then she said, 'I *am* grateful, Izzy. You go through the motions. At least you come and see me, you bring me things. You feel responsible, don't you? I do appreciate that.'

Those were her rational moments. At other times, she would warble on about everything and nothing. Increasingly, she slept. The nurses were always trying to get her out of bed, to get her to take some exercise. She swore at them. She had this walking frame, a great metal thing with rubber on its feet, that she pushed in front of her with a little wire basket hanging off it for her soap, and her flannel. The nurse pulled the covers back, and then it took her about ten minutes to move from a lying into a sitting position. The skin on her legs shone like rice paper; she had ulcers in several places, and the skin was mottled all red and purple, it looked as if someone had crushed strawberries and blackberries against them. They were swollen, too.

Then she tried to find her slippers, but she couldn't get her feet into them, because she couldn't look down at the same time as moving her feet, so I helped her with that. I gave her her dressing gown: her arms were like a stick insect's, and under her thin cotton nightie – made of a faded flowered seersucker fabric, you can't buy it any more – her breasts were nearly flat, like kippers. She was a young woman in the 1920s, when it was fashionable not to have breasts. You strapped them down so they didn't show. That must have caused quite a lot of deformity.

We'd got the dressing gown on, and then she stood up holding onto this walking frame thing. I had to do the dressing gown up for her. She was so misshapen by then that the hem was a good six inches higher at the back than the front. She held onto that frame like a baby monkey, fingers gripping its edge as though her life depended on it. And then she shuffled off across the ward. When she came back, she said she was too tired to eat any supper. She was determined to pay the nurses back for making her get out of bed.

At the end of visiting time, she always clung onto me and cried. I felt she was doing it to make me feel bad. She always wanted me to kiss her, to put my arms around her. She used to say that was the saddest thing about growing old, that no one touched you any more. I found that difficult. I knew she was disappointed in me, I was the only person she had left – my father disappeared years ago. As she said, her friends were all dead. It's important to remember that. Most of my life, apart from my childhood, that is, I hadn't had much to do with Mother. She was off leading her own life. We used to meet sometimes, for a cup of tea in some department store; or I would get a letter of a rambling kind telling me how happy she was, or whatever, and hoping I was all right, but she rarely gave me the chance to tell her whether I was or not.

The hospital reinforced her intention to die. One night she said to me, 'Isobel, I want you to bring Rebecca to see me. It is Rebecca, isn't it? I think I should see her once more before I die.'

I tried the 'Nonsense, Mother, you're not going to die' line but she wouldn't have it. 'Go and get her, Isobel,' she said wearily, 'I want to see Rebecca.'

That was awkward. I'd tried to take Rebecca with me to the hospital, but she wouldn't come. I've been having some trouble with Rebecca recently. 'She's *your* mother,' Becky said, when I asked her, 'I don't have anything to say to her.'

That night, when I got home, I went to Becky's room to ask her again. She wasn't in it, but all the lights were on, as usual; the blue lamp I'd bought in Venice, and the main light, with a 150 watt bulb in it. I don't know why she always left the lights on when she went out, but she did. I turned them off. She hadn't left a note or anything, but that wasn't unusual. I also noticed that her plants were dying, the soil around their roots was so dry it had sprung away from the sides of the pot.

I spoke to her the next evening when I came back from work (she'd been asleep when I got up) but she still wouldn't come with me to visit her grandmother. And then I had a bright idea. 'Why don't you go and see her without me, Becky? She might like that better.'

I didn't hear about it from Becky. Mother told me. 'She's all right, Isobel,' she said. 'You worry about her too much. Leave her alone. She's like me, that one. She'll make her way in the world.' I was suspicious. What had the two of them been talking about?

On September 15 when I went to the hospital, there were screens around Mother's bed. A nurse touched me lightly on the arm as I stood there wondering what was going on. 'I'm afraid your mother's not well today, Mrs Lennox,' she told me in a hushed schoolgirlish tone. 'She's had a little bleed, it often happens at this age.'

'What do you mean, a little bleed?'

'A cerebral haemorrhage.' The nurse, who was young, drew herself up to her full height as she said these words. 'She's unconscious. She may not recover consciousness. We were going to telephone you, but Sister thought you'd be coming up about now, anyway.'

Mother lay there like a wax figure; her skin had the jaundiced transparency of a waxwork. Her short silver hair (I still had trouble seeing her with that) lay in a kind of determined mess on the pillow. Her eyes bulged through the hoods of her eyelids; I could almost see the expression in her eyes, though according to the nurse there shouldn't be any expression in them now.

'Mother?' I put my hand on her shoulder. I could feel her breath inflating and deflating her body like a pair of bellows. But the sound it made was scratchy, unstable. I listened to that noise all the rest of that day. The nurses and the doctors came in and out. I had the feeling that they'd more or less decided not to do anything. But I didn't ask, and they didn't say anything. They were very busy just then, and there was only a young doctor in charge of her case, I didn't like to bother him. She was ninety, after all.

About seven o'clock I went to phone Becky and get a cup of

tea – I didn't feel like eating – and when I came back I got such a shock. I moved the screen aside, I was just going to sit down again when I saw that the sheet had been pulled up across her face. They should have warned me. It's not as though I were young and inexperienced and easily upset, but to go away and come back and find your mother's died while you've been drinking a cup of tea, that's not a particularly nice thing to happen. It was typical of Mother to have chosen that moment to die. I bet she noticed that I wasn't there, and she thought, okay, I'll die now, I'll give Isobel a shock. She liked to be the centre of attention, to feel everyone else was a minor character in the main plot, which was her life.

I thought you might ask me how I felt. Well, to be truthful, I never thought Mother would die. I'm not sure any of us believes in our mother's death until it happens. She's the one who gave life; she represents life, she *can't* die. Even on that last day, I thought Mother was just being awkward, she'd come out of it, open her eyes, and start complaining about me again.

When I was little, I used to try to imagine the universe. I mean, the universe as all there is; and the earth only a tiny part of it. But I couldn't. It was the same with my mother. I was unable to imagine life without her. Not at one, or six, or fourteen, or forty-eight. My age had nothing to do with it. Neither did need. I didn't need her. I didn't need her manipulations, her distortions, her constant inveighing against me. Without compunction, I could say from that point of view, I wanted her to die. My life, in that respect, would be better without her. I could also say that her own pain and wish for death made that event a good one for her. But I looked at her dead and I wished she wasn't; despite myself, despite my knowledge of her. I even doubted whether I myself should be alive without her. I found that thought particularly amazing.

The nurse said Mother's false teeth had disappeared. She seemed concerned about this. Perhaps she thought I would sue the hospital for losing Mother's dentures?

I saw the doctor who came to say she really was dead. He was young and desperately trying to appear professional. He saw me watching him. And when he signed the death certificate I saw him hesitate. Where it said, 'cause of death' he didn't know what to write. He should have written 'old age', of course. But that doesn't count as a cause of death any more. You have to call it something else, because death is a medical event.

The nurse gave me her possessions in a small suitcase. Then she put her rings into the palm of my hand, the two rings she always wore. Robert, the friend she'd had when I was a child, had given her one of them, the one with a large opal. I don't know where the other came from.

She wanted to be cremated. She'd even chosen her undertaker: W. S. McKintosh of Tunbridge Wells. Steven told me. He'd been visiting her every day. She preferred men to women.

Rebecca and I went to see her body. A policeman was putting parking tickets on all the cars outside. I felt there should be some exception for parking offences in the case of death.

A bell rang when you opened the undertaker's door. We went in. A woman with red lips in a black skirt and jersey came into the waiting room by the other door. 'We've come to see my mother, Mrs Kargar,' I said.

'Oh yes, Mrs Lennox,' she said. 'Have you got any matches?' Was she going to offer us a cigarette or carry out the cremation on the spot? Becky gave her her cigarette lighter. 'I've run out of matches, you see,' Mrs McKintosh explained. 'I was just about to pop out and buy some when you came. I haven't lit the candles in the chapel yet.'

She went off and did her business and then we were shown into this mean little room with green curtains, too short for the space, instead of a door. On the left was the lid of the coffin resting against the wall with a plate on it reading 'Molly Kargar'. Two white candles, already half burnt, danced miserably on a shelf. The open coffin lay beneath it. It seemed so small. She seemed so small, hardly bigger than a child.

She was unexpectedly beautiful. The skin of her face was smooth, without blemishes, stretched like silk over a perfect bone structure. Her high cheekbones, her correctly proportioned nose, her small flat forehead, her lips full and pink as they must have been in her youth. A lock of silver hair showed, combed carefully back into the white lace of the coffin's lining. There was lace around her neck and no more of her than this fine face could be seen, the mortal remains of Molly Kargar lit by secondhand candles and her granddaughter's cigarette lighter, in a small back room in Tunbridge Wells.

I didn't know anything about the management of death. When they teach you the facts of life in school, they don't teach you about death. They don't teach you much about life, for that matter. Mother had been what they call embalmed. I didn't understand until later what it meant. It meant that they'd taken Mother's body somewhere and they'd drained all her body fluids out of her – all the blood, the urine, and everything – they'd taken her insides out and put chemicals there instead. And then they'd brought her back so that I and my daughter could look at a body that wasn't hers any more, so we could say goodbye to a person who'd already gone.

Becky said that. She looked at her grandmother and felt me crying, and she took me in her arms and held me tightly and said, 'That's not her, Mum, that's not Granny, why does she have to be in such a revolting place? Let's get out of here,' and it was such a comfort to be held by her, to hear her speak such sensible words, to understand that I wasn't alone, that this agony of biological connection between women wasn't my private business, but every woman's; Rebecca's too, and Mrs McKintosh's, and the women Mr Jefferson put his hands into, out of which would come newly pink little girls struggling to do the right thing in their turn.

I went back after Becky had said we should leave. I had to have just one moment with Mother alone. I didn't know why; I still don't. I touched her face. It was, of course, cold, which I had known it would be, but not believed. To touch your mother's cheek and find it freezes your fingertips in the candle-light – now that is quite an experience. I wouldn't wish it on anybody.

The words 'I forgive you' came into my head. Again I don't know why. Why should I want to forgive my mother? That isn't what I said, though. I loved you, I said, I loved you, despite everything, because of everything, I loved you, and I will always love you, and my daughter will love me, though that isn't most of the time what she will say. Nonetheless, I know it now, it's part of the chain of connection – we, who are born of woman, not man.

I asked the young vicar Mother had recently got to know to take the cremation service. We had a long talk about Mother's unconventionality and lack of formal religious beliefs. He came to the house, her suffocating house, now more so, without her reigning over its crammed disorder, and I found the last bottle of her favourite wine, a light German substance bottled a decade ago, and we got slightly drunk on that.

He did a wonderful job. No reading from the Bible, no hymns, no forced prayers; just the simplicity, the poetry of the Christian language. Blessed are they that mourn, for they *shall* be comforted. My eyes were streaming, and Becky's too. I noticed then that she was entirely dressed in black; I wasn't. The young will revive our past, it's part of their rebellion against us. She, mothering me, gave me some Kleenex. I wasn't at all conscious of the people in the rows behind us. Fifty or sixty of them – I'd been through Mother's address book and rung everyone I thought she would have wanted me to. But as far as I was concerned it was just me, Mother and Becky and the vicar. And then the committal: that's what crematoria call setting the thing alight. The coffin slid off with only the two dozen white roses Becky and I had bought, and the doors opened and closed and it's gone, your mother is gone, and you even imagine a roar of red flames, the last judgement. The vicar turned most respectfully towards it as it slid away. 'We have but a short time on this earth. . . .'

A crematorium is a factory. A factory of death. One in, the ashes out: what to do with her ashes?

Mother made that one difficult, too. In her will she said she wanted her ashes scattered off Cape Cod in the United States where she had once spent some happy summers in a house in the woods by a Thoreau-type pond. I went there once, it was full of mosquitoes and some other insects that lay waiting to bite your ankles.

I didn't think the Americans would want her ashes. It might even be difficult taking them out of the country on an aeroplane. You might have to fill in forms saying whose ashes they are and why there isn't enough room for them in England. Also it would have been expensive, because I would have had to accompany the ashes. I couldn't just have sent them in a parcel with instructions to some anonymous courier to drop them in the right pond.

I told Becky about the ashes problem. For some reason she considered it funny. She told me about this novel she'd read in which the heroine's mother dies, and she takes the ashes and puts them round a plant in a shopping precinct, because her mother liked shopping, and it comforted her to know she'd forever be able to listen to women discussing the prices of cardigans.

In the end, I took them to the Lake District. I got a train to Windermere and then a taxi. I asked the taxi to take me to Waterhead, near Ambleside. We'd been there in my childhood, Mother and I. I remember being happy there. My best memories of her are in that place: I can see her there in a fur coat that Robert had given her, and a vast black hat with a rose at the side — she was a crazy dresser. Sometimes it worked, and sometimes it didn't. I can feel that silky fur now, resting my head against her side, looking out across Lake Windermere, at men foolhardily ploughing their sailing boats across the water in the October wind.

3

Talking to Mr Simons made me feel better, even though it did make me remember some painful things. I slept better too that night. In the morning when I came out of my room – its door opens directly onto a path leading up to the main house – I noticed for the first time a great bank of white convolvulus and yellow Michaelmas daisies.

Today is a brilliant day, with a cornflower blue sky. After breakfast, I take the path up the hill beyond the villa. It's impossible to walk quietly through the layers and layers of crunchy leaves on the ground, and I feel very self-conscious about the noise I'm making. But I tell myself it won't do, I've come here to relax, I have as much right to make a noise walking through the leaves as anybody else.

The path I'm on encircles the rocky promontory which houses the villa and its estate. A rail has been put at the outer edge, as in some places there's a straight drop to the lakeshore some four hundred and fifty feet below. But I stay away from the edge, walking as close as I can to the cliff face. And then after a few minutes I come to a little fortress in the woods, I can't imagine what it is, but while I'm standing staring at it Mr Simons' face appears at the window. He leans out, waves and says, 'Good morning, Mrs Lennox. Fine studio I've found, haven't I!' I don't know whether he's serious or not.

Round the next corner, I can see right down one of the lake's arms, further than from my room in the villa. The mountains here are vaster; is there more snow than yesterday on their tops? It makes me shiver.

All this walking makes me realize how little I do at home in London. My life in London consists of underground journeys and Saturday shopping trips round Shepherd's Bush Green to

Sainsbury's. Mother urged me to learn to drive, so did Becky, my friends, and Mr Jefferson: but I simply can't see myself behind the wheel of a car. Besides which, a car would be only one more thing to worry about.

Mine is a very regulated life. Up at seven, a cup of tea in my dressing gown in the kitchen, then my bath, a boiled egg and a cup of coffee. I take the newspaper (*The Independent*), with me on the train to work.

I get to Harley Street at 9.30. Let myself in: Dulcie, the cleaning woman, has already finished. I check the waiting room, to make sure the piles of *Woman* and *Vogue*, *House and Garden* and *Country Life*, are tidy, the chairs are at right angles, and the ashtrays emptied (a surprising number of our patients smoke). Then I go upstairs to my office on the first floor, which is a kind of ante-room of Mr Jefferson's. His first appointment isn't till 10.30. He goes to the hospital in Fulham before that.

Mr Jefferson sees patients at half-hourly intervals until five, three days a week, with a break of an hour for lunch. He's quite a popular doctor, there's no shortage of custom. I usually go shopping in my lunch hour, though sometimes I meet a friend, and we go to a small Italian restaurant. On the fourth day of the week Mr Jefferson has his operating session in Fulham, so I use that time to see that the accounts are in order. This can be quite delicate work, as a few patients don't pay up, even though presumably they've got plenty of money. You have to send them a note and hope that'll do the trick. If it doesn't, you can telephone, but that's difficult. I don't much like that part of my job.

On the fifth day Mr Jefferson doesn't come to the office in Harley Street at all. He stays at home in his house in Oxford-shire, where he's working on a new kind of gynaecological textbook. I'm typing it for him, as I type all his medical articles and letters. He's always writing letters to the medical press: just now it's a correspondence about the ethics of research on fetuses. A long time ago, I remember he taught me how to spell 'fetus': without the 'o'; apparently the 'o' was put there incorrectly by Isidore of Seville, who was a sixth or seventh century etymologist, and it stayed there for four centuries because nobody knew any better.

I do the typing on Fridays and I go home a little early because

I work through the lunch hour. I like Fridays: it's quiet, and it's awful to say so, but there aren't any patients to get in my way. I like some of them, but most of them I don't feel any great sympathy with.

I do respect Mr Jefferson, but in the end it's just a job. It suits me. Or rather, it did suit me when Becky was little, because then I worked part time and Mr Jefferson was very understanding about the days off I needed to take, when Becky was ill. After Gerald left there was only me to cope. I hadn't had a job since before I met Gerald, when I'd been working in an art gallery as a kind of general factotum – receptionist, saleswoman, plant waterer. I'd wandered from one thing to another after leaving school – a bit of art college, then a secretarial diploma, then the art gallery job. I never had any great vision of myself doing anything in particular. Some people are like that. We can't all be achievers or adventurers, can we?

Mother was seventy-two when Becky was born. She was living in France then with Maurice Rambeau, an art historian, but she consented to come over for the birth. I did want her there when the baby was born, though I was surprised in a way that I did. I suppose it was a bit of a shock, Gerald and I had been married for seven years, we hadn't ever taken any precautions, and I was quite taken aback to find myself pregnant at thirty. Mother had kept on asking why there was no baby: 'What did you get married for at twenty-three, if it wasn't to have children?' she'd demanded. And, 'Why aren't you doing anything with your life, if you don't intend to have any?'

It was nice being married to Gerald, it was a kind of excuse not to think about myself and What I Wanted to Do with My Life any more. Gerald was demanding enough for two of us. He was a writer. He'd wanted someone to organize life for him. I didn't mind, but I came to think of him as a child as well. I think that was one reason I wanted Mother there for the birth.

Rebecca was born at half past ten at night after a labour lasting most of that day. I didn't want to go into hospital, I'd never been in hospital in my life. So Rebecca was born in our flat in Kensington, the flat was in a house which always reminded me of the one in Noel Streatfeild's *Ballet Shoes*, bursting with talented little girls.

Mother arrived after breakfast on the day Becky was born

carrying a bag full of paperbacks and apples. We sat either side of the electric fire in the sitting room pretending to read while I endured the contractions. For once, Mother seemed more anxious than I was. 'I don't know much about this childbirth business,' she'd warned me. 'When you were born, I had a Caesarean. My doctor said I had a small pelvis,' (she seemed proud of this) 'so I don't remember anything. And then, when they brought you to me, of course I didn't recognize you!'

I only had a midwife for the actual birth. A capable woman, who wisely dispatched Gerald to his study. The birth was surprisingly easy. I felt pleased to see the little pink baby with its flapping fists and wet black hair. 'Did you want a daughter?' the midwife asked. 'Oh yes,' I said, though beforehand I'd only been aware of thinking how proud I would be to give birth to a boy. The child had odours of blood, of sweat, of the earth on her, which I don't normally much like, but on this occasion it seemed to be all right. But when I kissed her, I had a terrible sense of foreboding, I didn't know whether it was for myself or for the child. I remember trying to talk to Gerald about it afterwards: 'Don't be silly, Is; nothing awful will happen!' He was proud of her, proud of us.

So was Mother, who came to the door in an apron, summoned by the midwife to take a look at her granddaughter. She peered into Rebecca's face; 'Not like Gerald is she, thank God!'

'Mum!' I had to protest. But I didn't mind. Childbirth gave me for a moment a feeling of closeness with my mother: the union of women against men.

She'd prepared a meal for me then, which I'd been very glad of: scrambled eggs and salad and hot chocolate. The food tasted wonderful. But then she spoilt it all. I told her I'd made up a bed for her in Gerald's study, which should be comfortable enough.

But she said: 'Oh, I can't stay, darling, I must get back to Maurice! He doesn't like being alone at night.' I was shocked. This Frenchman, temporarily installed in a flat in Primrose Hill, had a greater claim on my mother than I did! Even now I can see Mother's self-satisfied face as she spoke of Maurice's reluctance to be without her. Going back to her Frenchman! Couldn't she leave men alone at all? It was surprising there hadn't been a man – or men – around at the end. I suppose the only reason was that all Mother's men were dead; she'd drained them of the energy they needed to outlive her.

I never know when I'm going to have to struggle against these thoughts about Mother. They seem to lead a life of their own, they just appear in my mind, and then I feel this terrible anger. I try not to, I feel guilty afterwards, but it's there all the same.

Biology. This problem of men. It was between me and Mother all our lives. I don't care to think about it. I'd rather think about the happier side of my own life with men. Gerald, in the period following Rebecca's birth: now, that was a happy time. Of course, I did all the work of looking after the baby, but I didn't mind, I understood how important it was for Gerald to go on writing. When he wasn't in his study, the three of us were together, a family. After Becky had started walking – which she did early, at ten months – we went on regular outings together, walking in Kensington Gardens, or in Hyde Park by the Serpentine, Becky in her very first pair of shoes – blue, made by Startrite in the same square shape as her own fat pearly feet. In the summers when she was one and two, Gerald walked beside her, or pretended to race her through the dry green grass, making her laugh compulsively at the heavy footed father beside her. Gerald enjoyed fatherhood – for a time. I enjoyed Gerald like that. But there were problems. After Becky was born, I hadn't wanted to make love; oh, I'd agreed to sometimes, because Gerald wanted it, but I didn't want it. I could have happily done without it altogether. I think most women can, if the truth be told: a baby is enough.

There were a few times in the early years of our marriage when we'd made love and I'd quite enjoyed it. I'd been able to relax: we'd been out for a pleasant dinner with wine, were on holiday, whatever. But even then sex made me feel quite panicky – panicky and empty, at the same time. What have I got to offer? Only an enclosure, an opening, a chance for someone else to relieve themselves into me. They might be grateful afterwards – though Gerald hadn't seemed to be, particularly, he used to leap off me after his own climax, as if with horror that he'd been there at all. No, I couldn't really suppose the activity would do *me* any good.

I'm clearly just one of those people who doesn't particularly care for sex. It doesn't bother me, except on the odd occasion when Mr Jefferson needs a chaperone, because he's got to do an internal examination on a woman who seems a little nervous, or perhaps flirtatious. He calls out to me then, 'Mrs Lennox, could you come in here for a moment?' and I always know straight away what he means. I go in, stand by the examination couch and try not to look. But the woman always seems to be looking at me when Mr Jefferson puts his hand up there.

I can't remember when I first became aware of the fact that Mother liked sex. Right back, when I was the age Rebecca had been when Gerald went, I'd assumed that the American Robert was my father. Of course, he didn't have the same name as my mother and me, but I had the same name as Mother which was what seemed to be important at the time. Robert came into and out of our lives all the time. He lived in Washington, but came frequently to London on business. Then he would stay with us as though he owned the place. I'd be sent to bed early, and my door would be closed, which normally it wasn't. I'd lie there listening to my mother and Robert laughing in the sitting room next to my bedroom. And then I'd hear their footsteps going upstairs.

I must have been about five when I found out. I'd brought home a painting from school, one of those bright splashy things, with unplanned lumps of dried powder paint on it, containing three figures, 'Mummy', 'Daddy' and 'Isobel'. I showed it to Mother proudly, but she frowned. 'I've got something to tell you, Izzy,' she said, 'I should have told you long ago.' She pulled me – I was a slight, wiry child – onto her knee. 'You like Robert, don't you?'

'Yes, of course I do. Why?'

'That's what I have to tell you, darling, Robert isn't really your father. He's very fond of you, naturally, but he isn't your father.'

'Who is my father, then?'

'Your father is a man called Evan Kargar. He's an anthropologist.'

'What's that?' I'd asked.

'A person who goes and lives in other countries and studies how different people live.'

'Is that where my father is now? In another country?'

'Yes, darling. That's where he is.'

It didn't make much difference, anyway, knowing that Robert wasn't my father. He was still there a lot of the time, he still behaved in a proprietorial way towards Mother. Much later, I uncovered the rest of the story: Robert had another family in Washington, a wife and two children, boys, of his own. For nine years he'd had a relationship with Mother, and all the time she'd known about his other family. As I got older, I became aware that a certain kind of dialogue was going on between Mother and Robert. They talked about jealousy a lot. Mother was jealous of Robert's wife, and Robert's wife was jealous of Mother, Robert was jealous of any other man who paid Mother any attention (and of me as well from time to time). The relationship ended when I was ten. Mother was very upset, but I couldn't really understand why. So Robert had let her down! So now she'd have to face life on her own. So what?

But Mother didn't want to face life on her own, and after we'd come back from a holiday in the States with Robert (which was the last time we saw him) she sent me away to stay with a friend. She did the most awful thing then: she swallowed pills and went into hospital. I was taken to see her a few days later, but all Mother did was cry. It was difficult for me to understand why a man mattered more to her than I did.

After she came out of hospital, Mother went on crying. She was often asleep in the morning when I went to school, but I didn't mind getting my own breakfast. I preferred it, really, to Mother fussing over me.

One Saturday afternoon, I heard Mother screaming and crying in her room. I went to find out what was going on. She was still wearing her apricot silk dressing gown, although it was four in the afternoon, and she was standing by the window cutting something up angrily into the wastepaper basket. She was cutting up photographs, at least the one I saw floating down into the wastepaper basket, of naked bodies against a background of creased white sheets. 'Bloody men! Why do they have to do this to me? Doesn't he understand what love is? Love, not fucking. Fucking is all he can think about!' She must have heard me open the door, and when I turned to go away, she ran after me, 'Izzy, Izzy, don't be upset, let me explain it to you, please . . .' But I didn't want anything explained. I didn't need anything explained, I was sure I would never be like my mother. Never! Never!

The memory makes me feel nauseous, even now, in Italy where I've come to put all this behind me. It makes me lean over the rail round the promontory as if I'm going to be sick. But my body remembers where it is just in time. I sink back into the creepers knitted onto the face of the wall, and allow my face to be touched by the sun. It isn't the brassy heat of August, but a calm concentrated end-of-season warmth that splays out over my skin. It's as though the sun itself is making love to me, but it's a caring kind of love, not a selfish and grasping one.

Movements in the leaves behind me make me suddenly spring away from the wall: there's a tiny lizard dashing through the red leaves, like a flash of lightning darting here and there – the more obstacles it encounters, a twig, some berries, a gap in the stone, the more it races. It makes me laugh, its scurrying such a comment on my – the human – condition: to travel is not better than to arrive. But sometimes there simply isn't any destination.

I walk back to the villa, and go into the reading room, *The Times* is three days out of date, it carries horrific pictures of the fire at King's Cross station. As I settle into the white arm chair by one of the tall windows, imagining that conflagration, Professor Goldman lowers his own newspaper, 'Good morning, Mrs Lennox. And how are you today? I hope we didn't keep you awake last night. I'm afraid bridge brings out the worst in my wife sometimes.'

'I didn't hear a thing, I can assure you.'

He folds the paper and lays it solicitously on the inlaid marble table. 'You don't play bridge, Mrs Lennox?'

'I don't play games at all,' I reply, and then, realizing that might sound rude, I try to smile at him, but he doesn't notice.

'This is an unusual experience for us,' reflects Goldman, obscurely. 'Caroline and I rarely get uninterrupted time together. To play bridge, to walk, take trips – there are some wonderful trips to be taken round here, Mrs Lennox. Have you been to Como? Or Locarno? Or to Venice? Caroline says she simply won't leave Italy without seeing the *Last Supper* in Milan.

She's been doing a course on the old masters at the New York Museum of Art.'

'That's nice for her.'

'What do you do with yourself during the day, Mrs Lennox? Back in London, I mean.'

'I work.' I say the word quite fiercely.

'Don't we all?'

No we don't, I think.

'What kind of work do you do, Mrs Lennox?'

'I work for a doctor.'

'How interesting. Doing research?'

'No, I'm a secretary.'

Goldman's face registers disappointment, but he's quick to switch this expression off. 'I have a wonderful secretary. Couldn't manage without her. She makes all the important decisions. Caroline at home, Nancy at work: good women run the world don't they? Ah, Mrs Dichter!'

Carla Dichter, armed with a tall campari, crosses the scarlet carpet. Goldman pats the white linen seat beside him, but Mrs Dichter deviates towards the compact disc player: 'Let's have some music, shall we? Any preferences?' I don't mind, I say.

'How about the Goldberg Variations?' suggests Goldman. 'I noticed they have the early Glenn Gould performance.'

'No, for such a beautiful day we should have something more lyrical, don't you think?' Mrs Dichter flicks a disc into the player and stands back while Gershwin's *Rhapsody in Blue* unexpectedly bursts into the room. I can't help noticing her wrists, which are exceptionally thin, and seem to fold back on themselves like hinges.

When she sits down next to him with her campari, John Goldman realizes he needs a drink too, and goes off to get a whisky. 'Can I get anything for you, Mrs Lennox? A grappa perhaps?'

He must have noticed me last night. 'Not at lunchtime, thanks, but I'll have a glass of white wine, if they have any.'

'I'm sure they do.'

'He's a little overwhelming, isn't he?' says Mrs Dichter when Goldman's out of the room.

'Just a little.'

'And patronizing.'

'Yes.' I grin. 'He doesn't approve of secretaries. Though he depends on them.'

'I heard that.'

'Well, I'm not going to be defensive about what I do,' I say. 'It's a job. I have to work for a living.' I mean it, as well.

'Me too. I teach at the university. Philosophy.' She tosses her long hair back to remove it from the vicinity of the campari.

'Your husband's a poet, isn't he?'

'He is.'

'Do they mix?'

'I'm sorry?'

'Poetry and philosophy.'

She sets her empty glass down on the table and crosses her legs a couple of times. 'Well, they are, of course, the antithesis of one another. Philosophers intellectualize life, turn it into a logical construction. Poets are interested in the opposite – in deconstruction. We have some healthy arguments, yes.' She does seem to use a lot of long words.

'What would marriage be without an argument?' Goldman comes back into the room obtrusively, and gives me my wine. 'I always tell Caroline I only married her for the fights.'

For some reason, the mention of fights makes me think I should phone Becky. Just to see how she is.

'Hallo, Mother, how are you?'

'I'm fine, darling. Can you hear me properly? This isn't a good line.'

'It's okay my end. Why are you calling?'

I'm always taken aback by Becky's directness. My daughter forces me to say things most people would have taken for granted. 'I'm just calling to find out how things are, dear.'

'Well, they're exactly the same as they were when you left, Mother. You've only been gone four days.'

'Are you eating all right, dear?'

'You left enough food in the fridge to feed an army.'

I thought comfortingly of the boxes and packets I'd stored on the freezer shelves to fill my daughter's stomach: vegetable pies, frozen lasagne, prawn curries, broccoli, spinach, raspberries, chocolate ice cream, wholewheat bread, extra butter. 'Don't forget your hydrocortisone cream, Becky.' My mind leaps up a metre to the tube of cream hidden among the eggs on the inside of the refrigerator door.

'No, Mother, I won't. But you know I don't have eczema at this time of year. Don't worry, Mother. I thought you wanted to get away from everything. I'll call you if I need anything, okay?'

Her self-composure is crushing. When I've finished speaking to my daughter, I feel more worried than before I called. I haven't after all asked the questions I really want to ask: do you have anorexia, Becky? Are you taking the pill? Have you been to your classes today? What do you think of me, really? But Becky's right, it *is* a relief to be away.

4

I knew it was her. She always rings me when she's away, though I tell her not to. But she never says what she wants to say, only asks about food and stuff like that. As if I minded having the house to myself. I know she thinks I'm doing all sorts of awful things, filling the sink with filthy saucepans and the house with heroin addicts and AIDS carriers, holding catastrophic parties, but the only person who's here most of the time is Mary, and my Mother even likes Mary.

I've never understood why mothers are so suspicious. At least, in that respect, my mother is like everybody else's. Like Mary's mother, for example. I admire Mary's mother, she's a crazy woman, she's always running around doing thousands of things – she has a job in a museum arranging exhibitions, she's mad about that, and then she has Mary and Mary's two sisters and her father. Her father's mad, too. I go round to their house a lot because it's so different from mine. Mum likes everything to be organized, she gets upset when it isn't, and I don't keep the rules all the time. It isn't a phase, either (my mother's favourite word) – it's just *me*.

Mary doesn't have the same problem with her mother as I have. Of course, her mother wants to know what she's doing all the time, but she's not inquisitorial about it. She trusts Mary. My mother doesn't trust me. Oh, I know she's had a difficult life, what with my father skiving off when I was three and leaving her without a penny, and her having to work all those years in that boring job for that awful Mr Jefferson, and having that hysterical mother of her own – but how much sympathy can you give someone for something that's basically their own fault?

That's the main difference between us, my mother and I. She

thinks she's a victim, and I think she brought it on herself. I think we all do – the mess I got myself in a while ago, for instance, that was my fault, I don't blame it on her. If I blame it on her, then I sink back into this huge morass of self-pity, don't I, and that's no help to me at all.

My mother's speciality is worrying. She thinks if she worries about something enough it won't happen. Unfortunately, that's not the answer – if it were can you imagine how easy everything would be? We'd all sit back in our little nuclears and worry about the big nuclears and everything would be alright.

I've felt the burden of my mother's worry all my tender young life. Like the polluted air, it's stunted my growth – the little green shoot got diverted and hardened, it reached out for other parts of the sky where it had a chance of breathing freely, but all for nothing. Dear Mum. You can't help but admire her determination – nothing stops her certainty that I am something to worry about. Of course what happened was that I gave her reasonable grounds for her unreasonable anxiety. Nothing very bad, not at first. A gentle suggestive untidiness in my room, for example. I used to be quite a neat little girl, and then these piles of used clothes and fungoid coffee: what did they mean? Not a lot, but I suppose they could have done. I started eating, too. My favourite place was in front of the refrigerator staring into it. The odd thing was, however full it was, it wasn't full enough for me. That's still true now – when my mother goes away, she goes to the supermarket and buys all this stuff she thinks I like and crams it in there. Usually I take it out and throw it away just before she comes home. I don't want to have a row about it. 'Becky, you haven't eaten anything! What have you been eating?' I can't bear her wittering away about the really trivial things.

She used to mutter on about how she'd like to send me to a private school. As if that were the solution! My school used to be a girls' grammar, anyway, it had kept some of the private school habits, which is why she chose it in the first place. She says she believes in state education, my mother, but I've noticed that a number of her generation say one thing and do another. I've heard it said that one shouldn't sacrifice one's children on the altar of a principle. Why not? I would. What are principles if they're not things to make sacrifices for? My mother couldn't afford a private school, anyway, not off what Mr Jefferson pays her. She could have got a better job, of course: she could have done something about herself, got herself a proper education, some more qualifications, she could have been ambitious for herself, but she never was. Poor downtrodden old Isobel. That's how she wanted everyone to think of her. My antics helped. She could point to them and say look what Becky's doing to me now, what have I done to deserve this? The sins of the mothers are visited on the daughters, Mother. In any case, the world's hardly a fair place. You're always telling *me* that.

I did get awfully bored with school. I came round to the view that schools are there as obstacles to learning. While we were being made to grapple with trigonometry or Jane Austen, there was a revolution in Cuba or wherever, women in China were being shot for wanting more than one baby, there were famines, other ecological disasters, including the ozone layer, but what did we learn of this? Absolutely nothing. I saw an advertisement in the *New Statesman* one day – I bought it as an antidote to all that romantic teenage stuff and to annoy my mother, but I only read the ads at the back. I saw this one for volunteer help in the office of a new, as it turned out, totally unsuccessful, revolutionary party – they were against meat eating, and a number of other things, possibly people as well. The office was in Hanwell. I used to go there and leaflet the local semis. Not because I thought they'd get converted, but because it made me feel important, as though I were *doing* something. The office was smoky and full of cardboard boxes and run by a superannuated hippie called Virginia, who wore long outdated Moroccan skirts. I lied about my age, said I was seventeen. They didn't care anyway. It didn't bother them who I was, where I came from, they weren't into responsibility at all.

I got Mary to come as well. For a while. Our school reports got worse and worse. And then, at the end of the term, when the parents came to talk to the teachers, they told my mother they hardly ever saw me. But where is she? said my mother. We don't know, said the teachers – why don't you know, you're her mother! To be fair, Mrs Rogers did try to see my point of view once, but it was a pretty feeble attempt. She said to me, pseudo-cosiness oozing out of every pore on her Helena Rubinstein face, 'It must be hard for you, Rebecca, having only one parent.'

'Not particularly,' I said. 'I have enough trouble with one, I can't imagine what having two would be like.'

The worst thing about all this was that my mother wasn't angry. She tried to be so bloody understanding. You know, Rebecca's little rebellion, it's just a phase she's going through, it hasn't been easy for her having no father around. The same line as old Bodger-Rogers. Then she said perhaps I needed to see someone? I didn't know what she meant at first. I thought it was an apparition or something. She meant a head shrinker. That's the solution of her generation, isn't it? To hire experts to listen to their petty little traumas. As if it made anything better. It just lets people feel more sorry for themselves, and it serves the additional suspect purpose of keeping another profession in business. You scratch my back and I'll scratch yours.

The crunch came when I landed up in Hanwell police station. My mother particularly didn't appreciate that. It sent her into a wild rage and naturally (but wrongly) she thought it meant I was committing all sorts of other transgressions as well.

Mary and I had been out doing a housing estate in W13. It was a sunny evening, we didn't feel like going home, so we bought some Wimpys and sat by the canal. It stank, and so did we: we weren't fond of washing at that time. 'This is all very tame stuff, isn't it?' said Mary.

'You're right. Let's do something a little wilder.' We went back to the office; I'd remembered noticing a can or two of paint at the back. Purple and green, real revolutionary colours. We lugged them back to one of the more middle class streets, where there was a good stretch of wall, by a C of E primary school, and we waited for it to get dark, meanwhile giggling a lot and consuming two cans of light beer. Then we inscribed 'Abolish Schools' on the wall, plus 'Education is the Opium of the Parents.' We were quite proud of ourselves for constructing this one. Unfortunately, the constabulary were passing at the time and saw fit to take us in to the local nick, giving us a bad fright as well as a cup of tea.

My mother took badly to being phoned by the police. I asked if I could do it instead, as she needed the news breaking gently, but this apparently wasn't one of my civil liberties. I only heard the sergeant's end of the conversation and I saw him hold the receiver a good distance from his ear, after the preliminary 'Mrs

Lennox? This is Sergeant Daly speaking from Hanwell police station, we have your daughter Rebecca here . . .'

She came to get me in a taxi, looking quite white, but only moaning about the cost of the taxi fare, and then being unduly polite and apologetic to the uniformed brigade. When we got home, she took me by the shoulders, 'Now, Rebecca,' she said – she always calls me Rebecca when she wants my attention or when she's cross with me – 'you must tell me the truth, I don't care what it is, but you must tell me the truth!'

Well, I knew *she* wasn't telling the truth. Of course she cared. If I'd been on hard drugs or having it off with some boy on the banks of the canal, of course she would've cared. But as it happened I hadn't been. All I'd been responsible for were a few graffiti. I told her that, I just said in a very self-controlled fashion, but Mother I only painted a few letters on a wall, I only skipped a bit of school. That's all I did. But she screamed at me, 'Rebecca, I've had enough! You're doing this to spite me, aren't you!' I wasn't, of course. I was doing it because I wanted to. I couldn't help it that she didn't like it, could I? I kept saying, but I'm not doing anything really bad. I'm not on drugs, I'm not screwing anybody (not at the moment), I'm not nicking things from Woolworths. But she didn't listen. She was somewhere inside her own fury about something that didn't have a great deal to do with me.

'You're lying, Rebecca, you're lying to me. You're making a fool of me, I'll never forgive you for this. After all I've done for you, you're doing this to me!'

What had she done? She'd looked after me when I was a kid, yes, but presumably she wanted to have me, didn't she? Why should I be grateful for that? She chose to be a mother. She chose to have all these worries and responsibilities, I didn't ask her to.

Myself, I'm never going to have children. I'm thinking of getting myself sterilized. The whole idea of children nauseates me. Not sex: sex doesn't worry me, not the way it apparently does my mother. In the whole time I've known her, which is the whole of my life, I've never known my mother have anything to do with men. Now I think that's really unnatural. She never ever delivered any facts of life speech to me. Not before I became acquainted with them, or after, for that matter.

My Dad did once. After he left us, I used to see him. Quite regularly for a long time, then he went to live in America when I was thirteen. He runs an arty magazine in Detroit, of all places. Since then I've only seen him a few times. His new wife didn't want to have me out there, and I don't blame her really. She went and had two little American boys of her own. She's called Pansie. Or maybe it's spelt with a 'y'.

It was just before he left the country. He took me out to dinner. Nothing posh. A fish and chip restaurant near Baker Street. He knew what I liked, he wasn't about to stuff all kinds of fancy material into me. I was in the middle of my skate when he said, 'Listen, Becky, there's something I want to say, you probably won't know what to make of it at the moment, but I don't know when I'll have another chance to say it, so I'd like to get it in now. Perhaps you'll just let me say it, and you can store it up in that clever little head of yours and make sense of it later.'

I went on eating. When adults say these things to you the best thing to do in my experience is to go on chewing.

'I'm sorry, Becky,' my father said, 'I'm sorry my marriage to your mother didn't work out. I especially don't want you to think I didn't love her. I did love her. I thought she was the calmest, most wonderful, most sensible person I'd ever met. Our first few years were very happy. But then by the time you were born I'd begun to realize there was something missing from the marriage. There was something your mother couldn't give me, something I needed. Passion, Becky. She had no passion.'

Well, of course I knew what he meant immediately. My mother is quite a frightened person. Anyone can see that. Fear stops her from feeling things. Or when feeling does get the better of her, like when she got hold of me after the episode in Hanwell police station, she can't deal with that either, she's really totally shaken up by it.

'Sex, Becky,' my father said. 'It was sex your mother couldn't stand. I tried to be gentle with her, I was careful, I was understanding, but in the end it didn't make any difference. She didn't want me, you see. Oh, she wanted to be married to me, she wanted the status, she wanted the escape, she wanted to share things, she wanted me to be her friend, she even wanted to talk to me, but she didn't want my body. It wasn't enough for me. I am a man, Becky. I have the natural feelings of men. I need a proper outlet for them.'

I didn't know where to put my eyes while this was being said to me. I think I appreciated him saying it – the impulse behind the confession, that is. He was being a bit over-confessional; relieving his own guilt, spilling it like vinegar over the fish and chips. I wasn't sure about the outlet bit, though. Even then I think I suspected men needed to think more about inlets and less about outlets.

'It's okay, Dad,' I said, trying to be reassuring. I felt he needed some reassurance at this difficult time in his life. 'It's okay: I forgive you.' And I put down my knife and fork and looked at him.

'Do you, Becky?'

It sounded grand, didn't it: I forgive you. I wasn't sure why I'd said those words then. I remember I was reading *Wuthering Heights* at the time, and I was full of Cathy and Heathcliff and it seemed a very Cathy-type thing to say: I forgive you, Heathcliff! My father wasn't Heathcliff, but I guess he was a kind of Heathcliff figure for me. Any absent father is. It's hard on the mother, though. She doesn't get a chance to grow in stature through absence. She's the one doing all the work and getting all the shit, while God the father's off having a good time.

Recently, though, I started to understand this thing about forgiveness. It seems to me kind of important that we should forgive our parents. First of all, for having us, which was probably a mistake. Secondly, for everything they did wrong, which was a lot. After that, what can you say? You need to forgive so you can stop blaming them for everything. Of course it was their fault – most immediately, that is, but not before that. Layers of responsibility. Like one of those *mille feuille* cakes: leaf upon leaf of incredibly thin pastry with all this sicky creamy stuff in between. You go through all the layers right down to the bottom one which is always much more solid than the rest, and there are the original sins of our forefathers, not to mention our foremothers.

Anyway, I said to my mother that day she got hold of me and accused me of lying, I said, 'You have to trust me, Mum. I'm telling you the truth.'

But she just started crying. 'Oh Becky, I can't cope with this! Please don't do this to me.' I wasn't doing anything. Not compared to what I did later. You see: my mother wasn't right about me then, but you know what suspicion does, it's infectious. If you live with someone who's forever questioning your behaviour, you can't help becoming devious yourself. After that incident, my mother almost didn't want to know what was happening to me. She didn't pick up the clues that I left around for her to see. I think she wanted to be alone with her worry in order to derive the maximum benefit from it.

I'm all right now, I've got it sorted in my head, but from fourteen to about seventeen I did do some fairly wild things. Parties, hash – never anything more than hash – boys, never anything more than boys! I never got into men. There aren't many of them where I live. I used to take money from my mother's purse to finance this lifestyle, that was one of the things she didn't notice. She didn't see the hash I grew in my room, either – well, she saw it, she asked me what it was, and I said it was an experiment we were doing in botany. 'Oh, how interesting.' She wasn't interested, except that the answer I gave sounded okay. As a matter of fact, we didn't do botany at my school, she should have known that.

It died anyway. It was about that time that I asked her to stop coming in my room. She was always poking around in there when I was out. It did get pretty shitty, I admit that, but so what? I never had her obsession about cleanliness. Fortunately. I used to think she'd pour a bottle of bleach over me if she could – it kills all known germs, and the ones she knew about were quite enough to warrant hydrochloric action.

By the time I was fifteen I had established the routine of lying in bed all day smoking, reading sweaty novels, and being rude to everyone who came near me, except Mary. Mary didn't go as far as I did with this performance, after a while she started going back to school. Both of us had grown somewhat disenchanted with the Hanwell Central Revolutionary Committee. Especially when we found out Virginia wrote slushy novels under a pseudonym to finance her Moroccan dressbuying. Mary's parents didn't make such a fuss about her little deviations. So she could afford to mend her ways. With my mother, though, it had got blown up into such a thing: I couldn't possibly give her the pleasure of toeing the line again.

There I was then, lazy, uneducated, and rather on the large side. Naturally I failed my exams. Except for history. I got an 'A' for that. I always think a historical perspective is so important.

Mother read all these books about eating disorders in young women, how it was all to do with a rejection of feminine identity. It didn't help her much, though, because I went on doing it. I'd be there in the kitchen stuffing my face with anything I could get hold of – bread, cake, tomatoes, cold baked beans, chocolate – and she'd be standing next to me trying to look sympathetic. I must say I do think parents are pretty pathetic the way they reach for a book when they can't handle their own children. The books are written by people who can't handle their own children either. That's why they write them. In fact, when you think about it, there's a huge industry in kids with so-called problems: somebody's making a lot of money out of us.

One of the things my mother said (she got it out of a book) was that I was getting fat so that boys wouldn't like me. I was surprised she couldn't see it didn't work like that. There were lots of boys around, there were some nice ones and some who were out for an easy screw, and some who were both. Why should a bit of excess weight put them off? I was still pretty – even I knew that.

She got the boys out of proportion too. I did sleep around a bit, but I always made them wear condoms, and when I'd done that for a while, I thought, right I know what that's like, I can move onto the next thing. I was careful not to leave evidence around of my doings during this period. For instance, I never asked any of them to the house. When I went out to meet them down the street, in the pub, wherever, I knew she was up there lining the curtains in her bedroom seeing what she could see.

When I went to see the old lady in hospital we had a conversation about that.

'How are you, Rebecca?' she asked, squinting at me from her white bed with her grey mess of hair all squashed out round her. 'You haven't been to see me, you naughty girl.'

Just like my mother. Why haven't you done this or that, not, look, you've actually done something right, for once. Why don't they understand it would help if just once in a while they made a positive remark?

'I don't know, Granny,' I said. 'I suppose I didn't come to see you because I didn't want to.'

She chuckled. 'That's right, Rebecca, speak your mind.'

It was horrible in that hospital. Like a factory: rows and rows of beds, awful iron things with the paint flaking off them, and the walls a dingy green, and these spotty nurses, with clumpy black shoes and hats like the paper they put on pork chops, clattered around endlessly with trays of metallic objects. I don't know why my mother put her there. Well, I know why, she didn't want to look after her: but we could have had her, she could have had my room, I could have slept in the sitting room, it wouldn't have been for long. Mum could have given up work for a bit – she's got all this money from the old lady now, so it wouldn't have mattered doing without Mr Jefferson's handout for a while.

'Why didn't you want to come and see me, Rebecca?' Nobody told me the old lady's mind was still working – it was cracking away like an expensive hi-fi.

I decided to tell the truth. When someone's dying, that's when you should come out with it, isn't it? 'I don't like old people, Granny,' I said, 'and I don't like the way my mother goes on and on about you. It just makes me think I don't want to have anything to do with any of it.'

'Hmm.' She was frowning at me from her nest of sterilized cotton. There didn't seem to be a lot of her left, she looked all shrunken, as if she was about to waste away into the mattress.

'So your mother complains about me, does she?' She sniffed and pulled a craggy hand from under the covers to give her nose a cross kind of tweak. I was worried, I thought she might break it off altogether.

Was she trying to make me feel guilty? There you are, if you tell the truth, they tell you off for that as well.

I decided to defend my mother for a change. 'It's not easy for Mum,' I said, 'she's caught between the two of us, isn't she? She feels responsible for both of us, but she's like a fish out of water, she doesn't really know what she ought to be doing.' I was quite proud of this speech, actually, it wasn't a bad analysis of the situation.

The old lady studied me thoughtfully, and while she was doing this, a nurse came over and shouted in her left ear, 'Have you moved your bowels today, Mrs Kargar?'

'It's none of your bloody business what I've done with my bowels,' she said, cackling. 'My bowels are not hospital property, contrary to what you might imagine.'

I couldn't help admiring her spirit. The nurse tried to exchange a knowing look with me, but my knowledge was different from hers.

'Well, Rebecca,' said my grandmother eventually, 'I don't think that I feel that sorry for your mother. She made her own bed. Now she must lie on it. We all must. I even must lie on this one.' She glanced round her in a cheerless way. 'She's not like me, you know,' she remarked then. 'Unfortunately, she's like her father. Which, fortunately, you are not.' I didn't know quite what she was getting at. 'Men aren't an awful lot of good as fathers in my experience,' she said offhandedly.

'No, I can see that.'

'But they are good for some things.' That laughter again. 'Are you a virgin, Rebecca?' The sharp grey eyes were watching me with a smile in them somewhere.

'No, Granny.'

'That's right,' she said. 'Get on with life. It's what Isobel never did. Tell me,' she went on, not bothering to lower her voice, 'tell me, Rebecca, do you like big men or small ones?'

I didn't know where to put myself then. I moved closer to her. 'Shush, Granny, everyone can hear!' I was surprised at my own embarrassment, I like to think of myself as someone who isn't bothered by these things.

'Well, I don't know,' she said vaguely. 'Perhaps not.' Her eyes wandered. Then they came back to me again. 'Do you think your mother loves me, Rebecca? Does she love me at all?'

She closed her eyes wearily. I didn't know how to answer that question. 'Of course she does, Granny.' That must be what she wanted to hear.

'Not of course, Rebecca,' the words hissed out from between almost closed lips. 'But never mind. I'm not being fair, am I? To you Rebecca. You're the future, I want you to do well. I'm not coming out of here, you know. I've come in here to die.'

I didn't say anything. Did she want me to contradict her? It was all getting a bit heavy. I thought I might go soon.

'So I want to give you something, Rebecca. It's in the bedside locker. Open it, please.'

I opened the stained brown door of her locker. There was a pile of things in there: shawls, slippers, perfume, folded night-dresses, some plums giving off a nasty sweet smell.

'At the bottom, Rebecca, there's a black zip case. Take it out.'

I did. 'Those are my diaries,' she said in a tone worthy of important announcements. 'I want you to have them. I want you to know about me. I didn't start them till after Isobel was born. Read them when you want to. I don't mind if your mother knows. But I did want to give them to you, Rebecca.'

'Thank you, Granny.' I held the case close to my chest. It was very bulky, there must have been a lot of words in there.

Her eyes were still shut. She could have been asleep. And then she started talking again. 'Mothers and daughters, Rebecca. The same flesh, we're the same, we come out of each other, but it doesn't help, does it? We're trapped. Because we don't have any power. Everything else can change, but *we* don't: we fight against one another, we're pains to each other all our lives. We're so busy looking at one another, measuring ourselves against each other, saying I'm not like her, or I am, my God, how awful, that we can't see anything else. Nothing else at all.'

She was exhausted. She opened her eyes and saw me looking at her holding her diaries like a baby. 'Oh, Rebecca! Kiss me, Rebecca! Please!'

Why did she have to go and spoil it by making me kiss her? I leant over and kissed her on her forehead. That was the best I could manage.

5

At breakfast Mr Simons talks about the book he's writing; he says he's come to the conclusion that the anger and conflict in some relationships only comes out in dreams. So I mention the dream I had about my daughter Rebecca last night. We're standing in the kitchen at home. I'm angry with her about something. I'm standing very close to her, very close to her face looking into her eyes — her eyes are huge and dark and very frightened — but there's such an expression of horror in them, I've never seen anything like it. The awful thing is, I know the reason for it, it's because I've been attacking her.

I only have muesli for breakfast and a white buttered roll. Professor Goldman comes in from running, as he does every morning, you can practically see the sweat on his track suit. He sits down next to me and says, 'I didn't mean to sound patronizing in our conversation yesterday, Mrs Lennox. I hope you didn't think I was.'

'Don't worry, Professor Goldman, I'm used to people thinking I ought to have done something different with my life. Where is your wife, by the way? Is she not joining us for breakfast?'

'Ah, no. Caroline gets her beauty sleep in the mornings. I'll wake her later. She's not the best companion before ten or so, though I say it myself.'

When Professor Goldman leaves the room to wake his sleeping beauty, Mrs Dichter says to me in a lowered voice, 'Mrs Goldman is unable to get up in the morning for another reason, you do realize that, don't you?'

'No. What reason is that?'

'Haven't you noticed how much she drinks?' I haven't. 'She's not happy, that one.'

'Well, would you be, married to Professor Know-All?'

Mrs Dichter laughs. She goes to the library after breakfast, claiming that even on holiday she gets withdrawal symptoms if away from books for too long. The dining room is empty then, except for myself and Mr Simons. He gets up and walks over to the window. The white bowl of the lake, spun about with maypole ribbons of mist, is framed in the white curtains. 'See how beautiful it is,' he observes. 'Each morning is different. But this view is also always the same, it's been here more or less like this for many hundreds of years. Doesn't it give you the feeling that nothing bad could ever happen at the Villa Cellini?'

I think about the dream again. I felt Becky's bones – she's very thin, now. I had her collar-bone under my hand and it was like a pigeon's. I could feel her ribs. I had this image of a skeleton, the sort medical students learn from, or which dangle in cupboards in films about ghosts. I think I wanted to kill her. She threatens me, she won't do what I want. She leads a wild life. I don't know what goes on in her head. I wanted to crush her to pieces, I wanted to take that body – that body which came out of me – and crush it into a pile of splinters, fragments of bone, I didn't want to see her standing there any more.

That afternoon we go on a boat for a miniature tour of the lake. Gina Lucca says it'll be cold on the boat, so I wear two extra sweaters under my coat, and take my mohair cap in my handbag.

When we chug off across the silver lake I feel it's a sacrilege to disturb its smooth surface for such a lowly purpose – tourism. 'Of course it's the deepest lake in the world,' booms out Professor Goldman. I go to the back of the boat to avoid him, and find Mr Moore taking photographs of the shore. He's leaning over the edge, and a lock of hair keeps getting in his way as he tries to position his camera – why doesn't he cut it, it must be a constant irritation? He tells me he detests being a tourist, but he does have an excuse none of the rest of us have, as he uses photographs for his paintings.

'So this is art, not tourism?'

He lets his camera fall on the end of its leather strap. 'That's right.' I notice he has incredibly long dark lashes round his blue-black eyes. He also speaks very slowly as though overcoming some speech impediment. I have the odd thought that if I were younger, I might find him quite attractive.

'Do you use oils?'

'Watercolours. Colours like water.' He grips the rail and stares hard at something in the distance.

'And you make a living from it?'

'I do. Isn't that remarkable?'

'I didn't mean to suggest . . .'

'I'm sure you didn't. I meant it *is* remarkable that people find enough in my paintings to want to possess them permanently. It's not a drive I admire particularly,' he adds.

'What isn't?'

'The drive to possess. All this for instance' – he indicates the platinum water flowing into the recesses of the mountains, the creamy light falling free from the sky, the vegetation, every leaf and berry and flower – 'we see this and we want to own it, we want to take it home with us, we want to possess it. Why? We should leave it alone, Mrs Lennox, we should leave it alone. It's our privilege to be allowed to look at it once in a lifetime. That should be enough.'

'I agree with you. But Mr Moore . . .'

'Dan,' he says.

'Dan.' I don't feel right using his first name. 'But why, then, do you want to paint it? Surely you have the same motive of possession?'

'Not at all.' He changes his position abruptly to face me, so the camera swings on its strap and nearly hits me. 'No, that's not it at all. When I paint I don't try to put down what is really here. How could I do that? How could I know? All I can paint is what I see. It's *my* representation. Only mine. I do it for myself.'

While we talk the coast speeds by. Cove upon cove of pastel-coloured houses, stepped up the sides of the hills like bricks in a children's game. I leave Mr Moore to his photographs, and find a place at the front of the boat where I can look straight ahead and think of myself heading out to the open sea.

Mr Simons comes up beside me, shivering. Without thinking, I take my mohair cap out of my handbag. 'Here, have this.' He pulls it down over the bald top of his head, his fringe of hair, his ears. He looks like a moose, very funny.

'See!' he points.

'What was that?'

'Oh, just another mountain. Probably not the tallest in the world. I don't know why,' he says cautiously, looking around him carefully in case someone's listening, 'I don't know why he needs to impress everyone all the time like that. It isn't as though he isn't clever. So what is he trying to tell us?'

'I can hear the Goldmans through my bedroom wall at night,' I tell him, 'they talk for hours.'

'And every time he laughs the tapestry on the wall loses some of its colour! Is he laughing at her?'

'No.' I see Caroline Goldman suddenly as a tragic figure, following her husband round the world, admiring his work, laughing at his jokes, washing his underpants. I haven't had to do that sort of thing for a man for a long time. When I did it for Gerald I did it out of love. Once the love had gone, when Gerald took it away with him, he took my duties off with him, too. 'He wouldn't laugh at her, he's too dependent on her.'

'I expect you're right.'

'Look! We're stopping. Where are we?'

Gina Lucca says: 'Could you please meet back here in half an hour? We have three more places to call at before sunset.'

I walk off in the general direction of what I assume is the centre of the village. I hear Goldman tell his wife, 'Queen Victoria of England stayed here in 1839, two years after she took the throne. She signed the hotel register as "the Countess of Clare".'

The village is deserted. Tall houses border steep alleys which draw one away from the water; there are flowers in window-boxes and washing strung between the houses. It's a little disturbing to see such disorder after the perfection of the Villa Cellini. I stop to look in a shop window mounted with silver and gold jewellery.

'They're pretty, aren't they?' Mrs Dichter peers through the glass, her aristocratic nose almost touching it. 'But at first I thought they were antiques.'

'They are, or some of them are.' I point out the antique rings to her – I'm surprised she doesn't know – and catch a wave of the scent *Ma Griffe*, that Becky uses. I feel suddenly faint at its musty, concealing adolescent odour and almost fall, but put out a hand to steady myself. I'm convinced Mrs Dichter's noticed, but she doesn't say anything.

'Do you like it here, Mrs Lennox?'

'Oh yes. And you?'

'I think it's wonderful. I came here as a child, so I have some vague memories of it.'

'You must be the only one of us who's been here before.'

'I think so. When I came there were few tourists here, mostly Italians, very upper class families.'

'Has the place itself changed much?'

'It's more commercial, of course. There are many more hotels. Have you seen the one along the waterfront that's being renovated?'

'The large yellow building?'

'That's where I stayed. As a child. I was brought here by my nanny − nanny is the right word? The woman who looked after me.'

'What about your parents?'

'My parents were too busy. I had been sick a lot that winter. They said, take Carla to the lake, the air will do her good.'

'And did it?'

She shakes her head gently. 'Airs, waters, places − yes, they can make things better for a while, I guess. I remember she − my nanny − used to tell me these stories about things that had happened here in the past. One in particular I remember, about an American heiress who left her husband and came here with a gypsy violinist. They rented a chalet and walked naked in the garden. Sometimes they took a big boat on the lake, and it was decorated with oriental rugs and leopard skins. He played his violin. I suppose she looked at him lovingly in the moonlight.' She sighs. 'I didn't actually want to come away now. But Hugo needed to get away. Poetry is different from philosophy − I need people to talk to, he doesn't.'

'Or men are different from women.' I'm surprised to hear myself say that.

'You could be right, Mrs Lennox.'

Our final stop is a little fishing village the other side of the promontory from the villa. From the harbour wall, you can see fish in the water; huge black ones, some smaller grey ones. I feel that if I just dip my hand over the edge, one of them will pop up and put its shiny head right into it. What odd images I keep having! Mr Simons says they're trout.

'Do you fish?'

'In London? God no. Only for souls!' The bad joke, modelled on the Americans, has to be laughed at.

We steam noisily across the lake. There are threads of pink behind the mountains and in the water. I feel at peace, glad to be here on this Italian boat, even glad to be sitting next to a psychoanalyst who's wearing my mohair hat. It's all very strange, not like me at all, but that doesn't seem to matter.

On the Friday, Susie Moore asks me if I'd like to come and see their apartment; they have a set of rooms down by the water-front, with a studio for Mr Moore to work in.

On impulse, as I'm leaving my room, I go back and pull a bright green scarf out of a drawer and tie it round my hair, admiring the effect in the slightly tarnished mirror. I like the way I look – spring-like, hopeful.

I find the place easily, and knock on the door. Susie comes to it, smiling. It's like visiting a neighbour at home, Susie will give me a cup of coffee, we'll pass an hour or so talking about nothing in particular. There is, indeed, a pot of coffee percolating on the stove. Susie opens another door. 'Here, here's the studio.' We stand at the top of another flight of steps looking down into a wide spacious room, full of light, with two long tables across the middle, on one of which Mr Moore is working. There's a pile of photographs and another of glass slides.

'Come in, Isobel. You said you wanted to see my paintings. Now's your chance.' I go down the steps and look at five or six pastel watercolours pinned to the wall on larger sheets of white paper. They have an almost feminine delicacy, reminding me of some of Mother's illustrations for a series of children's books featuring, as far as I remember, fairies and pale blue hydrangeas.

'I like these,' I tell him. 'They have a relaxing effect on me. I think you should recommend them to New York businessmen as a cure for hypertension.' We laugh. I'm even amused myself.

Susie and I go into the sitting room, which is much darker and has a large green plant in it. We drink our coffee.

'I've been finding out a lot about this place, Mrs Lennox,' she confides. 'You know, it has a fascinating history. For a long time

– from 1520 when the original house was built, to 1927 – it was owned by the same family, the Cellinis. A lot of history happened here.' Her young face is lit by this knowledge. 'And then, in 1927, there were no more descendants. The family was wiped out by syphilis.' A flicker of distaste might have passed across my face, which Susie must have seen, for then she says, 'not a nice thought, is it? The scourge of Venus . . .'

'What happened to the villa, after that?' I asked her. I'm getting interested now.

'Then it was bought by a man called Pietro Vereno, who added more buildings and relaid the gardens. Many of these trees – not the pines, but the others – were planted by him. He lived here pretty much on his own. Sort of a recluse. Nobody knew much about him. He died in what they call mysterious circumstances.'

'Where did you learn all this?'

'From a book in the drawing room in the main house.'

'And after Vereno died then what?'

Susie folds her hands in her lap. 'Vereno had a daughter no one knew about. She lived in America. After he died, she came to live here. Olivia was her name. That was after the war, in 1948. During the war, the villa was used by the Nazis. Italy was incorporated into the German Reich as an occupied region in 1943. They used the villa as a rest home.'

'Well, at least they got something right.'

'Yes, but can you imagine, Mrs Lennox, army officers in great boots stomping round here? Treading on the flowers. Blowing cigar smoke at the view!'

'Nasty things do happen.' I don't know what else to say.

Susie returns to her story. 'When Olivia came here the Nazis had gone. Of course she had to do a lot of work restoring the place. She built the swimming pool and she added the rose gardens and extended the vineyards her father had started. They made a good red wine here – still do, actually. She enjoyed drinking it. The villa had a reputation as a fun place – parties, endless parties, you could hear the laughter the other side of the lake!' Susie pauses. 'The whole area came into its own then – do you know Scott Fitzgerald's *The Great Gatsby*, Mrs Lennox? I imagine it must have been like that. Wild and wonderful. But some dreadful things happened as well. There was one rich lady, a Countess from Milan, who got tired of her lover's misbehaviour and flung herself in front of his car on New Year's Eve. He managed to avoid her. But a few days later, they were both at the same dinner party, she excused herself and went to the ladies' room and came back with her ermine muff and shot him through it. Right in the heart! The muff was used in evidence. That was the first time a diagnosis of temporary insanity was allowed in Italy. She went to a mental institution instead. It happened here, Mrs Lennox.'

'Really?' It occurs to me to wonder if Susie is making all this up.

'Olivia didn't have children of her own, but she adopted four war orphans – two boys, two girls. They grew up here, though I don't know how much she had to do with their growing up. She was very rich. Vereno made his money from tobacco and left it all to Olivia. She had dozens of servants – there were 26 men working in the gardens alone! And she never married. She led a wild life instead. Have you led a wild life, Mrs Lennox?'

I hardly expect this question, or know how to treat it. 'Why, of course I haven't. Why do you ask?'

'I like to think of people as dramatic,' says Susie, smiling. 'I like to imagine everyone has dark secrets, things they're hiding that they don't want anyone to know. I want to know about you, Mrs Lennox, you seem so serious, so self-contained.'

'That's interesting. But I'm really very ordinary, Susie.' I have to use her first name because of Susie's youth: she makes me feel so much older than her. She can't be more than a few years older than Rebecca. 'I've got a daughter about your age,' I tell her. 'You remind me of her. Why don't you tell me about you, instead?'

'There's only one thing that's important in my life,' says Susie immediately, 'and that's Dan. I love Dan. I think he's a genius. I've decided to devote my life to him.'

I nearly laugh at the absurd seriousness of her confession.

'I mean it, Mrs Lennox. By comparison with Dan, my life is totally without value. I feel that deeply. He has the most wonderful talent. I'm not particularly good at anything. Oh, my parents made me learn a few things – I can speak four languages fluently, I went to finishing schools in Scotland and Switzerland, I did a cordon bleu cooking course, that sort of thing – but nothing inspires me very much, except Dan.' Susie moves her hands round a great deal as she talks.

'I was married once,' I say eventually in response to this, 'I was married to a writer. I admired him, too. I didn't mind looking after him. It wasn't as though I especially wanted to do anything myself. Like you, really. Only I don't have your accomplishments.' I think for a moment about those times, the conversations, the silences, the meals, the getting up together, the climbing into bed at night, the solitude, the heavy feeling of Gerald lying beside me, and then later the mornings with Rebecca in bed with us. Gerald complaining and heaving the blankets round his ears to shut out the noise of his daughter's babble.

I'd almost got Rebecca used to staying in her own bed in the mornings when Gerald left us. 'I'm going, Isobel,' he said one day, and I'd thought he meant to the library, or to his agent's, or to meet a publisher, but he didn't mean that, he meant forever. 'I've met someone else.' And that was all he would say. I'd asked, 'What's wrong with me? What about Rebecca?' But he'd had this stormy face on him, and he'd packed a couple of suitcases and gone. I didn't see him for a year after that. Then he got in touch and said he was ready to see Rebecca again. I was furious. He'd had no right to walk out of our lives, then reappear claiming his rights.

When I refused to let him see Rebecca, he took me to court for something called access. He got it – a day every two weeks, two weeks in the summer – and I had to agree to it. In return I got something called maintenance. It didn't maintain us, it was never enough, and sometimes Gerald didn't pay at all. I hated handing Rebecca over; she was four then, and she went off for the whole day with her father, whom she hardly knew, coming back completely overwrought and exhausted. There was nothing I could do about it. But I did feel that no amount of genius on Gerald's part could ever excuse any of this.

I hope Susie won't be disappointed like that, and say so.

'I'm not going to have children, Mrs Lennox. I think Dan is all I can handle. I don't want to have a child, anyway. How do you know what kind of person you're going to get?'

'You don't.'

I feel quite exhausted after this encounter. When I get back to my own room, the maid's just finishing – 'Scusi, Signora' – she rattles away with her bucket and broom. The room is spotless, everything in its place. The windows are open, white curtains moving in the afternoon breeze. Three colours crowd the window – the copper of the horse chestnut, the navy blue of the mountains and the feathery grey green cladding of the olive trees. In the middle of the sky, the sun brings the three colours together in a brilliant jewel-like blaze. I can see an orange tree.

I take my pen and note-pad out of the drawer and get on to the grand white bed to write a letter to my friend, Margaret, an old school friend, who lives in Harrow-on-the-Hill. She has five children aged between ten and twenty-five. She gets up to town occasionally to meet me for lunch, and once a year she comes to stay for a few days to do her Christmas shopping.

I describe the Villa Cellini and its grounds, taking care to be as poetic as I can, without going overboard. Margaret read English at University and has an eye for style. Then I move on to the villa's inhabitants: Susie and Mr Moore, the Goldmans (who I can hear at the moment returning to their room next door, he's shouting to her from the bathroom), Mr Simons, Mrs Dichter, her stooping poet husband. I feel very sleepy, decide I might allow myself a little rest, lie back on the pillows and allow my eyes to wander across the navy mountains . . .

I'm a tiny child again in my room, the room with the cot against the wall, its red and blue blanket showing disordered tassels through the wooden bars. I see myself, a short, thin child in a red checked dress with white socks, and I'm standing facing the door of the room which is locked. I either have my thumb in my mouth or I'm shouting, 'Mummy, Mummy, let me out of here,' and there are salty tears running down my face on to the front of my dress, and I'm stamping my feet and kicking the door, so the paint is marked by the toes of my brown shoes and comes off in flakes onto the wooden floor.

If I stop all my noise for a bit, I can hear Mother moving around the house, quietly, doing things: arranging ornaments, flowers, tidying books, washing some cups, hanging up her nylons on the pulley above the bath next to her room. Row after row of weeping mauve-brown stockings bulging with the memory of Mother's legs, dangling from lines above the scratched bath tub, with its enamel worn off in places and showing black through the white. Mother never stops moving for more than a moment or two: it seems that she wants me to hear her. But she has no intention of letting me out. So why does she want me to know she's there?

'Mummy!' My voice is louder now, and more demanding. Not a protest any longer, a mere infant screaming, but a definite demand that something be done.

Footsteps down the corridor. The door is flung open and I fall back against the bedroom wall, frightened by the mother for whom I've so desperately been calling. She has a red look on her face. She's wearing bright pink rubber gloves because she's been washing her nylons. She raises one of these bright pink hands and hits me with a slap right across the face. And then again, and again. . . .

I wake suddenly, the smell of rubber in my nostrils, a quite awful smell, associated with the warmth in my cheeks which I feel now, brought in through the window glass by the yellow globe of the Italian sun. I'm relieved to find myself after all in this light, white place. What was all that nonsense I was dreaming?

Out of the corner of my eye, I see something horrible. A big black stain on the white bedcover. My pen! I must have put it down before I dozed off. It looks dreadful. I jump up and fetch some wet tissues from the bathroom. I touch the ink stain, and am horrified to see it spread rather than diminish. As I watch, it grows and grows, and fills up a large area of the bedcover, at least twelve inches in diameter, with concentric circles, blacker in the middle, a pale blue at the outer edge of the stain. I pull the whole cover off – it's enormous and very heavy – and rush it into the bathroom, where I fill the basin with hot water and dump the stained part of the cover in. A little of the ink immediately floats off into the water, but very little. Most of the movement is the other way, with the cover picking up the water, absorbing it, so that an area much larger than the stain is now wet, and I find myself dripping water everywhere while the evil eye of that blue-black stain stares at me from the basin. Of course I know that for the price I'm paying at the Villa Cellini, the stain on the bedcover doesn't matter at all. They have superb washing machines which will have no trouble with this stain. But what disturbs me is that I've allowed it to happen. I've been careless, it's so unnecessary, it isn't like me at all. To fall asleep, to dream, and, while dreaming, to turn this lovely Italian bedcover black – no, I'll never forgive myself.

What can I do about it? I look around the bathroom for something to scrub the stain with, but there's no scrubbing brush. My toothbrush, scraped across the top of the ivory soap, is inadequate to the task: all that happens is that its bristles crumple under the strain. My hairbrush! That, being more robust, ought to do it. I have a go with that and seem to have a little success, but by then I've been staring at the stain so hard that I can't remember what it looked like a moment ago. I need one of those Polaroid cameras that takes instant photographs so I can take one and then another and compare the two. I straighten up at the sink, my back's hurting. This brings another more useful mental image with it, of women eternally scrubbing clothes on stones in the river. I stretch the offending fabric carefully over the rim of the sink so I can see exactly where the centre of the trouble is, and I take my soapy hairbrush to it with a new wave of energy. I scrub and scrub, and it seems to be a little better. But, again, the problem is that I quickly lose my impression of what it has been like. I need some chemical help. I've noticed a maid's room downstairs, and now wonder if it might have been left unlocked. It has, so I take the glass from my room and fill it. I come back upstairs (being careful that no-one sees me), refill the basin with hot water, and tip in the whole glass of detergent. To my bare hands, the mixture feels unpleasantly slimy, but I don't mind anything so long as it works. I swish the cover back and forth in the slimy water for a minute or two, then scrub again. Leaving it to soak for a minute, I go back into the bedroom and look at my watch: four o'clock. I can't let the cover soak in the water for very long if I'm to have the whole thing finished and dry by six o'clock, when the maids come into the rooms to turn the beds down. I don't want the maids to know. That's why I'm in such a frenzy about it. Because, if the maids know, then Gina Lucca will get to hear about it, and that I couldn't abide.

I go back into the bathroom, squeeze out the cover and hold it up to the light. It still looks terrible. I try desperately to think of white materials which might be used to disguise the stain.

There's the little sewing kit I've brought with me – I could take some white cotton and sew over the mess – but I quickly discard that one, as the maids would certainly notice that some crazy English woman has been embroidering the bedcover. Toothpaste, perhaps? I take a little of the stinging fluoride toothpaste I use, and smear it over the inky surface of the cover, but the texture's all wrong, and the stain glimmers through the white with thin blue stripes. Then I have a much cleverer idea. I've brought with me some white powder for a fungus infection of the feet I get sometimes. I take the can of powder into the bedroom and, standing in front of the windows so I can see what I'm doing clearly, I tip some of the powder onto the stain. Being wet, the stain absorbs it. I turn the cover over and do the same on the other side. If you hold it to the light you can still see the stain, but now it's sandwiched between layers of white powder. If you look at it ordinarily, there's only a slight blue tinge, hardly noticeable.

I hang it over the radiator to dry, clear the loose powder off the tiled floor, empty the basin, rinse my hairbrush, and the detergent glass and sit down, relieved to have endured and got the better of the afternoon's crisis. I haven't finished my letter to Margaret, but I think that'll have to wait until another day now.

6

The hotel is unexpectedly full that evening, a party of Japanese tourists have arrived for two days.

The waiter gives me my gin and tonic, and I walk across the marble hall to the big two-level drawing room where the Bechstein stands blackly (like my ink stain) at one end, and the log fire hisses at the other. Behind me there's a sudden influx of people into the room: some of the Japanese, small figures in silk or worsted according to gender; Mr Moore and Mrs Dichter, and then Professor Goldman and Mr Dichter having an argument. 'Would you like me to give you a lecture on rheumatoid arthritis?' I hear Dichter angrily asking Goldman. 'Listen, Goldman,' he continues, 'I am in no doubt about your intelligence. Also, you know a lot, which is a different point. But so do some of the rest of us. I am not willing to be lectured on the poetry of Rilke by someone who has merely a superficial acquaintance with it, and is dragging this in to achieve social dominance. I have written a thesis on the poetry of Rilke, particularly about his *Sonnets to Orpheus*, of which I was one of the first critics. I have studied German literature for thirty years. But that is beside the point, too. The point is that you are arrogant.' Goldman looks quite white now, and is hunting the room with panicky eyes for his wife.

I tell Mr Dichter, who joins me at the piano end of the room, that he's very brave to challenge Goldman.

'It won't make any difference, but I couldn't stop myself. Why don't we walk on the terrace for a few moments,' he suggests. 'I need to cool down.'

We walk out into the dusk. Mr Dichter paces up and down. 'This place makes me nervous,' he says suddenly. 'It's the atmosphere. Don't you feel it, Mrs Lennox?'

I recall Mr Simons' remark that nothing bad can happen in the Villa Cellini.

'A sense of menace, no?'

'No. I can't say I've noticed.'

'Perhaps it isn't that, then. Perhaps I'm restless. I don't really like holidays, although I always think I need them to get away from things. But we take our problems with us, don't we, Mrs Lennox?'

Mrs Dichter joins us on the terrace. She's wearing a sapphire frock and her brown hair is coiled on top of her head like a snake. 'Hallo, my love,' says Mr Dichter, 'I've come out here to recover from an argument with Goldman. Mrs Lennox is kindly comforting me.'

Mrs Dichter links her arm determinedly through his: am I imagining the flash of suspicion in the look she gives me? 'I think we should go for a trip tomorrow, darling, right across the lake – I've heard there's a wonderful restaurant in Pirano.'

'What a good idea.' He pats her arm. 'Would you care to join us, Mrs Lennox?'

'No, I don't think so, thank you very much. I have some letters to write.' I don't fancy being the odd one out. The Dichters seem tense.

Dinner is fish, so we have to concentrate on eating. I study the relative degrees of skill my fellow diners have in avoiding bones: Susie Moore is the best – perhaps they taught her how to eat delicately at her finishing school. Next comes Mr Dichter, whose Germanic thoroughness means that he stops the bones before they get anywhere near his mouth. The Japanese are all very skilled. Caroline Goldman has the most trouble; she's continually reaching up with her ringed fingers to poke around in her mouth. Professor Goldman sits next to her, for protection, but appears to be back on top form again, treating poor Mrs Dichter to a treatise about William Wordsworth and the Romantic Revolution.

I tell Mr Simons about my experience with the ink stain. I make it sound funny, though, in retrospect. And I don't tell him about the weird stuff I dreamt about Mother. 'I suppose you think I'm very peculiar?'

'Not peculiar, individual.'

'That's better.'

'Nothing happens without reason, Mrs Lennox.' Why is it that he seems so old when he talks like this? I notice he's given up the cashmere waistcoat, it's far too warm. Now he wears light cotton shirts and either a yellow or a pale blue V-necked jumper. But the change of dress hasn't loosened the tightness of his manner.

'You sound so incredibly serious.'

'It's my profession.'

'If you say so.'

'Or a pose, an attitude; but what's the difference? Everything we do has an explanation. It's just that some of us do not have enough of an explanation of ourselves, and that's a pity.'

'Is it? Why?'

'Because to explain is to prevent.'

'I don't understand.'

'If you knew, Mrs Lennox, why the ink stain disturbed you so, you would be a wiser person now. And if you were ever to find the same thing had happened again, you would be able to prevent the same reaction. You would be able to choose what you did about it. You could scrub it, or not. You might call the maid on the telephone and explain and apologize for what you had done. Or you might never give it another thought.'

I say nothing.

'When I came here, the first night, I was walking down the hall out there, and talking to Tomaso, and he was so interesting that I leant back against that table, you know, the one half way down in front of the very large, very dark oil painting . . .'

'Yes.'

'It has two vases on it, you may have noticed. Large blue ones. Extremely valuable, I'm told by a certain person over there. So. I broke one of them. Leaning back, I pushed it over the edge and it cracked into a thousand pieces on the floor.'

I almost flush with embarrassment for him. He sees this. 'Don't worry, I've trained myself not to worry about such things. Why should I worry? We all perish. A broken vase will never be remembered. A broken life perhaps, but not a mere piece of pottery.'

'Are you trying to tell me something?'

'I never try to tell people anything. I just let them find out for themselves.' He chuckles. 'Anyway, the end of the story is, that by the time I came back down the hall ten minutes later, all the pieces had gone, been swept up, there was no sign of the crime any more. And there was another vase there, an identical one to the one I had broken. So, you see, I was right! Everything is replaceable. Don't worry, Mrs Lennox, I shouldn't worry about anything.'

The bells of the town ring out on Sunday, and I go down to see what can be seen. This time I take the path by Mr Moore's studio: the gate in the wall by the studio takes you out on the road that leads directly to the village. I pass a small cinema on my left, with posters advertising a Fellini film, and one called 'Full Metal Jacket', which I know Becky has seen. I rarely go to the cinema myself, there seems so little on these days that interests me.

Coming up the hill into the village, I meet crowds of people in their Sunday best, with linked arms, catching up on local and international news. Down an alley to the main piazza and west along the lakeshore, past the hotels – the Splendide, the Excelsior, the Metropole, even a Hotel du Lac.

At the main quay, men in blue overalls are energetically cleaning a large boat. A policeman draws up on a white motor cycle, dismounts, shouts greetings to the workmen – I suppose they are greetings, but the trouble about not understanding much of the language is that he could have been saying quite different things. Further on, there's a persimmon tree, unusual enough to be remarkable. I peer beyond it into the garden of some villa – not a hotel – to see if there are any others, and see instead something I do not mean to – two figures sitting at a table under an olive tree – Mr Moore and Mrs Dichter. There's a bottle of wine on the table between them; they lean forward in a mutually earnest posture. The green shrubs and hedges shroud them from the road, or would do, had I not noticed the persimmon tree.

I spring back from my vision with a schoolgirlish sense of excitement. I will, of course, say nothing to anybody. But what does it mean? My first impulse is to feel sorry for Susie Moore – for her misplaced dedication. The poor girl's probably up there in the villa washing Mr Moore's shirts at this very moment, while he's wooing Mrs Dichter down here under the trees. Without quite meaning to, I retrace my steps past the shrubbery:

– 71 –

yes, they're still there. He's taken his jacket off now, and has his hand on her shoulder.

After this I go straight back to the villa. Along the promenade, past the women in their fur coats – as though it really were winter.

At dinner that night – unexpectedly a curry – I realize that I need to take someone into my confidence. I shall tell Mr Simons about Mr Moore and Mrs Dichter, see what he thinks. So, after dinner, I suggest to him we go into the games room, which is a sort of annex to the main drawing room: a little dark room with a round walnut table patterned with fleur de lys, some Louis XV chairs, a stack of records, and a discreet telephone cabinet.

'You must have something *very* secret to tell me,' says Mr Simons, installing himself on one side of the table. I tell him exactly what I saw behind the persimmon tree – no more, no less. He laughs. 'So things are hotting up at the Villa Cellini!'

I don't like his reaction. 'But doesn't it worry you?'

'Not a bit. Why should it? I can't understand why you should consider this to be any business of yours, Mrs Lennox. It isn't your concern. These people are free agents. What they do with their lives is up to them.'

'I know that, but this is deceit. They're treating other people badly.'

'You don't know that,' he points out.

'I do.'

'How?'

'It's obvious.'

'To you, maybe. Not to me. I suggest you forget it. Forget you ever went for that walk, ever saw anything.'

Despite this advice, I can't quite rid myself of the feeling of responsibility that hangs over me.

From then on, I watch Mr Moore and Mrs Dichter. He isn't around much over the next few days. Susie carries reports to breakfast and lunch of how hard he's working on his watercolours of the village. He makes brief appearances at dinner, smartly dressed. I see him talking to Mrs Dichter once or twice, but I can't hear what they're saying.

Mr Dichter's begun to look rather haunted, or is that my imagination? One night he's summoned away from the dinner table after the soup by Gina Lucca, who's rerouted a telephone call for him to the cabinet in the games room. He's away fifteen minutes or so. Mrs Dichter's black eyes dart anxiously after him. I want to stroke her, as one might a nervous cat.

Mr Kraus sits down at the piano and starts to play, a Rodgers and Hammerstein song from *South Pacific*. His big strong hands beat the rhythm from the piano keys, shaking the walls of the Villa Cellini until they, too, begin to dance, perhaps remembering the old days with Olivia Vereno that Susie Moore was telling me about.

Martha Kraus, little, pretty pink Martha, stands next to her husband turning the pages and singing in a bright thin voice. I have no impression at all of her personality. She flickers like a candle shadow beside Kraus, is always behind him, or beside him, or not far away or doing something for him. Soon they're joined by the Goldmans, who sing Rodgers and Hammerstein in the way they do everything else — with a kind of pretentious competence — and by Susie Moore, who throws herself with unexpected vivacity into her singing.

'How's your book going?' I shout to Mr Simons. Oddly, I feel we're some sort of family now, united by this extraordinary setting, and by our own no doubt equally extraordinary individual motives for being here.

'As well as can be expected,' he shouts back. 'How are your dreams going?'

'Not badly,' I answer, thinking, this isn't the sort of exchange I'm used to having in Shepherd's Bush, or even in Harley Street. I still don't consider, as a matter of fact, that these dreams have really got anything to do with me. I don't know where they come from. Last night, for example, I dreamed I was home at Christmas time. Mother was there, and Becky. Through the window it was snowing — there was nothing but snow to be seen. In those circumstances, one would normally expect it to be all warm and cosy inside, but it wasn't. Inside the room, there was a white cold silence. I didn't find this remarkable, however, as something even worse confronted me. My mother's face and my daughter's face were covered in thick white powder, like the clown in the film *Les Enfants du Paradis*, thick white make-up clogging the skin, so it can't breathe. And round the eyes hard black lines and painted lashes giving the eyes a fixed, mournful look. Their faces were like the clown's. They couldn't smile. They couldn't afford to smile at me and nothing I did could make them. I offered them all sorts of treats – a Christmas cake with marzipan and royal icing on it, hot mince pies and cream, an old English custard tart, canapés with melted Swiss cheese and olives, roasted nuts, chestnuts with rich, mushy insides, but nothing made a bit of difference. So I just got up and walked away. Left them to it. I walked out into the snow, and once I was out there I could see all these other houses resembling igloos dotted about with pink lights showing inside them, and I knew none of them had clowns inside.

The next day the weather changes: the auburn tones of the landscape switch to grey, and water runs off everything. Gina Lucca brings out a crowd of colourful umbrellas and puts them in brass stands in the hall of the Villa. But no one feels much inclined to walk. Instead, we congregate in groups in the various communal rooms. Apart, that is, from Mr Simons, who tells us he is going to the library to read Jung's *Modern Man in Search of a Soul*, and Susie Moore who's in bed with a head cold.

I decide it's time I got to know the Krauses. I ask Martha Kraus if she'll play Scrabble with me. We set up shop in the games room, first putting all the lights on to get rid of the gloom. She seems nervously excited, as though attending a birthday party. I'm good at Scrabble, I've got the sort of mind that flourishes on rules and regulations. Martha Kraus, on the other hand, always wants to do things the rules won't allow. But she does achieve a high score with the word 'zygote', which I wouldn't have thought she'd known (I only knew it because of my work), placing the 'z' on a triple score square and not doing badly with some other such words, either.

After that, she seems to relax, and starts to tell me about herself. It appears that she knows words like 'zygote' because she was once a medical student at Brandeis University in New England. She was a very good student, all set for a five star career. And then something happened, she had some kind of breakdown and she went to a psychiatric hospital in New York and then to a private psychiatric home on Long Island, from whence Tom Kraus rescued her. The business of which he's managing director donates money to the home and Tom visits it and its director, a friend of his, regularly. Tom is twenty-five years older than Martha. They've been married two years. It's all quite fascinating. Now Martha keeps house for Tom in his Manhattan penthouse along with a set of domestic staff who are all older than she is. She's going back to her studies, but slowly, as she gets headaches if she does more than a hour or so a day. She definitely hopes to qualify as a doctor one day. The only problem is that this is Tom's first marriage, he wants children. How long do I think one can wait before starting a baby?

'I should think you would know as much about that as I would,' I tell her. And then, seeing her disappointed face, I go on to say, 'I was thirty when my daughter was born. I didn't plan that, it just happened. And my own mother was forty-two when I came along.' As I say this, I realize I never asked Mother if I was what they call a 'wanted' child. And now Mother's death has cut me off from knowing anything about my past. She didn't think of that, did she? I only have a few records – some letters and odd papers. Unless that is, my father's still alive in some equatorial rainforest with a memory for selected European events. Evan Kargar, the anthropologist, was sent packing by Mother. Soon after their marriage, he went to Africa and never came back. He was six years older than Mother, so he'd be ninety-six now. Considering the rigours of West African fieldwork – snakebites, malaria, hookworm – it's quite unlikely that he's still alive. I long ago got used to this ambiguous status of having a father who might, or might not be, alive. But I do prefer to think of him as possibly alive, there's no doubt about that.

'Would you like another game, dear?'

'No, I don't think so.' Martha Kraus doesn't seem quite sure. She glances sideways out of the window. 'Do you think we might go for a walk, Mrs Lennox?'

'In this weather?'

'I feel so shut in here.' She folds and unfolds her hands on her pink lap a number of times.

'It's English weather,' I say. 'Rain, rain, the sky's an overfilling tank. But I don't see why we shouldn't go out and tackle it.'

We pick up two of the house umbrellas – one red, one yellow

– and stride off into the slushy undergrowth. We make an ill-assorted pair. One, in middle age, with greying hair, a thick brown overcoat and pigskin boots of a respectable antiquity. The other, slight as an autumn leaf, dressed in a delicate grey raincoat and matching supple leather boots, the whole topped by a cap of creamy hair and apple blossom skin. Beside Martha Kraus, I feel terribly square and solid.

We choose one of the main paths away from the villa that climbs the hill at a gradual angle. The gravel glistens and squelches with rain. Because of the umbrellas – Martha Kraus has the yellow one – I can't see the expression on her face.

'What's your husband doing today?' I ask conversationally.

'He's taken the boat to Como. He has some business there.'

I find it hard to understand how anyone could be so wedded to business that they'd allow it to pursue them here. 'How do you feel about that? Do you mind?'

'Not really.' We reach a clearing. She shakes her umbrella and lets it down. 'It's stopped raining.'

'So it has.' We stand by the stone parapet and look at the great silken stillness of the lake, circles and swishes out in the middle suggesting strong currents underneath. A boat chugs methodically across it – a*chug*, a*chug*, a*chug* – it beats like the pulse of a large animal staggering through a wood.

'To tell you the truth,' says Martha suddenly, 'I'm tired of being married to Tom Kraus. Yes, I'm tired of it.' The clean pale look on her face suggests that this is the first time she's been able to reach such a conclusion. She smiles, a little one-sidedly. 'It might even be that the cure is worse than the disease.'

'I don't understand.'

'When I was in that place on Long Island I was in possession of myself, if you know what I mean.' She pauses to see if I do. 'Oh, I know I was crazy, but the craziness was mine. I created it.'

'Yes, dear . . . Forgive me if I'm being stupid, but what is the point of being in possession of a madness, when that madness prevents you from doing anything? As presumably it did?'

'What is there to do, Mrs Lennox?' Martha turns towards me, her eyes momentarily as wet as the lake. 'What is there to do? Take courses, pass examinations, get a job, get married, have children – or get liberated, don't get married and have children

– put the kids through school, and college, take out a pension and die? And all in a world where so much has gone wrong. So much!' Martha looks down at her little grey feet planted there in the Italian mud.

'It's not as bad as that, is it? There's pleasure to be had on the way, isn't there?'

'Pleasure?' The look on Martha's face says she's never considered that word. 'What pleasures have you had, Mrs Lennox? Is there anything that, in your life, you have truly enjoyed doing?'

Opening up doors in my mind one by one, I have a look. The first one I open is, naturally enough, my early childhood, but the room's hung with cobwebs and spiders and other crawly things and I shut the door again quickly. The next one's better: if I go inside the door a little, I have a sense of closeness to the warmth of Mother's body. Beyond the silky fur of Lake Windermere, there's real flesh, soft and throbbing to the touch. I can touch it. It's within my reach. I'm hungry for it, want my eyes to feast on it, my hands to be around it, my mouth to be full of it. What am I thinking of? What is this place doing to me?

'Well, there were parts of my childhood that were happy, I suppose,' I say at last.

'And after that, what else?' Martha Kraus watches me keenly.

I peek inside a few more rooms, but I don't much like what I see. After a while, I come upon Peter, and that's all right. He did kiss me eventually on another park bench after a promenade concert. 'I had some good friends,' I say.

'Including boyfriends?'

'One or two.' After Peter there was an anaemic sequence: I'm not even sure I can remember their names now. Adrian – he played the trumpet in the Salvation Army, and put something on his trumpet-coloured hair to make it as flat as a pancake. Paul: now Paul was the one Mother disliked the most, which was why I'd gone out with him for much longer than I'd wanted to. I met Paul on the way to school one day. He was leaning against a post box. His acne was almost the same colour as the post box. We walked to and from school together and went to see Hayley Mills in *Tiger Bay*. Paul came home with me and into the kitchen where I made us both tea. Mother wasn't in. We took our tea upstairs. We were discussing something very intensely, I can't remember what (with the door closed, to keep the heat of the small electric fire in) when Mother came back. 'Izzy,' she shouted up the stairs, 'I'm home.' I didn't answer. I suddenly thought I couldn't be bothered. So Mother had come cracking upstairs – her knees cracked on the stairs with some form of arthritis – and she opened the door without knocking and had looked surprised to see Paul sitting there with his acne and his cup of tea. It made me cross, the way Mother burst in on me like that. She had one set of rules for herself and another for me.

I shut the door of that room firmly. The next one had a label on it: 'Gerald'. 'And then I met my husband,' I say, watching the steamer dock a good half mile below us, under the overhanging trees. 'I met Gerald when I was twenty-two. That was in 1962,' I observe, precisely.

Martha Kraus is amused by something: '1962 was the year I was born!'

'Really?'

'The sixteenth of June.'

'How extraordinary! That was my wedding day!'

We exchange a look containing a whole row of exclamation marks like an avenue of poplars.

I think about my own wedding. Now that I did enjoy. For once I, and not Mother, was the centre of attention. I insisted on a church wedding. Mother said, 'What rot, Isobel, you don't believe in any of that,' which was true, but irrelevant. Gerald was a dapper bridegroom in his black tails and his smart tie and his black shoes polished, as Peter's had been on the park bench in Chiswick, and I ordered a cream satin gown from an expensive shop, and a headdress of roses with a veil as light as cobwebs. I'd walked up the aisle with Uncle Simon, now dead, and possibly not very alive then; and Gerald was standing there in front of the altar, waiting to make his promises to me.

Which he didn't keep. I make myself look back into the liquid of the lake, at its calm, its strong persistence against the twisting and turning currents of time.

'What are you thinking about, Mrs Lennox?'

I look at Martha's smoothly curious face, outlined against the dank woodland.

'I was thinking about my wedding.'

The ring, a wide gold one, glinting in the light of the seventeenth century church – Gerald's hand on mine, 'I, Gerald Anthony Samuelson, take thee, Isobel Miranda, as my lawful wedded wife . . .'

I'd thought things were right with the world then. After those years of wandering from one thing to another, putting any notion of a career out of my mind, searching for the right man to make promises to, to run away from Mother's untidy, unfaithful life with: Gerald, my saviour!

In a blue silk suit, far too hot for the greenhouse June day, I got into a car with Gerald Lennox and we bumped tin cans over the roads to a seaside hotel in Norfolk, where the waves had pounded on the rocks all night, and Gerald slept beside me in absolute silence. That was at least one of my anxieties taken care of: he didn't snore. I'd had this picture of men as snoring creatures. I'm sure Robert had snored. The a*chug*, a*chug*, through the ceiling like the paddle steamer across the lake.

'Do you like men, Martha?' I turn to Martha suddenly, as this question comes into my head and leaves it as quickly, before I've had time to catch it and lock it up.

'It's not up to us to like them or not to like them,' remarks Martha with a daring simplicity. 'We have to live with them. We might as well get on with it.'

I feel I might agree with this sentiment. I'd been going to say, 'I'm not quite sure what men are for,' but this one I'd stopped in time, recalling that night in Norfolk, the very thing it was all about.

'I don't think I'm going to like this,' I'd confessed to Gerald on June 16, 1962. 'But perhaps it's all right if you do,' I'd added, seeing from his face that I'd said the wrong thing.

'There's nothing to worry about, Izzy darling, nothing: I'll take care of it all. You just lie there and relax.' Afterwards, when I'd started working for Mr Jefferson and been called upon to chaperone during internal examinations, I'd understood why Gerald had told me to relax. For that's exactly what Mr Jefferson says before he plunges in there with his hands or a metal instrument. It seems that men are programmed to utter the command 'relax' when they're about to do something intimate to a woman. It must be part of their maleness, like growing hairs on their faces, or the way they fly at their boiled eggs, decapitating them in the mornings.

Mother had tried to talk to me before the wedding. 'I know you're a virgin, Izzy, but you won't be able to keep it up for much longer. But if you haven't practised it, Izzy, do you at least know the *theory*?' (What theory?) 'Here, I bought you this.'

'This' was a book by a woman called Dr Janina Foxwood, and it was called *Sex for the Uninitiated*. Rather to the point, that title. So was the book. Full of technical words and phrases, the total effect of which was to make you feel you didn't much want to do it after all, you might end up as a piece of machinery. There were numerous drawings of different coital postures. They all looked equally uncomfortable. I felt a special revulsion for the one which had the man one way up and the woman the other. I didn't imagine it would be particularly nice to smell a man's bottom.

Mother also wanted to talk about contraception. This was 1962. There were only three real choices: the Dutch cap, durex, or a baby. Something called withdrawal wasn't recommended. 'Though I didn't find it so bad myself,' remarked my mother, laconically and obscurely. She referred me to a doctor who 'fitted' young women. I had a number of practice goes squeezing my cap, wriggly with jelly, round Dr Beacon's consulting room, and putting it anywhere but in the right place – I was quite put off by being told that my cervix felt like a nose. It immediately made me feel I couldn't breathe, which didn't help with the relaxation.

Gerald, my husband, had, on June 16 1962 in Norfolk, I suspect, done his best. His best obviously wasn't what was required, however. 'I don't want the light on,' I'd said, considering that we'd get nowhere if I didn't say what I wanted. He asked my permission to draw back the murky brocade curtains and let the light of the moon in. The man on the moon. Oh well, why not?

I shut my eyes most of the time. When I opened them Gerald, who wasn't a bad-looking man with his clothes on, shone with the slight blue tinge of cinema light. I looked sideways for the girl with the tray of icecreams, but her time hadn't come yet.

Gerald took off my nightdress and folded it up carefully. That struck me as incongruous. Then he touched one of my nipples as though it were a button. I flinched, not being used to having my nipples pressed like that. Gerald noticed and changed his technique, instead using his whole hand to massage my breast. I tried to concentrate on the niceness of it all. Gerald parted my legs, and started looking for something else. This was really embarrassing. He licked my ear, like a dog. 'Gerald?'

'Yes, darling?'

'How long is it supposed to take?' I'd noticed Dr Foxwood hadn't given any information on this point. Luckily, Gerald interpreted my question as juvenile curiosity, rather than mature impatience. Eventually, as the man in the moon grinned at me from behind Gerald's head, he pushed himself inside me, telling me to relax again. It seemed about as intimate an act as Dr Beacon's prodding and pulling and manoeuvring to fit the Dutch cap. Nonetheless, I'd agreed to let Gerald in.

'I love you, Isobel,' said Gerald, unexpectedly.

'I love you, too,' I'd replied, hoping that the attachment of this phrase to the physical coupling that was going on down there would turn the mechanics into a proper union: mind and body, souls on wings, together for eternity. But shortly after that, Gerald shuddered and leapt off me, and the mocking face of the man on the moon through the window seemed to say, I told you so.

'I'm not sure I do,' I say to Martha Kraus, having replayed this episode from the past. 'Like men, that is. Not especially.'

'Did you love your husband, Mrs Lennox?'

'Do you know,' I reply, suddenly clear about something for the first time, 'I don't think I actually care for that question. It's not that I mind you asking it, you understand, or that I'd be shy about answering it, I just don't think it's the right question. It's the question men want us to answer, isn't it? Do we love them? How much do we love them? I wonder what question we would ask, if we had the chance? Let's go on walking, shall we?'

Martha is silent for a bit. Then she says, 'You're probably quite right, Mrs Lennox. Do you know, you've made me realize something. You've made me realize what I've got to do!'

'What's that, Martha?' Her troubled face seems suddenly animated.

'I've got to go back to where I started and begin again. I didn't get it right the first time. So I must do it again. Go back to the place where at least I knew what I was feeling – so much so that I was put in an institution for it. I married Tom because I wanted to be saved from myself. He did that, but it wasn't the right thing. Don't you see, Mrs Lennox – my marriage to Tom was a mistake!'

She's so convinced she's right, and she looks so happy that I have to agree with her. I put my arm round her, which I couldn't have done earlier in our walk, when we'd been encumbered by the two red and yellow umbrellas in their upright positions. Beneath my arm, Martha's delicate frame brings to me the dream I had of my daughter Rebecca as a crushable object. I think about the question Martha asked me: what pleasures have I had in my life? I have had pleasures, but they haven't been fully-grown ones; I haven't allowed myself to lie back, relax and enjoy them. I smile at my own private joke. Just relax, Isobel. The person who needs to say that to me is me! No one else. Pleasure is to be had in freely choosing something one really knows one wants. I pause on this sentence, struck by something odd about its formulation. But no, I can't put my finger on it. Then I repeat the sentence out loud without meaning to.

'I have never experienced myself as being free, Mrs Lennox.'

'Few people have.' Is this true? I don't know. We walk on for a while, companionably kicking the russet leaves together. Then the Villa Cellini comes in sight round the corner of the cliff path. Beyond the villa, down both arms of the lake, the weather is clearing. Instead of menacing slate-grey, the sky shines with a pure chromium light, across which there are fingers of duck egg blue and daffodil yellow.

7

At dinner that evening, Martha Kraus looks happier than I've ever seen her. Her big bear of a husband sits across the table from her, his wineglass in his paws. At the head of the table Carla Dichter sports a novel hair style: her hair's tucked in all round the nape of her neck with diamanté combs. She has a fragile swan's neck. Her husband, opposite, neither smiles nor doesn't smile.

'I saw you walking in the rain this afternoon,' remarks Mr Simons, looking (I think) at both Martha and me. 'I commend your bravery!'

'It wasn't brave, it was necessary.'

'Nothing is necessary.' He smiles cynically into his pink wine. 'Not even life itself.'

'Oh, for God's sake!' My intolerance surprises me: I want to tell him to stop making these fathomless remarks of his. At first I think I was rather impressed by them; I'm not used to psychoanalysts. But now I find them irritating.

'Tell me,' I ask him (being a little more provocative than usual), 'is it this place that attracts people with problems, or do the people here have no more problems than anybody else?'

'You want my professional opinion?'

'I want an opinion. I don't care how professional it is.'

'My opinion is that these people, the kind who can afford to come to the Villa Cellini, are those who can also afford to have problems. There are no particular struggles in their lives: they don't have to combat poverty, they don't need to search for beauty, illness doesn't threaten, so what else can they possibly occupy themselves with? They're too selfish to worry about the world's problems – about unemployment, nuclear war, the famine in Africa. So they look into their own souls and see knots and tangles there and worry about them, how to get rid of them, and, most of all, what would be left if they did. The pursuit of paradise.' He appears to sigh deeply.

I can see the waiter advancing with a tureen of soup. 'It's the psychic sickness of our age,' continues Mr Simons, oblivious of these culinary manoeuvres. 'Carl Jung, you know, said, when talking about the spiritual problems of modern man, that he knew a great deal of the intimate psychic life of hundreds of educated persons, but this only told him half of what he wanted to know. Because as well as the inside psychic life there is the outside one – the cultural ambience. It's the cultural ambience of our age to be concerned with our own mental health to the point of absolute obsession. Something to be pursued and worried about like a dog with a bone. That's what these people remind me of, spaniels and labradors and spoilt poodles.'

'It doesn't sound very nice.'

'It isn't. But I'm as much a part of the culture as you – as they are,' he flicks a psychiatric eye round the table. 'Instead of being concerned about my own psychic disorder, I've decided to be concerned about other people's. That's what I shall confess when I meet my judge in the underworld!' He laughs a little. 'That I haven't committed the crime of worrying about myself too much.'

'What are you talking about?'

'I'm sorry, Isobel,' – did I tell him he could use my first name? 'I'm being more than usually obscure. According to ancient Egyptian tradition, when a dead man meets his judges in the underworld he must confess in detail all those crimes he hasn't committed, not those he has.'

I find this idea entertaining, and briefly wonder what I myself would admit to not having done. The crime of not being passionate occurs to me, as does that of not helping Mother to die.

During the main course, *bollito misto* with green sauce and fruits glazed in mustard, Caroline Goldman talks at me, telling me about her husband's lecture in the medical school in Milan the next day, and about their recent sojourn in the Smithfield area of London during the famous hurricane of 1987. The chef passes through the dining room in his white skyscraper hat and is applauded for his pleasing efforts. A moment later, just as the conversation has resumed, the lights in the dining room go out. In the blackness, everyone *oohs* and *ahs* and wonders whether to be alarmed or not. Then, from the direction of the kitchen, a point of light. A solitary candle, on an apricot cake, carried by the chef to the head of the table, to Carla Dichter, whose birthday it apparently is. The look on her face in the restricted light says that she hadn't known what was about to happen. We sing 'Happy Birthday', and then Carla is exhorted to cut the cake and to wish: the first is easy, but the second seems more difficult for her, she spreads her hands in front of her eyes and leans back in her chair.

Mr Moore watches Carla Dichter with gruelling intensity during this procedure. Hugo Dichter's face looks a little concerned, I think. And there is Isaac Simons next to me watching me watching them: the whole room is peopled with a nervous surveying energy. Only the Goldmans, stuffed with their own silly knowledge of the universe, can afford to sit back and allow other people to get on with their own lives without trying to spot the places where they might stumble themselves.

I draw the curtains and unlatch the green shutters, pushing them outwards with the palm of my hand, so they clip into their niches on the wall either side of the window. Amazingly, almost all the mountains across the lake carry snow; it must have happened in the night, I knew nothing about it.

I get dressed quickly in comfortable trousers, the blue sweater I wore yesterday, then my coat. I grab my mohair cap and gloves and then go out into what I think of as the snow, only it isn't to be experienced, except in the sense that the landscape is totally altered by it — the sky is white above the snowy mountains, there are rings of white cloud, and the lake throws the whiteness back at the sky. Only the green of the pines, the olives and the fruit trees, and the pink-red tiles of the houses make a difference.

A truckload of gardeners on their way to work passes me, and Gina Lucca whizzes past in her Datsun, off to purchase treats in Como. I myself am going to visit the cemetery outside the village. Various people have told me it's worth looking at, but I don't want to go with them, because I can't imagine looking at graves and trying to be polite and amusing at the same time.

The cemetery's set on the side of the hill, sloping gently down to the lake shore. Though it's full of plain grey and black marble, the first sight one gets is flowers – an immense profusion of red, yellow, pink and white flowers decking every grave. It makes me feel quite guilty about Mother, consigned to Lake Windermere, which wasn't even where she wanted to go.

A small enclosure to the west of the main cemetery is for foreigners. A couple from Sheffield: an old lady from Bloomington, Indiana. I've never been to Bloomington, Indiana, but I suppose to be buried here is preferable. Another one: 'In loving memory of Clara Elizabeth, daughter of Edward and Mary Ann Pembroke of Blackheath, England, who Departed this life 13th April 1886 Aged XVIII yrs. Blessed are the pure in heart for they shall see God.' But most sentimental of all is the grave of a young man from Cheshire, who saved his brother from drowning in the lake, and died in this very act nearly a hundred years ago. 'The White Flower of a Blameless Life.' Does such heroism automatically cancel sins? Or was Sydney Herbert blameless anyway? I walk over to the main part of the cemetery, which is given over to more purely native remains. The dead all lie in one direction, North to South, not East to West. But as the heads all point to the walls, so their feet point to each other.

Apart from the flowers, many of the slabs have a little lamp containing something that glows. A candle perhaps? On closer inspection, a wire leads out of the top of the lamp, runs across the marble for an inch or two, and then disappears into it. So the dead are wired up to the electricity supply, in death, as in life, dependent on the power of others.

It must be the memory of the evening before, when we were all so intensely watching each other, but suddenly I have this image of myself looking at myself. One figure in a woolly hat and big overcoat looking at another, looking at a collection of dead people. Curious. It makes me wonder why I've come to the cemetery. For the same reason as I've come to Italy? Because of death? Or more simply just to see the sights?

I search in my mind for the thing that was worrying me yesterday. Now I feel quite certain I've got the answer, but I've forgotten the question. Someone famous, I recall from one of the witty Villa Cellini conversations (most of which are far above my head) once said on their deathbed, 'so what is the answer?' And when no one, out of deference to the dying, dared answer, he went on to remark, 'in that case, what is the question?' There's a whole art in this matching of questions and answers. What the dead want and what the living can provide; what one generation gives and another takes away; the greediness of some, the redundant unselfishness of others. The food one person puts into the refrigerator and the food another person wishes to take out; the affection that some give with difficulty and which gets stuck awkwardly halfway out in others.

I think of my daughter Rebecca, alone in the house in London without a mother to watch over her. Surveillance, out of place in this Italian resort, is surely part of the art of mothering. I've always felt I've failed Rebecca, that I've given her too much of something and not enough of something else, but I can't for the life of me work out what they are, or in which order they come.

Thinking about Rebecca makes me remember Martha Kraus and our odd conversation yesterday, and this finally enables me to dig up the question to which I've now got the answer. I said something to Martha about pleasure. That it requires both free choice and proper knowledge of one's own desires. The question was, where did I get this piece of wisdom from? I feel sure it *is* derivative, I'm not nearly clever enough to have thought of it myself. It's like an electricity shock from one of those funny little lamps on the graves when I realize that the person who said this was my own mother.

'When *my* parents died,' says Mr Simons, 'I had the feeling there was nothing between me and death any more. Death is liberating.'

'That's a neat line for a psychoanalyst,' replies Caroline Goldman, brightly. 'I would have thought you made your living off the *un*-liberating nature of death: the unresolved problems, the complexes, the neuroses.'

'Would you? Would you indeed have thought that?' This from Martha, the quiet, composed, pink and white Martha. 'Sometimes I wonder,' she says deliberately, 'whether you really know anything about anything, Mrs Goldman.'

Professor Goldman draws himself up to his full biochemical height. 'What is this, an inquisition?' He tries to beam over his aperitif glass.

'I just wondered,' says Martha, mildly, 'what kind of person your wife really is. What she can do that's useful to others. Can she make puppets, for example? Or type theses? Or suffer? Do you suffer, Mrs Goldman? Do you know that poem of Sylvia Plath's, the one that refers to glass eyes and rubber crotches and stitches to show something's missing, and inquires whether you're our sort of person? Well, I don't think you are. I must say,' she gets up from her chair and strolls calmly across towards the compact disc player, 'that I don't think she is. I have no patience these days for people with rubber crotches!' She laughs then, almost politely, and stomps out of the room.

The Goldmans break the silence: 'I thought she was under stress from the first day I saw her,' pronounces Caroline Goldman nervously. 'Why, anyone can see their marriage is in difficulty.'

'Poor girl,' says he, 'I gather she was once an extremely bright and promising medical student.'

'Who told you that?' I turn on him sharply.

'Tom Kraus. We had a game of tennis the other day. I asked if Martha could join us – Caroline was keen to play – but she said she had some studying to do. It was then that Kraus explained.'

Mr Simons puts down the *New York Review of Books*: 'When someone speaks the truth,' he observes, 'they get punished.'

'Naturally.' Hugo Dichter is listening too. 'Because the world keeps going on a pack of lies.'

'Well, not quite.' Mr Simons drains his Virgin Mary and sets it down on the table. 'No, I wouldn't say so. The world keeps going on lots of different packs of lies. We each have our own. Our own individual, unique, bungling nonsense.'

'History is not what happens,' says Goldman suddenly, 'history is what it felt like to be there when it happened.'

We all look at him.

'Said by a famous diplomat once. Here, as a matter of fact. What do you think of it?'

'Unduly subjective,' comments Mr Dichter.

'But Dichter, you're a poet, how can you say that?'

'There are poets and poets,' objects Mr Dichter gloomily.

'I'm going to make sure Martha's all right.' I feel someone should.

Martha is in the games room looking at the Scrabble board. 'Fancy a game, Mrs Lennox?'

'Are you feeling all right, dear?'

'Never better.'

She's moving letters fiercely and haphazardly around on the board. 'I've got an awful feeling I'm going to take my own advice.'

'To go crazy again?'

'Yes. You see, Mrs Lennox, I'm really a witch.' Martha flicks up her white lambswool jumper and points to a spot below her left breast. I can't see properly without my glasses, and I start struggling to get them out of my handbag. 'See that, Mrs Lennox? That is a supernumerary nipple.'

'Oh, really?' I can't see it, but I'm sure she's right. She was a medical student, after all. I don't know how I'm supposed to react.

'They used to burn us at the stake for that. Women who knew things. Knew how to heal, how to care, how to deliver babies. This was a sign, you see, of our craziness. For which read our wisdom.'

'Did you learn that in medical school?'

'I learnt nothing in medical school, Mrs Lennox, for the simple reason that they don't teach you anything there. They require you to absorb facts, I became full of facts, Mrs Lennox, they started coming out of my ears, I had them at my fingertips and when I put my fingers into my cunt I found facts there as well. Lots of little red ones all crowded up together, fighting to get out. Do you put your fingers up your cunt, Mrs Lennox?'

This is terrible. I have to leave the room before she says anything worse. I pace up and down the marble corridor, thinking what it would be best to do now. The only people here with medical knowledge are Professor Goldman and Mr Simons. I can't imagine Martha letting Professor Goldman near her in a professional capacity. And though I don't know much about psychoanalysts, I don't imagine Mr Simons knows anything much about really crazy people.

During dinner, Martha behaves perfectly — nothing out of order at all. I begin to think I've imagined the whole thing. I go to bed feeling uneasy and as I'm drifting off to sleep, I hear that awful word 'cunt' ringing like a bullet through the air around my bed.

8

Halfway through my holiday at the Villa Cellini I agree to go in a boat across the lake with Susie Moore and her husband. It's a cloudy day, so we can't see much. Loud pop music is playing, we're the only cargo on the boat, apart from a lorry piled high with wooden planks, and the lorry driver and his crew. I pass the door of the crew's quarters and see a man in navy blue in the middle of eating his dinner. As we dock at the village on the opposite shore, he lays down his fork entwined with pasta, springs onto the deck, seizes the rope, throws it to another man in navy blue on the shore, puts down the metal gang plank, and then springs back to the cramped dining table, where he picks up his pasta fork again.

The Moores insisted I come with them, I couldn't get out of it, even though I thought they might be feeling sorry for me, spending so much time on my own. But I don't mind spending time on my own, I'm used to it.

'Nothing happens here in winter,' complains Dan Moore when we walk around the small deserted town.

'What would you like to happen?' Susie takes his arm, lays her cheek against his. I shiver, though it's not particularly cold.

We have some lunch and talk about what happened the previous evening. It seems we all think Martha's quite right about the Goldmans, but we all feel she shouldn't have said it. I do mention that she said some even worse things in the games room afterwards, but they don't ask me about this. We pay the bill, and take the next ferry back. Some of the clouds have cleared, so Mr Moore is able to take a few photographs.

As the three of us walk in a friendly silence up the drive to the villa, Gina Lucca calls out to us from the gates below. 'Mrs Lennox! Mr Moore! Susie!'

We turn round and wait for Gina to catch up with us. 'Have you seen Mrs Dichter?' She's quite breathless. 'Mr Dichter hasn't seen her since last night. She went out for a walk in the late evening. She hasn't come back. Tomaso and I have both been looking for her, and the staff as well, and Mr Dichter of course. I'm going to take a photograph of Mrs Dichter to the police now.'

I think little more of this, have a bath and listen to a tape Mr Simons has kindly lent me, of Gustav Mahler's *Das Lied von der Erde*. He told me it was a setting of seven out of eighty-three Chinese poems, which are all about the anticipation of death. Sections of the score recommend wine as the answer. I myself have only brought Mozart's *Elvira Madigan* piano concerto, some John Denver, Yehudi Menuhin playing Beethoven's violin concerto, and the film music of both *Out of Africa* and *Death in Venice*. I didn't realize *Death in Venice* was Mahler as well, but this encourages me to try Mr Simons' tape. In the event, I find it quite moving, especially the two syllable word at the end – *ewig, ewig* – the way it trails off into nothing. It's sung by someone called Christa Ludwig, who has a very good voice.

I dress for dinner, somewhat more smartly than usual – my black dress, a green necklace, a light shawl round my waist. I feel I'm really getting into the swing of things here now. I could get used to this kind of life, it's spoiling me for Shepherd's Bush! Mr Simons compliments me when I arrive in the drawing room, which makes me wonder if this was why I'd dressed up a little more than usual. To get his compliments. This would be ridiculous wouldn't it, me, a woman of forty-eight, him, a man of? I don't know how old he is. Under the influence of one drink I ask him.

'Forty.' I can't make up my mind whether he looks it or not.

'Very few people ever look their age,' he says, as I ponder this. 'But, since we all die at different ages, we can hardly be expected to. Ageing is idiosyncratic. I will age differently from you, because our life spans will be different.'

'One should aim to be a woman in Iceland these days,' observes Professor Goldman from the periphery of the room, where he's been using his interfering antennae to pick up what everyone else is saying. 'Seventy-nine point three years in 1980,' he drones on, 'It'll be eighty point six by the year two thousand. And the weaker sex, us men – we are biologically weaker, you know – we're about six years behind the ladies. Not in Bhutan, however, in Bhutan we're actually ahead . . .'

We ignore Goldman. I feel strangely flirtatious tonight. 'How old do you think *I* look, Mr Simons?'

'As old as you want to be.'

'You're not answering the question.'

'I am. Your appearance depends on your intention. Sometimes you wish to appear old; sometimes young. Sometimes you feel you must be a mother, sometimes a daughter.'

What an extraordinary thing to say!

'Tonight,' he goes on, 'you are a daughter; tonight you want to be gay and seductive.'

As had happened before in these odd conversations of ours, Mr Simons' use of a particular word – here 'seductive' – surprises and confuses me.

'I'm not married,' he goes on to say, though I don't understand why, 'but I have had a number of important relationships with women. Just now I am in love with one of my patients. That is inevitable, but distressing.'

The words are selected with great care and uttered without much emotion. I hadn't thought much about Mr Simons as a person. I'd considered him mainly as a kind of sounding board for my impressions. But here he is, practically forcing me to take him on board as an individual, telling me about a most intimate and delicate situation in which he's involved. I don't really want to know, it's no business of mine what he does. I don't say anything. I look out of the window, and try to think of a change of subject.

'But I don't want to talk about it,' he says, to my great relief. 'I wanted to say it because you haven't asked a single question about me. Did you know that?'

'What?'

'You haven't asked me any questions the whole time we've been here. No personal questions. You have, after all, just been through a profound experience,' he says. 'One of the deepest and most difficult experiences any of us have to handle. You haven't been in a position to inquire into my circumstances, or anybody's: you've only been able to receive certain kinds of information, haven't you?'

I thought about the conversations I'd been having since I arrived at the villa. With Susie Moore in the studio, while her husband looked at his photographs; with Carla Dichter about the mismatch between philosophy and poetry; with Martha about the craziness from which Tom Kraus had rescued or stolen her. I had thought these people were using me for their own purposes: as a listening ear, or an agony aunt. I must admit I hadn't seen myself as using them for mine.

'Isobel,' says Mr Simons then, almost casually, 'I suppose you realize your mother isn't dead yet? You are busy imagining her death. You've come here to prepare yourself for it, haven't you?'

I feel terribly faint, it must be the heat of the fire behind me. I think I would have fainted if at that very moment I hadn't seen Gina Lucca coming through the doorway at the other end of the room, looking extremely agitated. 'She has been found,' she says, 'Mrs Dichter has been found.' She pauses. 'She is dead. She fell over the cliff on the eastern side of the promontory. She must have slipped in the dark and the rain. Her neck is broken.'

Carla Dichter's swan-like neck: I can see it now as I had the other night, preening at the head of the table. Three images join together in my memory: that one – the visual metaphor of the swan preening itself, the polished antique table acting as the satin-smooth surface of the lake; and then the conversation by the jewellery shop the day we went to the fishing village; and, thirdly, the scene Carla didn't know I'd witnessed: her and Dan Moore enjoying a bottle of wine behind the persimmon tree. No one now will ever know the meaning of that scene. Unless either Mr Dichter or Susie already does, of course.

Everyone at the Villa Cellini is naturally very upset at the news of Carla Dichter's death. We all want to know exactly what happened and why, but for a number of hours, no one dares to ask. Mr Dichter doesn't come to dinner – it must be so awful for him. I think about going to tell him how sorry I am. But I don't imagine he'd want to hear that. We do see him in the hallway later. Is there anything we can do? 'I don't think so,' says Gina Lucca, who seems by now to be managing the whole affair. 'There will have to be an inquest, of course. There is the question of whether it was an accident to settle.'

But if it hadn't been an accident?

The next afternoon I go up to the path where Carla Dichter fell. I know it's not a very nice thing to do, it's like going to look at motorway crashes or air disasters. But somehow I must do it. The path is the same one that Martha and I took the other day, when we talked about madness. I can almost feel little Martha beside me as I walk. She's still asking me for advice – who am I? Who should I be? What will a child do to me? What did it do to you? Voices ring in my head, some out of history, some not. I round the corner to the rail one leans on to obtain an unencumbered view of the lake. Today the lake's merely a grey sheet spread out below; everything is grey, has merged into a funereal obscurity – water, cloud, snow, light, stone.

I rest there for a few minutes, trying to remember this same view as I saw it only a week or so ago: golden and blue, full of colour and optimism, a sort of paradise. Death hadn't lurked there, nor self-knowledge; doubt and distress had been can-celled by the sunlight, by the moving of light over stone, across water, through leaves.

Then I go on further up to where there's no rail and looking down (if you can manage it) feels quite risky. The drop to the sharp shore of the lake is terribly steep. It seems clear to me as I stand there that this is where Carla Dichter had been, and looked down and had perhaps chosen to fall. Maybe it's an awful thing to admit to, but I felt perhaps she might have chosen the form of her own death.

'It's quite terrifying, isn't it?' The voice behind me nearly makes me fall myself, but with it comes a hand on my shoulder which restrains me. Push and pull; advance and retreat; the future and the past: always this competition. 'Imagine what it's like here at night and in the rain.' So Mr Simons has come, too, to see for himself what might have happened to Carla Dichter. 'Do you think someone pushed her, Isobel? It wouldn't have been difficult. Just a light shove on the back, why I could have done that easily to you just now, couldn't I?' Instinctively, I step backwards, his words make me seek the haven of the promon-tory's edge. 'I came up to have a look, I expect we've all done that,' he goes on, in a light conversational tone, as though discussing the price of tea. 'I saw Hugo Dichter himself come up here this morning. I wondered if I should come with him, but then I thought no, we all have our own unfinished business, it wouldn't be right to interfere. He needed to find his own answer. Shall we walk on, Isobel?'

He puts his arm in mine then. I don't ask him to, he just puts it there. What are we, a married couple out for a Sunday afternoon walk or something? I want to get rid of his arm, but I don't dare just to push it away, in case he understands I'm uneasy to have it there. I'm afraid of his anger. But with each minute his arm becomes a growing preoccupation. I even think I can feel the muscles in that arm, behind the thick dark material of his overcoat. His hold on me seems to tighten.

'Do you remember what we were talking about last night, Isobel, when Gina Lucca brought us the news of Mrs Dichter's death?'

His arm is pressing against my body now, he must be able to feel the outline of my hips, a breast, even. Why did he use the word 'seductive' last night?

The path becomes steeper and narrower. For some reason I notice things with a particular intensity: the orange-red of the cotoneaster berries, the placid dark green of the ivy, a shoot of yellow grasses tumbling out of the rock. Some cyclamen and a display of little blue flowers tight on the ground, the common speedwell. I feel breathless, that Mr Simons is propelling me in front of him. 'We were talking about my relationships with women,' he continues.

'*I* wasn't,' I point out.

'Correct. I was. Because we'd decided you didn't want to know anything about me, hadn't we, Isobel?'

'Well I . . .'

'It's all right. Don't protest. As I said, you yourself believe you are going through too much to be truly responsive to anyone else's needs.'

'Believe?' I manage to drag my body away from his now, I'm angry. 'You're talking nonsense. I've never heard such nonsense in my life!' I start to run away from him. But he calls out to me through the greyness of the day: 'I want to tell you about this woman, Isobel, the woman I love!'

'Don't bother.' I feel terribly menaced by his wish to impose something of his on me: knowledge of him, of myself, of happenings at the Villa Cellini. But Mr Simons doesn't hear what I say. 'She's like you, Isobel,' he calls, 'the woman I love is exactly like you! I love her, I love her, I'll tell you why I love her, Isobel,' the words go on flying at me, 'it's because she knows nothing, she understands nothing, so everything I tell her is bound to be true.' He stops in his tracks. I can hear the footsteps turn into silence. 'Bound to be true,' he repeats the words. 'I like that. It's all bound to be true. Whether she likes it or not.'

I turn round and look at Mr Simons' face quickly. It's a mottled deep red. It reminds me of Mother's legs before she died. He sees me looking at him, the eye contact seems to bring him back from somewhere else to his situation now with me on this hill. He begins running towards me. 'Isobel, come here, want to talk to you. You've talked enough to me, it's my turn now!' I take off again, but round the next corner there's a tunnel cut in the rock. I go into the tunnel because there's nothing else I can do, no other way to go. It stinks and is dark, I can't see where it ends, all I can see is the grey light on the sides of the grey rock, the crumbly surface I'll have to get across to escape from Mr Simons, all I can hear is the abrasive sound of his feet on the dead leaves and gravel, and the slow plod of water falling in the distance from the tunnel's ceiling.

It's a changed landscape now. The sun's out, not in the undergrowth on the promontory itself, but a long way further up, on the upper slopes of the mountains enclosing the lake. It touches the mountains gently, making of the thick snow a pale lemon colour: lemon and pale rose pink, the colour of icing on cakes at children's parties. The sky itself no longer bears a metallic sheen, but is painted with cottonwool balls of white against a blue as clear and honest as any painter could wish for. All around me, if I keep my eyes on that fixed point up there, is a sanitary stillness, the perfect gloss of porcelain that nothing is able to stain or mark: an absolute, unchangeable wholeness.

At the same time I can feel in my body that something has happened. The superior vision of sunlit mountains must have been awarded to me as a result of something I myself have undergone. Something spiritual, but not purely spiritual; indeed spiritual only because corporeal. My body is changed in some way. I know this, also that I don't know how. In bed – my own bed in the Villa Cellini – I move one limb and then another, testing each to see if they function in the ways to which, over the forty-eight years of my life, I've become accustomed. Everything works, except that in one arm and one leg there's some stiffness and a feeling of being bruised. To turn my neck is also painful. This brings instantly to my mind the memory of Carla Dichter and what happened to her, and where I most recently had been going, retracing Carla's last journey; up that path to look over the cliff's edge, then further up, running pursued by footsteps, into the tunnel cut through the rock with the sound of rain dripping. . . .

I feel dizzy and I hear the horrible beat of my heart again. Like the footsteps in the leaves: hunting me. I turn on my side, the side that doesn't hurt, pushing the memory away. So it had happened in the tunnel? 'It?' It seems both important and silly to observe that I have survived. It's like the ink stain all over again, only much, much worse.

9

While Isobel Lennox sleeps, downstairs in the Villa Cellini the Goldmans are telling jokes again partly in order to relieve tension. It would have been difficult for them not to be aware that a number of sinister events had occurred lately in the Villa Cellini. First, Carla Dichter's death. Second, poor Mrs Lennox's collapse while out for a walk. Third (though it had started happening some days before), Martha Kraus's incipient craziness. Goldman himself had been the person to take Tom Kraus on one side and advise him to get some medication to calm his wife down. A local doctor with excellent English had been summoned, and a prescription obtained. As a consequence, Martha now also sleeps, though not peacefully, beneath a fifteenth century tapestry depicting a leopard in flight.

Tom Kraus has examined his medical insurance carefully, in case he needs to have Martha committed to a psychiatric institution in Italy. Goldman warned him — and Simons had echoed this — that psychiatric diagnoses are different in Italy from elsewhere. Italians are much less prone to administer — or receive — a label of anxiety neurosis than many other nations; which doesn't stop them swallowing some twenty thousand sets of tranquillizers, hypnotic and sedative agents every year. These figures are supplied by Goldman, who goes on to speculate about the lack of consistency in international diagnostic and prescribing patterns, and particularly the fact that diseases of the digestive system are four times as popular in Italy as in France.

The inquest on Carla Dichter has been held: death by misadventure. As Tomaso Lucca said, 'There was no evidence to suggest that anything else had happened'. The Luccas have been marvellous, doing all the communicating with the police, going with Hugo to the mortuary to identify the body, and now helping him to make funeral arrangements. The Dichters live in West Berlin. Carla's broken body will be transported there, where her husband's family will gather to mourn her passing, and even more cogently the fact that none of them had taken any trouble to get to know her. Her life, exquisitely formed and with such promise, has been wasted.

And then poor Mrs Lennox. Hugo Dichter and Isaac Simons had found her; they'd both been out walking separately on the promontory that afternoon. She'd apparently been lying unconscious in the tunnel Olivia Vereno had had constructed in the rock as one of several follies that gave the estate its air of careful grandeur. Simons had run down to the villa to get help; Dichter had stayed with Mrs Lennox. She'd come to, before the house staff arrived with the stretcher (as its brochure said, the Villa Cellini was in every way well-equipped). Dichter had told the Luccas what Mrs Lennox had said – that Isaac Simons had attacked her. Neither he nor the Luccas had mentioned anything to Simons. Hugo was locked in his own personal tragedy: he couldn't really be expected to lose himself in another. The Luccas were shocked. Mrs Lennox had seemed such an ordinary, nice woman, Isaac Simons, the epitome of the English professional man, courteous, charming, sensitive, cultured, wise. They had noticed (as everyone had) how Mrs Lennox and Mr Simons had increasingly sought each other out. However, they had supposed this to be natural. These two were the only two single people there, and they were both English.

'What do we do about this?' Tomaso had asked his wife. 'Do we tell Simons? Do we call the police again? What will all this do to the Villa Cellini's reputation?' There had already been a stream of reporters up the hill in connection with Carla's death. Even a German national newspaper had been in touch with the Villa Cellini office.

'We'll put her to bed,' said Gina Lucca, 'with a sedative. Call Dr Lorenzo again.' They did, and he prescribed more pills. 'And then perhaps,' said Gina wisely, 'perhaps she won't remember what she said? Or perhaps she'll say something different.' It is in such practical ministrations that Gina expresses her maternalism, having chosen to be salaried for it rather than procreating herself, as her fecund family have done. The more progeny they have, the more she cares for the historical estates of the Villa Cellini, feeling hers to be a more authentic contribution to the future than theirs.

Tomaso takes himself off to church at this point. He hasn't been for some time, and he has the feeling it won't do any harm to go to confession now. He finds Gina's sagacity disturbing, not enough of a refuge for his own anxious concern about what's really going on.

That night in the Villa Cellini, the Goldmans get into their queen-sized bed and decide to have sexual intercourse as a change from the other kind. It isn't a common event for them. 'Never mind, dear,' sighs Caroline, helping John Goldman to climb off her. With all this death around she's becoming frightened of exertion anyway. She rearranges her nightdress and falls asleep almost immediately, thinking about how nice and safe she is lying here next to her husband. Who himself lies awake for some time. The impotence doesn't trouble him particularly; it would if Caroline minded or anyone else knew about it. One can't have everything. And he has a lot: wit, humour, intelligence, a distinguished career, a large verandahed house in Santa Barbara; Caroline, the golden Caroline as his wife: a son about to finish medical school. Josh fancies neuro-surgery. His parents are gratified.

No, other things are causing Professor Goldman's insomnia. The menacing chain of events at the villa; does some sort of curse hang over the place? Even as he formulates the question to himself, he says in response: absurd! He, a man of science, considering a curse! Besides which, there's distinct evidence to the contrary. Hasn't he just been reading Manzoni's *The Betrothed*, an account of how they kept the bubonic plague away from these parts by dint of determination, good management, geography and the luck of the gods? Of the three events that have happened in the villa recently, Goldman is most perturbed by what happened to Mrs Lennox. Such a sane, balanced, albeit boring woman. In the time they've been here he's seen her relax, get into the swing of things. But then she'd been through a hard time with her mother's death. Caroline had told him she had a daughter with problems, too; that her husband had left her when the child was very young. It couldn't have been easy.

What was that he'd overheard Isaac saying the other night? John Goldman overhears most things, he regards it as his mission in life to tune into all available dialogues on the chance that he himself might be able to enrich them.

He thought he'd heard Isaac Simons say that Mrs Lennox's mother isn't really dead. Perhaps that was some kind of clever psychoanalytic comment: 'the mother in you is your mother surviving', for instance. Mrs Lennox does have this strange aspect to her. Sometimes she looks so maternal, sometimes her whole stance and bodily and facial expressions suggest someone still considering whether to grow up. No one has been very clear about what happened this afternoon to Mrs Lennox up there on the promontory. Gina Lucca said she'd had some sort of nervous collapse. Dichter and Simons had come down with the stretcher to the house. They'd looked like funeral attendants – but then that's what Dichter is at the moment, he supposes.

Next door, Hugo Dichter paces up and down his room. He's halfway through a bottle of the best cognac the villa has – courtesy of Gina and Tomaso Lucca, who are being so kind to him.

He'd loved Carla, but she was so restless, a roaming soul. He suspected she wanted something from him he couldn't give or didn't even know about. The night of the accident she'd been upset, distracted – no, upset: after dinner, she hadn't been able to settle to anything. They'd started a game of poker with the Moores in the library, but she'd got up after half an hour complaining of a headache. She'd tried some Schubert on the compact disc player, and then the novel she was reading, Julian Barnes, *Staring at the Sun*. Being a philosopher, she was fascinated by the idea of TAT – the absolute truth. She'd turned to him, 'What's the absolute truth about us, Hugo?'

'How do you mean?'

He'd been sitting at the desk in the window correcting the page proofs of his next book of poems.

'Are we happy, Hugo?'

He'd suppressed a feeling of impatience. He wanted to get on with his work. But he'd put his pen down and looked at her and said carefully, 'Of course we're happy, darling. I love you. You love me, don't you? We're having a wonderful time here. We have no obvious problems. We have a nice flat, you have your job which you enjoy. You may be having a few problems finding a publisher for your thesis, but you'll find one in the end. It'll be Christmas soon. You like Christmas, don't you: remember last year, when you saw the Christmas lights in the Kurfürstendamm for the first time?'

She'd put *Staring at the Sun* down on the bed. 'Well, I'm not happy, Hugo. I'm not happy at all!' And she'd started to put her coat on and he'd said, 'Where are you going, can I come with you?' And she'd pushed him away and walked off into the night.

He'd worked on his poems until about three. She hadn't come back, but he'd known her go off like this before. Her bouts of instability endeared her to him, actually. He'd even slept, waiting for her. But he couldn't now. Sleep would elude him for some time, he imagined. The hardest part was to believe that Carla's death had been accidental. She wasn't a careless person. She knew, she always knew, exactly what she was doing. He wasn't denying that she was upset – no, her distress was quite genuine, but she was consciously constructing something of it, turning it into an episode that would lead her out into the night and then back again probably for an argument and then some kind of reconciliation. She'd probably even use it for some philosophical dispute. It was like being married to a novelist, he never knew when something he said or did would be reborn in one of her speeches. That's what he'd expected: that she'd come back and they'd have a drink or two and she'd shout at him (he worried about the Goldmans hearing, the walls were like cardboard) then it'd be over – until the next time.

He goes over to her side of the bed and pulls back the pillow. Her blue nightdress lies there, folded by the maid the morning before last. He picks it up and buries his face in it. Its scents, redolent of her, make him feel quite sure that she hadn't meant to do this to him. No, someone had caused her to fall over that cliff. That's it: someone else had done it. Isaac Simons? Hugo thinks of Isaac because of what Mrs Lennox had said, when he'd had those few moments alone with her on the promontory. 'He attacked me,' she'd said. 'Isaac Simons attacked me. I went out for a walk, I wanted to see where Carla had fallen, and he came up behind me . . .'

Hugo has taken a dislike to Isaac Simons, but it isn't personal.

He merely has a thoroughly Germanic dislike of anything to do with Freud. Still, it wouldn't have occurred to him to consider Isaac Simons a pusher of women over cliffs or into tunnels. That's where he'd found Mrs Lennox, in the tunnel. He'd come into it from one end and seen a figure against the light at the other end; you had to walk halfway along it until it curved sufficiently for you to see the light. The figure had been Isaac Simons, standing over something on the ground which, it transpired, was Mrs Lennox. The man had acted quite naturally, saying, 'Look what I've found, something has happened to Mrs Lennox, we must get help'; but then, in retrospect, perhaps there had been tell-tale signs of guilt? An underlying panic in the way the words were aspirated, a few beads of sweat rather than condensation from the tunnel roof, on Isaac's forehead. There was the question of motives, which didn't bear thinking about, for how could Isaac Simons possibly have a reasonable motive for killing Hugo's own wife and then attacking Mrs Lennox? The only motive could be an insane hatred of women. Who was Isaac Simons, anyway?

In the room below, Isaac Simons sits at his desk in front of his portable computer admiring the aquamarine words on the screen: 'The viability and credibility of an autonomous existence is contingent upon conflict and competition characterizing one's relations with others.' After considering the words for a moment, he moves the cursor back to 'credibility' and presses the delete key. He then types in 'happiness'. This sets him off on another line of thought: is happiness a technical word? Can he use it as such? If so, perhaps he needs to devote a separate chapter to it. He makes a note on the pad next to the keyboard. Every now and then, he looks up at the unshuttered windows of his room and the ebony night beyond – the dripping pines, the wet, red-berried shrubs, the hedgehogs inching their way across the paths that humans now feared to tread. He himself is glad to say he experiences little fear, either of open or enclosed spaces. Except for the enclosed spaces of the mind, perhaps. The fear and the desire to get in there: these motives guide him like the Bethlehem star to uninhabited and disorganized spaces, disused mental cathedrals full of the debris of wars and innumerable failed coalitions. The Villa Cellini has turned out to be a perfect place to pursue these interests. He'd seen from the start that the psyche that interested him the most here was that of Isobel Lennox. He was attracted by her psychological naivety, by her incapacity or unwillingness to acknowledge psychological drives and motives, not only in herself but in others. He could have taught her a lot. He had taught her some things. But sometimes a person like that, caught in a spider's web of their own defensive construction, needs something to happen to get them out of it. He's therefore glad, on Mrs Lennox's behalf, about the recent turn of events – the drama and mystery of Carla Dichter's death, the ludicrous inappropriateness of Martha Kraus's madness, and Isobel's own sudden hysterical collapse.

Interesting that he'd been trying to tell her about Andrea when it had happened. Andrea Collins, his patient, his beloved. He'd thought of bringing Andrea here, but decided he would work better if she stayed in his mind, so that he could rouse her before him at times of his own convenience. About her being a patient he feels no stirrings of conscience at all. For long ago he'd concluded that curing could only be accomplished by caring: and how better to do this than by the nutritive embraces of the sexual act? This sets him apart from the psychoanalytic establishment, of course. But his charisma yields sufficient income, and the residue of his parents' estate provides what else he needs to maintain a reasonable lifestyle.

Around one, Isaac Simons undresses and gets into bed. He leaves the shutters as they are so he can continue to observe the night. He lies on his back and breathes deeply, rhythmically, resisting the fantastical stimulation of Andrea's flesh and considering himself both lucky and clever to be able to do so.

The Moores sleep too, though Dan only thanks to one of Susie's sleeping pills. Susie sleeps like a baby, curled up fetally. She even sucks her thumb sometimes. Occasionally, Dan wonders from which planet Susie has come.

The only good thing to be said about Carla's death is that an obsession has been removed from him. Well, of course, the obsession will possess him for a while longer, but the removal of its object gives it a limited life span. Carla! He'd wanted to paint her at first – of course; didn't they all? That was what she had said. He simply thought her the most aesthetically perfect representation of womanhood he'd ever seen. And after the painting, he'd wanted to touch: was her flesh warm, was it made the same way as others? Her beautiful wandering eyes, so different from Susie's, had spoken to him across crowded rooms and boats and terraces with carved peacock trees, and had said, reach out for me, and we'll light a flame together. Some flame: half a dozen or so meetings down in the village, out in the night; one hurried coupling in his own room when Susie was out looking at a church with Mrs Lennox, another in Carla's when Hugo had gone for a day's hike with his poems on his back. It had all had to be furtive adolescent stuff; and how, apart from these constraining circumstances, would they have been able to know whether their passion was capable of enduring?

The last time – he'll always remember the last time. A bright day, with summer colours, almost. They'd made their individual excuses and met in the woods, by the statue that had the words 'Hic Tragedia' inscribed on it. She'd been waiting for him, decorating the statue with a bunch of oddly purple berries she'd found. 'This man,' she'd said, tucking a clump of dark berries behind his ear, 'knew what was important in life. He founded a library and a public baths. The cleanliness of the body and the cluttering up of the mind. He kept his own mind clear by having an absolutely quiet dark room, so that when he woke in the morning he composed whatever he was going to write in his head before dictating it to his amanuensis. I think I'd like to have one of those.'

'An absolutely quiet dark room?'

'No, an amanuensis.'

'How come you know so much about this place?' he'd asked her.

'I've been here before. In another life!'

He found her sense of humour weird, exciting. Oh Carla! How would he ever be able to understand that he'd never hear her laugh nor feel her flesh again! They'd walked, and the sun had shone and they'd said to each other: this is the present moment, this is all we want, who cares about the future! Carla had said: 'I'm used to the artist–intellectual conflict, I have that with Hugo, but Hugo's so hung up on words! With you, it's the pure feeling, the image. . . .' And he'd echoed this, telling Carla there was more mutuality of experience and attitude with her than there'd ever been with Susie, whose very belief in his genius had obstructed, rather than facilitated, his art.

That day they'd found a kind of shelter in the woods, high up, near the thousand-year ruins of the castle from which ancient Italians had defended this startling bit of earth. The shelter seemed to have been used once as a studio of some kind. There was a desk, a chair, and an old stuffed chaise longue. There they had made love with more leisure than the other times, more freedom from reminders that they weren't free. Carla had said to him – was it true – that she'd never had an orgasm with Hugo, or with the other three or four men she'd slept with: only with him. It was hard to believe, but the authenticity of her response left him in no doubt about what she'd experienced with him. That day in the woods he had nearly lost himself in her, he had wanted to stay there inside her for ever, looking into the true blackness of her eyes – so dark the pupils were nearly invisible except to him when he was close to her, and could see how huge they were with sensual pleasure. Who killed Carla Dichter? The wind, her own stumbling, or another's hand? Whatever the answer he, Dan Moore, feels he isn't even free to ask the question, for his own illicit involvement in her life makes him an interested party to the answer. It doesn't matter, anyway, who did it, how it happened. She's dead. She had been alive. These are the only two facts that matter to him.

But Martha Kraus, the witch, knows the answer. Sedated by large doses of diazepam, she still knows the answer, she has it inside her like a flashing diamond, an encoded secret. Nothing can take the secret out of her except her own desire to let it out.

Isobel is dreaming. Because she'd seemed not to remember what had happened on the promontory, Gina Lucca had told her that she had been found on the floor of the tunnel by Hugo and Isaac Simons simultaneously. Doctor Lorenzo, now becoming accustomed to his frequent visits to the villa, had examined Isobel, and had pronounced her bruised, no bones broken. He'd prescribed rest. 'Probably nervous strain,' he'd said, taking Gina on one side, 'as a result of the young Mrs Dichter's body being found. Is she highly strung?' Gina hadn't known how to answer this, for she hadn't paid a great deal of attention to Mrs Lennox. She'd understood her reason for coming to the Villa Cellini.

But, as to understanding the woman's character – well, if she tried to do that with all the Villa Cellini's house guests, she'd never have time to do anything else.

But what Isobel remembers in her dreams is not the events that had caused her to fall in the tunnel on the promontory. She first of all imagines that she hears the telephone ring, and then her daughter's voice on the line, faltering, blurred by long distance cadences and crossed lines; but eventually Isobel makes out what Becky's saying, and the words are, 'this is a house of death, Mother.' Becky is immensely distressed – hers is the sobbing of early childhood, alone in a darkened room, left with a stranger, lost in a crowded shopping mall. It isn't like Becky today at all: in control, taut, impervious. And she, Isobel, needs to force out of Becky what's been troubling her. The dream wakes her, she wonders if the phone has been ringing, if there is news she needs to hear. She stumbles across the room to the lavatory, forgetting where the switch is, but finding it by the light from the small square window. Then back to bed. To sleep? She isn't sure whether what happens next is fact or fiction, not at all sure. What happens next is that she becomes aware that on the bed next to her lies her dead mother. The form is statuesque, it's been taken straight out of its coffin, so it lies there with extreme neatness and decorum – the decorum of one who wants to give as precise an impression as possible of who she is. Doubts after death: who wants those? Or about death? About death there can be no doubt. Death is absolute. But life is relative. That's the problem, the weakness of the whole arrangement.

Isobel stares through the darkness at the figure next to her. She has this electric impulse, which has to be fiercely resisted, to cuddle up to it, to find the welcoming curves of her mother's body and fit herself to them. She wants to be held. She wants to be connected. But her mother had always seemed to demand love, not to give it. Isobel had never had the experience of bearing her mother's love as a snail carries its house on its back: the essential burden of maternal love. This was what her mother hadn't chosen to give her, but she wanted it, she was a needy child, like Rebecca on the telephone just now, 'this is a house of death.' So now her mother had come to tell her this, after death. The timing was most important. In presenting her dead body, she recreated the desolation of the original invitation: 'come to me, I'm your mother, I love you. But come only when I say so, on my terms, when I've got time for you.'

Oh, Mother! And all the time saying you were trying to lead your own life, that I would respect you for that. I won't, I never will. You should have put me first. I was yours as nothing else ever was. You made me. At least, you started out making me, you did the outline, as it were, but then you gave up, you left me empty; and then you had the extraordinary cheek to notice the emptiness and complain about it. 'Love me, Isobel! Why don't you love me? Kiss me, Isobel, why won't you kiss me?' I'll kiss you now, Mother, because it's safe now, it's safe for the very reason that you won't know I'm doing it. I can pay you back for your resistance to me in life. It's no good you lying there dead accusing me of this and that, I won't have it any more.

The figure rises from the bed and hovers above Isobel for a moment, then melts through the painted Renaissance ceiling.

Goodbye, Mother! Isobel might have waved quite cheerily, were it not for the fact that she feels so angry. Those other dreams she's been having: they aren't dreams, either. She's remembered here in the Villa Cellini what it was like to be a child. She's reinstated herself in a place of violence. It wants her to know about it. Her mother's physical abhorrence of her, the child Isobel's emergence as a separate being; the clash of wills resulting in a clash of flesh. The pink rubber hand with its awful smell on her cheek. And worse, worse: the hours of solitude without knowing why. Let me out, Mummy! Mummy, I won't do it again, I promise I won't! But what was it she had done? It's difficult to promise a blameless life in the future if she doesn't know where the first blame is. 'The White Flower of a Blameless Life' – achieved after death, not before.

Her mother used to make her chocolate semolina pudding. At five or six, she'd eaten it and heard, felt, the nasty stony scrunch of the sugar scattered on top. She had noticed that, whatever benevolence her mother had bestowed on her, there had been gritty obligations involved. The chocolate semolina pudding image was rapidly exchanged for another. Her mother skinning a rabbit at the sink. It was wartime: rabbits were scarce, good food. Her mother, though, didn't want the rabbit's nourishing meat. She only wanted its fur, to make a coat for herself. She skinned a dozen rabbits that summer, and hung their skins in the pantry to dry.

Rotten flesh, strips remaining on the interior surface of the rabbit's skin, dangling like worms. Isobel had been sent to the pantry sometimes to fetch something, and had seen them there. Mortality mixed with raisins and shortbread squares and gravy powder.

Goodbye, Mother! No wonder you never stopped complaining about me. I couldn't do things right, because I simply never was what you wanted. You didn't want a child, a living, breathing, fighting, laughing, being; you wanted a puppet, who would dance when you pulled its strings, or a mechanical toy, that you could wind and set down on the floor. Then, when it had done its little act, you would put it in the cupboard. But children can't be put in cupboards. I'm not talking about discipline, you understand, I'm talking about an abuse of power. Which you got away with because it was an accident. An accident of the place and person: your personality and mine, that abhorrent union you had with a man you said was my father, and, not content with that, whom you summarily dispatched to an African forest never to be heard of again. I do not, actually, believe that such a man could have been my father. Though perhaps what I'm saying is that I do not actually believe that such a woman as you could have been my mother. I wanted an ordinary woman as my mother, the sort other people have. The sort that smile and make cakes and sleep with their husbands in silence for half a century. Why, Mother, oh why, couldn't you have been like that? Couldn't you have done it for me? Just for me?

Now her mother has gone from the room, having failed to get the last word, Isobel is possessed by a new feeling; that of being parentless, an orphan, of having nothing between her and the black void, oblivion, heaven or hell – death; the universe in its limits and its partiality. She, Isobel, has become the last generation. She is now an ancestor. Whatever she knows is all there is to know. God help the mothers, when they have no mothers to help them. But just to make sure, when she gets back to England, she'll go and see the Kargar family, from whence she got her name and, according to her mother's account, half her genetic inheritance. She needs to be sure now that she has no living father. Old Lady Kargar died before Becky was born, but Evan had a sister ten years younger, who may be alive still, somewhere. She'll find her, ask her. Get the answer.

This resolution pacifies Isobel and she drifts off to sleep again. She thinks she might see her new landscape once more; the mountains with their pink and yellow slopes, reminding her of the idyll of Heidi in the Swiss mountains with the cowbells and the flowers and the old man who reared her. This was a favoured children's book when Isobel was young. Heidi the innocent, the free one, living in an enchanted world.

And so Isobel does see a glimpse of the scene she is coming to think of as her own particular paradise. It's so quiet up there, and clean, with a matchless clarity of light streaking the snow crystals. The air shines with a meteoric brilliance, encapsulating joy. Isobel is at peace. But not for long. She is startled by a creak of the floorboard, caused by the expansion of the central heating pipes. The mysterious notion and operation of cause. As she moves, she's aware again of the violence done to her own body. Caused by the stones on which she fell? That was plausible. But why had she fallen? Again the pounding of her heart as her mind goes backwards and then forwards with Isaac Simons on the path around the promontory, arm in hers, the menace of his monological presence. Isaac, whom she had liked and favoured with her confidences, her company, her upswept hair on the night Gina had announced Carla Dichter's death. Had she, Isobel, then simply fallen? Had it been because of the news of Carla's death, the sighting of the funeral parlour of the lake's edge a thousand metres below? Isobel didn't consider herself a nervous person. She wasn't given to depressions and undue anxieties (except about Becky, but that, naturally, was different) and she certainly wasn't prone to fainting fits. No, there was something else. Someone else following her. She could remember it if she tried. If she wanted to.

Isaac Simons! He comes after her into the tunnel. He seizes her wrists, pushes her against the rock face. The angles of the rocks project themselves painfully into her back. Her feet are forced into a pool of fetid water. He knocks her to the ground. He wrenches her skirt up to her waist, he pulls her tights and her pants down. What is he doing? He's doing what Mr Jefferson does, all the time. He's looking at her private parts. To see if there's anything wrong with them. Are they stained, odoriferous, mutilated? Do they bleed unduly? Martha Kraus's words: 'do you stick your fingers up your cunt, Mrs Lennox?'

10

It's nearly the end of their time at the Villa Cellini anyway. Martha Kraus, still on her medication of 15 milligrams of diazepam p.d., stands staring out of the window. A strong wind has been blowing, then it rained, now it's begun to snow. Thus it becomes December, no longer autumn but winter. Through the changing seasons, the landscape of lake and mountains and trees and terraces offers its consolations to the inhabitants of the villa up there like a yellow crescent on the hill above the town, where the bells chime and the boats come and go with a language of constancy and perpetual motion far more soothing to the human condition than any diazepam tablet.

Tom Kraus puts a coat over Martha's shoulders. 'Come on, Martha, let's go down to the town. I need to go to the post office.'

Obediently, she turns and goes. He guides her down the steps to where the vista of red rooftops appears, and further out of the side gate and down the Salita Cellini to the lakeshore, where tourist shops, even in this declining season, hang out their objects of desire. Red inflatable ducks for children; giant-sized Pinocchios and other puppets; delicate silver, silk and the tang of leather burnished with gold. Martha's eyes are unseeing. Tom is glad to have her back. He plans to return her to Manhattan where she'll see a psychiatrist friend of his, whom he's already phoned to make an appointment. Kraus's office in New York has changed their flights. They'll go home early. Martha's mental health is not to be taken lightly.

He goes into the post office, leaving Martha outside. There's a fair-sized queue; he waits, listing in his head the things that still have to be done. Call their housekeeper so that the apartment will be ready for them. Pay the bill at the villa: cash some more traveller's cheques; buy some expensive gift for the Luccas, to reward their kindness.

Martha, outside, watches people coming and going, accompanied by small children and dogs. An invisible wall is between her and them, she keeps hitting her head against it. Still it occurs to her, watching the women passing busily backwards and forwards with their shopping baskets, that she might have business of her own to do while her managerial husband is in there doing his. She possesses some consciousness of having started something she needs to finish. It's chiefly a feeling of having been prevented from action. She moves out of the shelter of the arcade of shops into the open ground between the shops and the quay, needing to feel the cold fresh air on her face – the tonic the doctor hadn't ordered. That's better. It helps to clear her head. She walks fast, away from the town centre, out towards the lido and the large hotels that are being restored for the next season – or the one after that. She walks faster, round the back of the lido and up a road which climbs the opposite side of the hill from the one she had come down with Tom. Now she's able to look down on the rooftops, but there is no Tom beside her. How wonderful to be alone! Now she's alone, she can get back inside herself to where she'd been when this whole nightmarish thing started. Now she knows her destination – she has to get to see Mrs Lennox, poor, wonderful Mrs Lennox, who's having a bad time of her own.

She comes out by the back stairs of the villa, the external stairs leading directly to the second floor. She knows Mrs Lennox's room – she'd been there to borrow some aspirin. She takes her shoes off, and creeps along the glossy beige carpet holding her breath so no one will even be able to remark on the noise the air makes as it enters and is expelled from her body.

She opens the door, goes in carefully. It's a large room, with a big white bed facing two windows. The windows are closed, but not the shutters. The white curtains resonate with the stirrings of snow outside.

'Mrs Lennox!' Martha's voice is urgent. Isobel is in a deep sleep. Martha touches her cheek: 'Mrs Lennox, wake up! I need to talk to you!' The voice inside her telling her what to do is a great deal more insistent now.

'Martha!' Isobel is pleased that Martha should be there. She doesn't even feel apprehensive about Martha's newly loose tongue. 'Why are you whispering, dear?'

'Mrs Lennox, I want to tell you that I know what's been going on here. I think you do, too, but I want to make sure before I go.'

'Are you going, dear?' Isobel's eyelids begin to feel heavy.

'Mrs Lennox, don't go back to sleep, please, not now. In a minute you can, but not now.'

Isobel shuts her eyes. 'All right, I'm listening. But you must forgive me if I close my eyes, I'm very tired, you see.'

'Do you remember Olivia Vereno, Mrs Lennox?'

'How could I remember her? I never knew her!' Isobel's voice is quiet, unemotional.

'Yes, yes.' Martha's getting impatient now. 'But you know who I mean? The woman who owned the Villa Cellini. Forty years ago. You know the story, I'm sure you do!'

Isobel does remember Susie Moore telling her about Olivia Vereno in their studio apartment by the waterfront where the white duck occupied the lake. 'Yes. Go on.'

'It's her,' insists Martha urgently. 'She was a witch, too, like me. She's making these things happen.'

Isobel opens her eyes. 'Now, why would she want to do that? Why on earth?' It did seem an extraordinary idea.

'Olivia wasn't only a witch, Mrs Lennox. She was a healer. The two things often go together. Gina Lucca lent me an unpublished book about the villa – not the one in the library upstairs, that doesn't have any of the interesting stuff in it. This one's the work an American student did for his doctoral thesis – *Time out of Place: Four Hundred Years of the Villa Cellini*. There are boxes of letters too, other documents. Gina let me look at those as well.' Martha stops for a moment to check that Isobel's paying attention. 'You see, Mrs Lennox, Olivia was a healer, but in order to heal, first the spell has to be cast, and then people must confront in themselves what it is that prevents healing. All a witch can do is to help people help themselves.'

'Like God,' whispers Isobel, sleepily able only to think in clichés, 'God helps those who help themselves.'

'Women *are* gods,' says Martha clearly. 'But we resent the vision. Do you remember our walk, when I realized I had to go back into my craziness, because that's the only place where I'll find out who I am? You told me I was right, Mrs Lennox.'

'Did I really, dear?'

Isobel turns her head and sees Martha, agitated, assertive, no longer quite so little and pretty, in fact rather formidable. Martha's insistence on the truth of the matter rouses her thoroughly at last: 'All right, Martha,' she responds distinctly, 'I'll tell you what you were going to tell me. That in order for any of us properly to survive, to live, to get on with our lives, we must take out our pasts and look at them, and make peace with what happened. But we won't do that unless something makes us. Here, at the Villa Cellini, it's Olivia Vereno who does that. She won't let anyone get away with pretending any more: she wants us to have the vision.'

'You too!' Martha speaks gently. 'It's so calm and beautiful up there, I do so love looking at it.' The two women smile happily at each other. 'But you haven't got it quite right, Mrs Lennox.'

'No?'

'Olivia Vereno isn't interested in everyone who comes here. She doesn't care about the men. She doesn't mind them going on with their dissembling, their lies. She lets them carry on, but she uses them to extricate us: to release us, the women, from our histories, to make us whole.'

'Yes,' says Isobel, 'but why?'

'Why what?'

'Well, I don't understand why Olivia Vereno doesn't care about the men. Isn't that rather unfair of her?'

'I'll tell you why, Mrs Lennox. Olivia Vereno adopted four war orphans.'

'Yes. I remember Susie Moore telling me that. Two boys and two girls. They were brought up here. What happened to them?' Isobel recalls asking Susie the same question and not getting an answer.

'One of them is the doctor – Dr Lorenzo. In the village. The one who gave me my pills. The one who came to see you.'

'How interesting.'

'He isn't, particularly. Olivia's not pleased with her "son". She thinks he's acting against her. The use of medicine to treat distress, for example: that isn't right. It blocks the very process she's trying to encourage.'

'What about the others?'

'The second son, Dino, became a painter. I don't mean a painter of pictures. I mean a painter of houses. He lives in Naples.'

'Does Olivia approve of that?'

'Oh yes. He preserves the shells which house us; if we're to sort out interiors, someone must take care of the exteriors, mustn't they? People say, though,' Martha moves away from Isobel's bedside and starts walking the room with some agitation, 'people say that Dino never managed to do anything more than paint houses, because he could never get over what happened to his sisters. They killed their mother, you see. In 1958 they poisoned Olivia with one of her own concoctions. Vincente made the accusation. They were tried and found guilty. They were executed. That was the law then in Italy. You do see, Mrs Lennox,' Martha turns and faces Isobel, 'that the Villa Cellini is one of the few places in the world where we find ourselves in the midst of the first drama of the human condition. Not fathers and sons, not Oedipus. The myth of Oedipus is the second drama; but the world is ruled by men, so they say it's the first. The first is really what happens between mothers and daughters. It's terribly simple, really.'

'Is it?' says Isobel. She isn't sure.

'Women give life: women mother. Women are the mothers of both men and women. In order to give life, we must want to give life. Only our mothers are able to make us want that. Oh, I don't mean,' goes on Martha hastily, 'I don't mean just getting pregnant and delivering the baby. That's not the important part. The important part is the tending, the caring, the feeding of body and soul: the whole lifetime of mothering.' She stops talking then, and is suddenly a great deal calmer. She returns to Isobel's side, takes her hand and looks into her eyes. 'I wanted to tell you that, Mrs Lennox, before I leave. And something else; thank you for mothering me. You have given me life. What you have helped me to understand has set me on the right path. I know which direction to take now.'

Isobel remembers Carla Dichter's death.

'She was the one victim, Mrs Lennox. There always, unfortunately, has to be a victim. Did Carla tell you she came to this part of Italy as a child? Her eyes looked into this lake, at these same mountains, she was drawn into it all then. It was just waiting to get her back, that's all. But you will find her reincarnation somewhere. In what happens to you, perhaps.'

Martha leaves the room, suddenly, and Isobel closes her eyes. The feeling of tiredness comes back to her again, overlaying everything that Martha told her, returning her to sleep.

The next day, Martha and Tom Kraus set off for Switzerland en route for the States. There are strikes in Italy paralysing the transport system. The Krauses hire a car to take them to Berne in Switzerland, whence they can pick up a flight back to New York. Tom keeps a careful eye on his wife throughout the whole tedious journey; he doesn't want any more wanderings.

Hugo Dichter has already taken Carla's body back to West Berlin. The arrangements, which were complex, had fortunately been made before the full effects of the strike were felt.

On December 13, Isobel gets out of bed feeling as though her strange ordeal has come to its natural conclusion. With Gina Lucca's help, she changes her own air ticket, so as to leave the Villa Cellini a few days earlier than planned, but after the end of the strike. Isobel wants very much to see Becky again – and also her decision to establish the mortality or otherwise of her father makes her want to get back to London and get on with things.

She joins the others for dinner that last evening. Only the Moores, the Goldmans and Isaac Simons are left. It's the first time she's seen Isaac since the incident on the promontory. Susie sits one side of her, and Caroline Goldman the other. But what do they know of what happened? Susie is kind to her and chatty, under the circumstances. She mentions that Dan seems depressed – his paintings aren't coming along well. She refers to Carla's death as 'that awful tragedy', but asks no questions about Isobel's own collapse, for which Isobel is grateful.

Caroline Goldman behaves as though nothing at all has happened. She talks about cultural life in London, where, as everyone already knows, she and her husband had been briefly before the Italy trip. According to Caroline Goldman, there are only a half a dozen movie theatres in London. This is appalling to one who lives in New York. Also, does Mrs Lennox realize that the *zuppa inglese* which they're presently eating for dessert isn't *zuppa inglese* at all? Does Mrs Lennox know how the true *zuppa inglese* is made? She goes on rapidly to discuss with Dan Moore a meal she and Professor Goldman have recently eaten in Bergamo, of larks' beaks, enlivened with yellow corn. Tomaso Lucca had told them that the killing and eating of larks is a criminal offence in that region of Italy, and they had consequently both had indigestion.

'So.' Isobel looks across the table at Isaac Simons. 'How are you, Isaac?' She feels considerable charity towards him, now he's there in front of her. A real person. Not an imaginary friend or foe. It's also plain that *she* will have to take the initiative in speaking to him, or they will never talk again.

'I've finished a draft of my book,' he tells her, safely.

'That's good, isn't it? That's what you came here to do. Will I get to read it some day?'

He puts down his fork. 'I'll send it to you, if you like.'

'I'd like that.'

'How are you, Isobel?' he asks then in return, after a pause.

'I'm better,' she says, firmly. 'Much better. Quite a new woman, in fact.'

The only available flight back to London is in the afternoon, though Isobel would have preferred to leave in the morning. She has coffee with the Luccas, who express a wish that she'll return to the villa one day. Perhaps she'll bring her daughter to see them? They like to keep in touch with old clients. Isobel says she'll write. The stay has been good for her; the collapse probably inevitable, and facilitating her return to health. Her last image of the Villa Cellini is of the Luccas standing in the main driveway waving her off from under a big yellow umbrella.

Halfway through the flight, the pilot, who introduces himself in an obsequiously familiar way, tells them that the sun is setting on one side of the aircraft and the moon rising on the other.

On her left, Isobel sees the rosy infusion of the sky as the sun slides down beneath the field of clouds. Ribbons of red and orange and yellow join one another, a new coalescence of a rainbow, in a celestial blueness that's never the same when seen from earth. To her right, an identical field of white fluffiness floats by, but at its edge, the moon peeks up, even as she watches, a crescent and an eye of ivory whiteness at first, then a half moon, then the whole resplendent orb, winking like a pearl at her, bringing to her mind a picture from long ago, the man in the moon voyeuristically watching her first congress with Gerald. How long, Isobel, how long! How many moons! How much more you understand now – not of the moon and the universe, how pearls are made, whether larks should be eaten, or the name of the Italian wind that rages round the head of the lake and the promontory from which, and on which, women fall, but of how you yourself are made and what you are able to make of it, of life! Her mother saying she was boring. Her daughter that she is stupid. The two of them talking to each other, exchanging secrets about her. Women gossiping about each other. Gossip: the stuff of life. You don't need three nipples to know how important gossip is! Isobel laughs and the moon laughs back. But the man in the seat beside her shifts nervously within the constraints of his seat belt, and considers the woman beside him, laughing to herself, probably crazy.

11

I met her at the airport. Since that first fussy phone call I hadn't heard from her again – except for a couple of postcards. Then I had this really strange phone call from a woman called Mrs Lucca, at this villa place she was staying in Italy. This Mrs Lucca said I ought to know my mother had had some sort of minor nervous breakdown, but she seemed to be back on her feet again now, and it might be a good idea if I came to meet her at the airport, instead of letting her stagger home on her own. At first, I thought interfering bitch! But then I worked my way through that one and I thought, hell, she's probably trying to tell me something important. Why would she moralize to me? She doesn't know me from Adam.

She came through the sliding doors with a load of stuff in the luggage trolley. She looked tired. I hadn't seen her for nearly a month, it felt like meeting a stranger. She didn't know I was there, so I rushed round to intercept her on her way to the underground. I suppose she was going to struggle onto a train with all that stuff. I never understood why she didn't take taxis more often, but the concept of a false economy isn't one my mother has heard of.

She was really pleased to see me. Gave me a big hug. Made me feel self-conscious with all those people around us. 'Come on, Mum, let's get out of here.' The same words, actually, as I spoke in the undertaker's when we went to see Granny's body. It seems I'm always extracting my mother from emotional situations.

I was quite affected by my grandmother's death, in fact, though it didn't really sink in that she was dead until we went to this absolutely revolting place where they'd taken her. Mum was fussing about the policeman who was putting parking tickets on cars outside the undertaker's, as though death should be an exception to the normal business of life – but death's a part of the capitalist enterprise just like everything else.

This snotty woman in the undertaker's borrowed my cigarette lighter. I could see Mum didn't have a clue what was going on. We went into this little room, and there was this doll in a white lace ruff neatly tucked into its coffin. I knew right away it wasn't her. I said so to Mum. Mum was bending over it saying, 'I loved you, Mum.' I'd never heard her call her 'Mum' before. I had to drag her away. 'Come on Mum, let's get out of here.' I clung onto her, she was really shaking. I thought this is really odd, three generations of women at the undertaker's. One dead, two sobbing. If the old lady could've seen us, she would have liked it: she'd caused a reunion by dying. I bet she never thought that would happen. I doubt it was her intention at all.

I had a problem at the funeral, thinking of her being transformed into dust. Brown dust? Grey dust? That vicar: our days on this earth are numbered, or whatever. Mother crying. Everyone watching this box with Granny in it being conveyed to an oven. It does strike me that there must be a better way to deal with the dead. Poor Granny. Still, at least she was unconscious at the time. That's not easy, though, for the living. So long as a person's body's still there, you think they might just be in it somewhere. Lurking in a vein, or in a corner of the liver. And then, even when you know the body's gone, you get this thing about the ashes; the person might be hiding in there, mightn't they? You need to consider that.

Well, I got my mother to take a taxi from the airport. That was my achievement for the day. It cost all of £12. I told her about the phone call from Mrs Lucca. She looked a bit disappointed then, as I clearly hadn't come to meet her of my own volition, but I made up for it by saying, 'I was worried about you, Mum, what were you doing having a nervous breakdown on Lake Como?'

'I'll tell you about it later, Becky,' she said.

We had a bottle of wine for supper. I don't drink much myself any more, but she obviously wanted to. She made spaghetti carbonara, and tomatoes stuffed with garlic and herbs and breadcrumbs. Under the Italian influence, you see. 'It's good to have you back, Mum,' I said, 'At least I'll get to eat some proper meals now.'

'Oh *Becky*,' she said, and we both laughed, knowing she was about to launch into her nutrition lecture.

'Listen, Mother,' I said, 'I've got something to say to you.' Have you ever noticed how if a young person says that to a parent, their ears always open and flap around wildly, whereas the other way round results in deafness? Anyway, 'Now you've been away a whole month,' I said, 'you must be able to see things in perspective at last.'

'Quite right, Becky. But how did you know?'

'You don't give me any credit for being wise,' I complained.

'Quite right,' she said again.

Her eyes had started looking a little moist and pink. I was getting fed up with all this; it didn't feel right for me to be right all the time. But I had to carry on now I'd started. 'Listen, Mother, what I wanted to say is that I think you should give up being obsessed with me now. I'm a big girl. Why don't you just consider me an adult person and leave it at that?' She stared at me. Her face looked as though this was an entirely novel idea. 'No more of this fussing like a mother, then,' I went on, anxious to make sure she'd grasped my point. 'It never got you any-where, anyway. It always sent me running in the other direction to do the opposite. I'm much more likely to do the right things if you leave me alone. Let's call it quits, Mother. About eating, certainly. Also about leaving the lights on in my room. And am I on heroin? And will I ever learn to clean a toilet? Actually,' I went on reflectively, 'it might interest you to know that while you were away I did clean the toilet. Funnily enough, it wasn't all that bad. Quite an illuminating experience. Not to say purifying.' I laughed at my own joke. She didn't – it always took my mother ages to see the point of jokes. When I was younger, I found it irritating. Now I find it sort of endearing. When everyone else has got on to the next subject of conversa-tion, there's my mother staring into space wondering what the joke was. The bit of her brain that deals with humour – also crossword puzzles, that's something else that's completely for-eign to her nature – is absolutely one hundred per cent missing.

'To you, Becky!' My mother raised her glass of wine. 'It's wonderful to be home. And to have you as a daughter.' I don't like too much emotion at a time, so I interrupted, and asked her again about the Villa Cellini. It certainly looked a fabulous place on the postcard she sent me.

'It's a long story, Becky,' she said. 'I'm not too sure what happened myself.' But then she went on to tell me. It sounded amazing. After a while, I began to wonder if she'd invented it? Perhaps she'd really been to some respectable little pension in Siena or somewhere, where nothing had really happened at all – but she'd got stuck into an immense daydream which included all these characters. She's had quite a boring life, my mother, she certainly needs to make up for it, and why not by using her imagination for the first time in her life?

I particularly didn't believe this part about this American woman called Martha being a witch. We did witchcraft in my history class; it's definitely a historical phenomenon. The other thing that happened, this Italian-German lady going over a cliff, seemed to me quite simple. Her husband probably tipped her. He couldn't stand her having it off with the painter. He wanted to get on with his poems.

She didn't say much about her own so-called nervous break-down, though. Just that she went out for a walk the next day to see where this Dichter woman had gone over the edge – that's a bit morbid, if you ask me, like driving to look at a motorway crash – and she'd gone into this tunnel with a shrink from England – that's a bit off too, who'd want to go into a tunnel with a shrink? – and woken up in bed covered in bruises. Mind you, he could have attacked her, I suppose. Shrinks are known for that sort of thing. It's a bit like *A Passage to India*, isn't it? When Adela Moore passes out in a cave and you don't know whether Aziz screwed her or not. Maybe this shrink even screwed my mother. If he did, she certainly wouldn't mention it to me. She doesn't think screwing is a normal activity, my mother doesn't. Well, I suppose it isn't, in a tunnel with a shrink. I hesitate to use the word rape here. That would get me into a whole political discourse I'd rather stay out of. She did like him in any case, didn't she? She said she did.

I wanted to ask her questions. But I didn't. Wisdom again! 'Come on, Mum, I said, it's time for bed. Enough emotion for one day. I mean, I've had enough. I don't know about you. I wouldn't presume to make a judgement on your behalf.'

12

The weeks following my return from the Villa Cellini are very busy with Christmas. Of course, I'd intended to do the important shopping in Italy, but I simply didn't get round to it. So I've got no alternative but to join the crowds in Oxford Street, and fight my way to enough counters to purchase gifts for Becky, my friend Margaret, four or five others and a few multi-purpose presents which will do for neighbours or people who turn up unexpectedly. I hate every minute of it, not only because of the last minute circumstances in which I have to do it, but because somehow the energy I usually have for such things seems to have left me. I'm in Selfridges, looking at handbags, when I discover myself wondering what to buy for Mother. Not a handbag, but perhaps a bright new purse? The jewellery counter catches my eye and I wonder about a flashy gold chain necklace. I have to find a chair and sit down when I realize I'm considering these gifts for a dead person. This is the first year of my life when I don't have to think about what to do about Mother's present, what she might expect, what might please her, how she'll always find something to criticize about it. Last year, for example, I gave her a soft wool shawl, blue with stars on it, to wear in bed, but, although this was what Mother had asked for, when she got it, the material wasn't right, it irritated her skin, and the stars were very inconsiderate of me, in view of the fact that the only play she, Molly Kargar, had ever been in that had been a total flop had been called *The Moon and the Stars*.

On Christmas Eve Becky goes to a party, and I watch television. I don't mind Becky going out, I don't mind being alone, I feel I'm merely getting back into my old habits. The only problem is, my heart isn't in them any more.

I write to the old Kargar home in Sussex, not knowing to

whom I should address the letter, but deciding to risk 'Dear Elizabeth Kargar'. Of course she's likely to have changed her name, the way women have a habit of doing. But I have no way of finding out what the new name might be. In my letter to Evan's sister, I put the case simply: does Elizabeth know what happened to my father, is he dead or alive? What was the last they heard? Have they had any news of him recently? I didn't contact Elizabeth when Mother died, because Mother left explicit instructions that she didn't want the Kargar family – what was left of it – to be told. She said they hadn't taken much interest in her life. So why should they have the privilege of being notified about her death? I'm not sure I agree with that opinion, but I suppose she did have the right to keep them away if that was what she wanted.

Christmas comes and goes. Towards the New Year, it snows quite thickly. My friend Margaret in Harrow-on-the-Hill invites me to lunch. It's a steep climb from the station, reminiscent of the pathways in the grounds of the Villa Cellini. I stop for a moment, looking at the lunar landscape, and imagine I can see the Villa Cellini instead: watching, full of secrets, whispering about me. There might be snow in the grounds there now too. The winter in that part of Italy is short, but they do have one. Against the whiteness, the profusion of holly berries would stand out like clots of blood. Like the ink I allowed to leak onto the white bedspread that day when I fell asleep and re-entered my childhood, quite as painfully as anyone who ever fell in a holly bush.

I go back to work on January 2nd. Becky's college doesn't start for another week, but she's locked in her room most of the time, reading and writing essays. Her social life seems to have been much contracted. Mary comes round, and a male friend, Jason, is there once or twice a week. I can hear the gentle rise and fall of conversation from Becky's room. When they listen to music the volume's low as well – so low that most of the time I can't hear it at all, but I can make out one particular song they keep playing, it's got the tune of an old hymn and words which, once heard, continually chase each other in my head:

'Love must always change to sorrow
And everyone must play the game

Because it's here today and gone tomorrow
But the world goes on the same.'

I find myself humming it in Sainsbury's between the aisles of lavatory paper and baked beans.

Relations between Rebecca and myself are much more amicable these days. I sometimes do ask her to do more in the house, there's a token grumble, but then she obliges. She now informs me she wants to go to university. Without saying anything to me, she's already applied and been offered a place at St Andrews to read English. She says she hopes I won't mind her being so far away. But if it's what she wants to do, how can I say anything?

Harley Street, and Mr Jefferson, are just the same, except that Mr Jefferson now strikes me as a rather boring, pompous and unimportant little man. Not little in size, but lacking the stature one looks for in human beings. That I now look for. Now I see the women who wait, reading *Country Life*, as victims. I decide to wait a week or two and then give in my notice. It's time I did something else with my life – nothing dramatic, but I've still got some time left.

Something's beginning to concern me, however, something about myself. I'm putting on weight, I feel tired all the time, my breasts hurt, I'm terribly hungry. At work one day the phone rings and a woman I don't know requesting an appointment with Mr Jefferson describes exactly the same symptoms as I have. I put the phone down, my coat on, and leave the office. (It's a Friday, Mr Jefferson isn't there.) I tour the streets for a while, and then, because it's cold, I go in the side door of the British Home Stores. In the lampshade department, where I'm pretending to be examining a new kind of desk lamp, I realize that, as a result of events in the Villa Cellini, something material might have happened to me: I might be pregnant.

My periods have been erratic for several years, so a gap of three months or so isn't a reliable guide to anything. But I do definitely feel queer. I go back to the office and write myself into Mr Jefferson's appointments book for the following Monday: '10.30 Mrs Lennox'. Before I leave work I even fill in a standard medical history for myself and take a specimen bottle from the drawer.

On Monday morning, when Mr Jefferson looks at the book, he says, 'Isobel, what is this?'

'I need to see you. Professionally.'

'Are you sure?'

'Oh yes. Better the devil you know than the devil you don't.' I smile placatingly at him. 'Am I sure I need to see a gynaecologist? Well, I suppose you'll give me the answer to that, won't you?'

We sit down. He picks up his pen. 'Tell me the symptoms. Why you booked yourself an appointment.'

'I've already filled in a medical history.' I point at a chart on his desk.

'Oh yes. Let me see. Breast tenderness, lethargy, unusual appetite, weight gain. See, she knows the technical terms! Well, it looks as though it may be something hormonal. Last menstrual period October 24. Irregular menstruation for three years. We'd better do an examination, hadn't we?'

I hand him my little container of yellow liquid. He takes it to the other side of the room, where he keeps the urine testing equipment. I know about these urine tests, having on occasion been asked to do them myself and quite quickly learning not to think of it as any kind of intimate fluid.

'Hmn. How old are you now?'

'I wrote it down on the chart.' I'm not going to cope with his nervousness as well as my own.

'Forty-eight. It isn't likely. It isn't at all likely.'

'What isn't?'

'Pregnancy. But I'd better examine you, if only to rule it out.' He seems extremely loath to do so. I think to myself: there's no chaperone. He can't call for me. I can't be my own chaperone, can I? Yes I can, why not? 'You don't need to worry,' I say firmly, 'we've known each other long enough.'

'Yes,' he replies, not looking directly at me.

I go behind the screen and take my clothes off. On the examination couch is a neatly folded gown: I put it there myself. I arrange myself on the couch. 'It's all right, Mr Jefferson, you can come in now.'

He comes in, coughing slightly.

'Oh, have you got a cold?' It seems only polite to inquire.

'No, I . . .' The telephone rings.

'I'm afraid I'm not in a position to answer that.'

He goes back to his desk. I hear him saying, 'Yes. No. Why not? Okay. All right, put her at the end of the list.' Then he comes back, not coughing this time.

I lie back on the couch. I close my eyes and think of the Villa Cellini. The lake, under a blue sky. The iced slopes of the mountains. The olive trees; hard green olives falling and being trodden into the ground.

Mr Jefferson clanks around with his instruments. He approaches me with one gloved hand. 'Just relax,' he says, 'just relax.' I'm able now to follow his instruction. I continue to think of that Italian landscape – the magnificence of the villa, lemon trees backlit by a rising sun. He withdraws his hand and exchanges it for a speculum. As he gazes at my interior, I gaze at my own, a different part of it, and I'm not at all displeased with what I see.

'That's fine, you can get dressed now, Isobel.'

I replace my clothes methodically and join him at the desk. He's writing something. 'What did you find, then?' I ask.

He looks up. 'I assume, Isobel, the possibility of pregnancy is a real one?'

'I don't understand the question.'

'Have you been having intercourse?'

'No.'

'So. Well, the uterus is enlarged to the size of a ten or eleven week pregnancy. The cervix is soft. It's bluish. The urine test is positive. All of which suggests pregnancy. But if you say . . .'

'I didn't say that,' I interrupt him. 'No, I didn't say that at all. I said I hadn't been having intercourse. But there are other ways to conceive, Mr Jefferson, aren't there?'

'Are there?' He looks awfully puzzled. 'But at your age IVF . . .'

I let him drivel on for a bit, and then I settle myself more squarely in my chair and concentrate hard on the words as they come out of my mouth. 'I went to the Villa Cellini for a month, Mr Jefferson. At your suggestion.' I remember him pushing the brochure into my hand. The fact that it had been raining at the time instantly brings back to me my final view of the villa with the Luccas under the yellow house umbrella. 'It was exactly the right thing to do. The best thing that could have happened to me. I'm very grateful to you for making the suggestion, Mr Jefferson. But one or two interesting things happened there. With some consequences. This may be one of them.'

'I still don't understand, Isobel.'

'You don't have to. Some things pass our understanding, and are meant to. Life and death are mysteries, don't you think, Mr Jefferson? I've never approved of science. Of course I've never said so to you. It hasn't been my place to offer opinions. But science in my view is only an excuse. So that we can avoid the responsibility of being puzzled. I don't require an understanding from you. I require a diagnosis. Treatment, perhaps. And by the way, I'm resigning from this job. I've done it for long enough. You've been good to me. I think I've done the work reasonably well. But other things are demanding my attention now. I hope you don't mind. I don't think you'll have any trouble getting a replacement.' I finish a little more lamely than I would have liked. But, still, I've said what I think. And in the matter of my physical condition, it's true that I'm the only one who need be concerned about the question of cause. Either something has happened or it hasn't; Mr Jefferson's task is to establish the answer to that question. But as to what happened and why: well, those questions belong to me.

Mr Jefferson says, 'I'll be very sorry to lose you, Isobel.'

At first I think he's talking of my demise. 'It's not a fatal disease,' I observe.

'Resignation? No, indeed.'

'Conception. I meant conception.'

'Well, my dear, at your age . . .'

'I don't need a lecture on my age, Mr Jefferson. I realize I'm far too old to have a child. When I did have one, I was too young: now I'm too old. That's the way it is. Biology is no respecter of human convenience, is it?' I get up. 'I think we ought to end this appointment now. I've got some work to do. I assume it's acceptable to you if I work out the month? I wouldn't like to leave you in the lurch. I'll even help you find the next person, if you like.' I imagine a woman with red manicured nails, the colour of the holly berries in the gardens of the Villa Cellini. Maybe a little prickly even. From time to time.

13

My mother's been acting really oddly. Goes to bed at nine. Eats all the time. But her face looks younger, her eyes kind of sparkle. On my birthday last week, she gave me a gold watch. A real one. I didn't like it at first. Then I thought, but she's only trying to give you something memorable. So that when I'm an old lady I can look at it and think, my mother gave me that when I was nineteen and she was behaving oddly.

At the same time, she gave me a large brown envelope. 'That's my will, Becky. I know this isn't the proper time to give it to you, but I don't know when is. After Granny's death I wanted to sort out everything for you, so it's all clear, you know what to do when I die, it's as simple as it can possibly be.'

'Well, thanks Mum.' Did I say that? I think I said, am I supposed to read it? Now?

'No. Not unless you want to. Just keep it somewhere. Oh, and by the way, it includes instructions about what to do with my body, that sort of thing.' She laughed a bit tensely.

Naturally, I took it to my room and read it straight away. The financial part was straightforward. She left everything to me — well, all she has, which isn't much. She left a painting my father had bought her to her friend Margaret. About her body, the will said it ought to be cremated, but insisted that before the cremation it shouldn't be embalmed and no one must look at her after she was dead. I sympathize with this — I wouldn't want to be wrapped in someone else's nightie and be turned into a boxed china doll, either.

I was a bit taken aback by what my mother says about her ashes. She wants them transported to that villa place she went to in Italy. She wants someone to take them down to the edge of the lake there and chuck them in. I guess chucking ashes in lakes is becoming somewhat of a family tradition. I'm not sure I'll do the same. I might consider leaving my body to medical science. I've often wondered what happens if you do that. Is there a department somewhere with freezers full of bodies left to medical science that no one can be bothered with? Perhaps there is a superfluity of such bodies. In which case, I wouldn't want to add to the problem.

I had a letter from my father, too, on my birthday. My mother saw it, she said, 'Well at least you have got a father who keeps in touch with you, even if he didn't exactly behave in an exemplary fashion at the time.' It's possible she's feeling the non-existence of her own at the moment. I mean her mother's death could've brought that home to her. She said something to me about trying to find out what happened to him. I'm in favour of that.

Is it coincidence, or is it destiny that both my mother and her mother got abandoned by men and left with daughters to bring up? I've mentioned that to both of them, actually. Just to get their versions of events. Granny said — it was when I visited her in hospital — she said, 'Don't be taken in by the apparent similarities, Rebecca. They weren't the same at all. I got rid of Evan, he was a useless sod. I didn't plan to have a child. The whole thing was — not exactly a mistake, but an accident. Don't misunderstand me,' she went on, because I was certainly in danger of doing so, 'I don't regret it. I don't regret any of it. Your mother's given me a lot of pleasure. Even if she has been a disappointment as well.'

All this matched up with what I subsequently read in her diary. I haven't shown my mother the diary. I wonder if I should? It might shock her. I wouldn't want to shock her. It seems like she's had enough shocks recently. If she were more broadminded, I'd risk it, but I really think she might never recover, particularly from the bit about how she got conceived.

When I asked my mother the question about coincidence or destiny, she came down squarely on the side of destiny. 'There was this awful American at the Villa Cellini,' she told me, somewhat obscurely, 'he really was quite the most dreadful person I've met. But he did say a few wise things. "Women rule the world", he said one day, referring to his wife and his secretary. They do, Becky. It's the women who carry the responsibility. That's why men can come and go, but the world goes on more or less the same whatever the men do.'

'Did you love my father, Mum?' I didn't respect myself for asking this question, but she didn't seem surprised by it.

'I'm bound to say, what is love, Becky? I thought your father was the answer to everything. I enjoyed the time we spent together. I remember him best running beside you in Kensington Gardens, laughing.'

'And it was spring time and the sun was shining . . .'

'Not exactly.' She grinned. 'But you've got a point. It was the image I loved. Of a man and a woman and a child sharing life together. Being happy.'

'I don't think Granny felt like that,' I said slowly.

'I'm sure she didn't. Your grandmother was always better at the reality than I was. It's taken me a long time to sort out the facts from the fairy stories.'

It occurred to me then that what ought to happen is that mothers inform daughters about this kind of thing. So none of us needs to be duped, and then uncover the naked truth on our own. But the passing on of such knowledge appears to be a rather difficult thing. On the whole children don't want to know. Whenever my mother starts up, 'There's something you ought to know, Rebecca,' or 'I've been alive a good deal longer than you and . . .' I shut my ears. Not because I distrust what she's going to say, but because I'm not interested. It's my experience I'm interested in, not hers.

I didn't mind so much listening to Granny, though. Perhaps that's the custom – the knowledge has to skip a generation. But Granny was a pain as well. I used to find it a bit difficult when she launched into her attacks on Mum. I mean it's my prerogative to criticize my mother, nobody else's. She is my mother after all.

That's it, isn't it: you only have one mother. Generally. So it's better not to be careless with her.

My father said in this letter I got on my birthday, that he was planning a trip to Europe with his son. My half brother. He's fourteen. I'd say that was a bad age for a boy. He's probably already breaking out into acne. Not to mention dandruff and unpredictable vocal activity. Anyway, could my father meet me somewhere when he comes to England? Catch up on old times?

No, I said to myself, you won't be able to do that. The old times are gone. But I don't mind seeing you again, I don't object to the chance to take another look at a bit of my genetic inheritance. I wonder if little Charlie looks like me? I sincerely hope not. I don't want to resemble a youth full of milkshakes from the midwest.

On January 25th I had trouble getting back from my English class. When it snows, everything in England gets paralysed. The roads, the trains, the airports, the looks on people's faces. It happens every year practically, but it seems this doesn't make any difference. We can't get ourselves geared up to deal with it.

I struggled in late, around nine. I actually had to walk from Hammersmith station. I'm not much in favour of walking. I think it's an overrated activity. 'I fancy an Indian meal,' my mother said when I trooped in the door, dripping grey slush everywhere. 'How about a chicken tikka, Becky?' Pretty amazing. She never goes to Indians.

I had a look in the fridge. It was absolutely empty. 'Mother,' I said, 'what's going on here? Are you developing anorexia? Or have we run out of housekeeping money?'

She already had her coat on. 'Change your shoes, Becky. There are some wellingtons in the cupboard. We'll go up to the Star of India.'

She ordered practically everything on the menu. Plus a pint of lager. My mother hates beer. I had a salty lassi. Much healthier. 'I've got something to tell you, Rebecca,' she said then.

Normally I would have shut my ears at this point, but she was paying for the meal, wasn't she, and I was kind of stuck there with her. Also, I was mildly intrigued by this new personality that seemed to have come back on the plane with her from Italy.

'Two things actually.' She was still chewing on her stuffed chapati. 'The first is, I've given up my job.'

I should have said, that's great, Mother, it was a dead-end job, I can't think why you've stood it all these years. But instead of saying that I had this awful mature practical response and I said, 'But what are we going to live on, Mother? Where's the money to come from?'

She appeared to find this quite comical. 'Well, I'll get another one, I expect. Or I may do an Open University degree. What do you think of that as an idea, Becky? We can always use the rest of the money Granny left. We could invest it, or whatever.'

She sounded frighteningly vague. 'I think it's time you got yourself a proper education, Mother,' I said. This was obviously the right thing to say. 'I'd like you to have all the chances I had. But why didn't you take them when you were my age?' I'd never been clear about that.

'Reaction, Becky. Reaction. I didn't want to do what my mother wanted me to do. I didn't want to be like her. So I decided to go for something safe. Respectable. Actually, I didn't decide. It wasn't a decision. I simply allowed it to happen.'

'I know what you mean.' I did. My years of dropping out of school and getting wrapped up in screwy activities – that hadn't been a decision. More like a natural change of weather I couldn't do anything about. The hurricane just had to blow itself out. 'Do you really mean that about the Open University degree?'

'I do. I've been thinking about it a fair bit recently. I've got the prospectuses. There's a course on the Changing Experience of Women, I might do that.'

'It could change your life, Mother.' I had to say it.

'My life is already changed.' She developed a severely meaningful expression then, and went on to say, 'The second thing is something I need your help with, Becky. I've thought a lot about whether to tell you this, and I've decided you can probably take it. More than that, I think you'll know what to do, and I certainly don't.'

I pushed my plate away. I couldn't finish the food. Absolutely stuffed I was. 'That was fantastic, Mother. Thanks a lot.'

'Rebecca, please listen to me!'

'I am.' I was.

'I'm pregnant.'

'You're *what*?' If I'd had any idea of what she was going to say, I definitely hadn't thought it would be this. I thought it would be something educational or domestic perhaps: should we get a dishwasher, maybe? How about repainting the sitting room? I didn't think it would be reproductive. Especially at her age. It was quite a shock, I can tell you. It seemed kind of indecent.

How did she do it? Get pregnant I mean? Like in the Bible, where it says, 'Mary knew not a man.' '*What* did you say?'

'Would you like me to spell it for you? P-R-E-G . . .'

'Shit!' I was afraid people at the other tables would hear her. Pregnancy confessions from mothers to daughters in the Star of India on Shepherd's Bush Green don't happen every day. There might be someone who knew us picking up the odd word while masticating their ladies' fingers.

'Am I embarrassing you, darling?'

'Yes.' I think I'd gone red. I needed time to get used to this.

'Sorry. I'm really sorry.'

'It's okay, Mum. It's not the first time, nor probably the last.' I was discovering a new maturity in myself, now. Clearly I had to rise to the occasion, I had to take things in hand. If I didn't, nobody else would. She was putting me in charge.

'Was it this analyst fellow? The one you said attacked you?'

'This may be hard for you to accept, Becky, but actually I don't know. Because I don't know what really happened. It could have been him. It could have been the German, the one whose wife died. I don't know who it was. I wasn't conscious, so I don't know who caused it to happen.' She gave a sarcastic semi-smile. 'Maybe it was an immaculate conception.'

'Just what I was thinking, Mother.'

She started fiddling with the cutlery. My mother has a habit of doing a Uri Geller act on spoons.

'Listen, Mother, the pregnancy I can deal with, but I can't have you destroying the cutlery.' I took the spoon away from her.

'I expect you think I'm crazy. You do, don't you Becky? Crazy and irresponsible and immoral – all those things. I don't want you to think ill of me. But I'm glad I've told you. It's a relief.'

'I need a cup of coffee,' I said.

She waved the waiter over and ordered some.

'Could we go back to the beginning for a minute?' I said. 'First of all, are you sure you *are* pregnant?'

She gestured at the remains of the Indian blowout all around us. 'Have you ever known me eat like this?'

'No.'

'This is what I did when I was having you. I couldn't stop eating.'

I didn't like being reminded of my fetal existence. In my experience, it tends to lead into gruesome birth stories.

'I've had a test,' she went on. 'There is a slight chance it could be a growth or something. But I don't think so.'

'I didn't know you could get pregnant at forty-eight,' I said.

'Last year in England and Wales there were fifty births to women over fifty,' said my mother authoritatively. 'I went to the library and looked the figures up.'

'All right, then. If you are, what are we going to do about it?'

'I don't know, Becky. What do you think I should do?'

I must say, this did rather make me flip. 'I think you should take a while to consider your position, Mother,' I said, noncommittally.

She did. In the morning, she came to me with a drained face, I thought she'd contracted food poisoning from the large quantities of Indian she'd put away the night before. 'I got it wrong, Becky,' she said, 'I've started to bleed. It was all a mistake. It must be the menopause. The time of life, you know.'

She seemed really embarrassed. Both about the mistake and about the menopause. I was glad about the embarrassment, it returned us to normal, to my mother's normal reticence. But the time of her life – yes, she'd definitely had that, there's no doubt about it. I was glad it all had a natural ending, though I couldn't quite bring myself to inquire how she felt about it.

14

To bleed is a relief, as it always has been, but also a disappointment, as though my body's no longer able to hold onto the secret knowledge of what happened at the Villa Cellini. Secrets pour out of me, red and black, clot-ridden. Perhaps I really was pregnant?

I feel enormously tired and sleep nearly the whole of the next day. In the evening, Becky brings me a boiled egg and a cup of tea, and puts the television at the end of the bed, and then I'm off again in a thick dreamless sleep.

On Friday there's a letter from Elizabeth 'Kargar' in reply to mine of a few weeks ago.

> Dear Isobel,
>
> I was sorry to hear of my aunt's death. We had lost touch, as you know. She must have had an interesting life. We read about her in the newspapers from time to time.
>
> It was good that you were able to be with her at the end. I should like to donate some money to charity in her memory. Perhaps you could let me know of a suitable one, when you have time?
>
> In answer to your question about my brother, I have not heard from him for a number of years. There are, however, some letters and other documents here that might interest you. I wonder whether you would care to come for a short visit? The weekends of March 12th or March 19th would suit me. I live alone here now, as my husband died of a stroke five years ago.
>
> If you could possibly make the March 19th weekend (engagements permitting) my daughter would also be here, so we could have a little family reunion. It occurs to me that

your own daughter – Rebecca? – might like to accompany you. She must be quite grown up now.

I should be very pleased to see you.

Sincerely yours,
Elizabeth Whittington (née Kargar)

I tell Becky I'm planning to visit the Kargar establishment on March 19th: would she like to come too? She declines. 'It's your trip, Mother. You're the guest. I think you'd better do it on your own. I've got my own father to cope with, remember?'

I get on the phone to Elizabeth immediately. It's extremely odd to make contact again, after all these years. The voice is condescending, but I remember that as the Kargar manner.

British Rail takes me for my reunion with the Kargar family through the Sussex landscape I'd always found most unpicturesque. The nearer we draw to places like Polegate, Normans Bay and St Leonards (Warrior Square), the more the redbrick terraces and the blank chalk walls eat into my spirit.

'I washed it, you know.' The voice of the dumpy smiling woman opposite cuts into my thoughts. The woman pats a white furry heap beside her, I think it's a dog, but it's actually a hat. 'It's come up really well, don't you think? I got it in a jumble sale for £1. Well, the price of hats these days, I'm not paying £17 or £18 for a hat!'

I smile politely. The Sussex trains are different from the London ones. Now tuned into the conversational tones of ageing women, I overhear two in the seat behind me keeping up a relentlessly miscellaneous dialogue.

Elizabeth Whittington, née Kargar, would have been incapable of this sort of dialogue. Her mind's too crisp, she has too clear a view of how everything's related to everything else. She meets me at the station. A tiny woman, with neat grey hair, wearing a black cloak. From beneath this she brings out a black-gloved hand to shake mine. 'We last met in 1951,' she says, with precision. 'Your mother brought you down for a few days. You must have been about ten or so.'

'Eleven,' I said mechanically. 'Odd, I don't remember it.'

Elizabeth laughs, like a well-trained horse. 'I'm not surprised, my dear. There wasn't anything memorable about it. Of course, I wasn't living in the house then. My mother was still very much in charge. Frank and I had the cottage on the estate. Andrea – do you remember Andrea? – was only three at the time.'

I can't retrieve any relevant memory, the file seems to be locked. The white Daimler is chauffeur-driven. Elizabeth sits in the front seat, I sit with my small suitcase in the back. I remember none of the countryside between the station and the house until we come to the driveway, where the two weather-beaten lions that guard it are familiar, but seem smaller now, less worrying, with particles of green slime on their manes. 'I try to maintain the place,' says Elizabeth from the front seat, 'but it's difficult. It's not just a question of money but of standards. Getting people to do the work.' She sighs.

I make a sympathetic clicking noise.

'Here we are.'

We grind to a halt in front of a great wooden door. Elizabeth waits for the chauffeur to come round to her side of the car to let her out. I, meanwhile, am fumbling, looking for the handle. I've found the ashtray and the handle that winds the window down, but escape eludes me until the chauffeur touches the door on the outside and it springs smoothly open, at the same time as the door of the house, which emits another small old lady clothed in a maid's uniform. 'This is Janey,' announces Elizabeth. 'Janey's been with us for forty years.'

Janey says nothing at all, just looks me up and down. I wonder if I've passed the test, but am given no way of knowing.

My room's on the corner of the house, with views in two directions. Both show rolling parkland, one a stream with some sort of generating equipment, and the other a large copse of trees; as I let my eyes rest on this for a minute, a score of white birds rise and fill the colourless sky.

'Well, my dear,' says Elizabeth later, in the main drawing room, in front of a resplendent fire and among Jacobean furniture that's been in the family for generations, 'it *is* nice to meet again after all these years.' Elizabeth has changed for dinner, and is now wearing a black velvet dress with green laurel leaves embroidered round the shoulders and the hem. 'How have you been keeping?'

I feel much as I did all those years ago, exposed for brief periods to the rituals of my father's family. Mother was always very rude about them, maintaining that the surface politeness concealed a serious incapacity underneath: none of the Kargars could feel anything, and that included my father, who, according to Mother, had merely wished to please his own mother by getting married. Marriage meant he could collect his inheritance and scarper off back to the jungle. So I feel like a fish out of water still, but I've come here for a purpose, and therefore must play the social game well enough to accomplish my mission.

We eat dinner beneath candelabra definitely inferior to those that hang in the Villa Cellini. The company at the Villa Cellini – even the Goldmans – seem to me more of a family than this one: I shared more with them, more comedy, more tragedy, more communication. The late Frank Whittington's brother and his wife have joined us, the one a retired stockbroker with a carved light ginger moustache, the other a kind of antique Cindy with cream lacquered hair. There's also another couple from the village, a Colonel and Mrs Harper. The Colonel looks like one, and has a habit of delicately picking at his ear as he speaks. Mrs Harper wears red, which doesn't suit her, and bubbles keenly on about their recent golfing holiday in the Peebles Hydro. The last guest is Elizabeth's daughter, Andrea Collins. She lives in London, and seems a much quieter personality than her mother. Andrea has a pleasant, open, slightly worried face, and a slightly worried manner to go with it.

We're served clear vegetable soup, quails, lemon sorbet and a Stilton soufflé by Janey, who talks to herself throughout in a manner to which everyone except me is clearly accustomed. But when I say to Elizabeth in a voice sufficiently low, I hope, not to be audible above the rest of the conversation, 'You know, I don't remember my father at all; he left us when I was a baby,' I'm relying on the concealing effect of Janey's mutter as she passes round the vegetables.

'Evan was a bad boy,' says his sister quickly. 'We never understood why. My mother used to say he was a wonderful baby, cheerful, sleeping ten hours a night. Always ready for sleep was Evan, used to doze off whenever his attention wasn't occupied. Even at dinner sometimes. We'd be talking about something and then you'd notice that Evan was off. If you didn't kick him awake, he'd snore.'

'At the table?'

'At the table.'

It strikes me that Elizabeth is talking almost affectionately of Evan. 'You must have been fond of him, though,' I observe, 'I mean you were so much younger, it wasn't as though you were in competition with him.'

Elizabeth laughs a little cruelly. 'Oh, my dear, when I was a young girl, I thought Evan was wonderful. There were ten years between us. When I was ten and eleven, I remember being taken by Nanny to Oxford to meet Evan in his college for tea. It was a perfect summer day. And there was Evan in his scholar's gown, with the sunlight behind him, a magical figure. Those were the days! Days of innocence and splendour!' She raises a finger at Janey, who's muttering in the corner of the room by the carved Jacobean sideboard. Janey comes over and refills Elizabeth's wineglass, and then those of the others. 'Evan left Christ Church under a cloud, you know. Oh, he got his degree all right, but he was caught *in flagrante delicto* as they say with a town girl. Her father ran the tearooms on the corner of the High. From then on it was downhill. He never could settle to anything. My mother despaired.'

'But what was he supposed to settle to? I mean he wasn't *so* bad, was he?'

'He was the son. He was needed to run his father's business. But instead of that this anthropology nonsense took him over. Once he'd been to the Far East, that was that. He had the obsession in his blood. I was twenty-five when he came down here and told us he was going to get married. That was the good news. The bad news was that they were going to do it in a registry office in London and she, your mother, was already pregnant. You did know that, didn't you?' adds Elizabeth quickly, catching, I suppose, a flicker of surprise on my face.

'No I didn't, actually. But it doesn't matter.'

'They met in the British Museum.'

'Please tell me, Elizabeth, what *happened* to him.'

'He died in 1970 in Fernando Po. That's an island off the coast of West Africa. He died of something we now think was probably AIDS. That was the news that finally killed my mother. We had a visit from a young missionary. He just turned up one day, rang the doorbell, no warning, nothing. He asked to see Lady Kargar. My mother was bedridden by then. Janey asked who she should say had come to visit her, and the young man said, "A Mr Foss." He went in and told her he'd been there when Evan died. He'd contracted some infection, a mysterious virus, from a local woman: of course some people say AIDS had been endemic in that area for years, but so have other sexually transmitted diseases. They don't get cured there as they do here, you know. As Evan was dying, apparently he said, "Tell my mother I love her. I forgive her for what she did to me." And this young man had come all the way here to relay that message.' Elizabeth stops for a moment. 'I hope you're not shocked, dear. It's not a nice story. But you did want to know. Of course what killed my mother wasn't the news that he'd died, so much as that sentence, "I forgive her for what she did to me".'

'I don't understand,' I say.

'She had done nothing. Evan had forgiven her when there was nothing to forgive. She was so angry at that. She wanted to get hold of Evan and take him by the collar and shake him, but he wasn't here for her to do that. She had an aneurysm that afternoon.'

How odd, I think. I tried to forgive my mother, too: but I didn't say it to her. I don't suppose she would have liked it, either.

'I've put a folder in your room,' goes on Elizabeth. 'It contains letters from Evan, copies of his birth, marriage and death certificates, also a copy of my mother's will. Things that might interest you. You don't need to read them here, those are copies for you. I had the letters copied as well. I thought you might like to keep them. I always think one's history is so important, don't you?'

'That's very kind of you.' It's very hard for me in the middle of all this to really take in what she's told me.

'To know where one came from,' continues Elizabeth. She turns to her daughter. 'Of course Andrea never knew Evan, did you, dear?'

'I heard about him. People always lowered their voices when they talked about him. I got the distinct impression there were things I wasn't supposed to know.'

'There were things my mother didn't like to have spoken about in this house. We had to respect that.' Elizabeth folds her napkin and rises from the table. 'Let's have coffee in the orangery, shall we?'

On the way to the orangery I ask Andrea where in London she lives. 'Hampstead – Fitzjohn's Avenue. We have a house there.'

'Isn't that where the Tavistock clinic is?' I remember one of Mr Jefferson's patients telling me about her trips to the Tavy, which, combined with her gynaecological encounters in Harley Street, constituted a full time job.

'I remember you, you know,' says Andrea suddenly. 'I must have been very young, but I remember you coming here with your mother. She had a splendid hat, with roses at the side. She sat me on her knee and I smelt her perfume. It's a very strong memory. I've smelt that perfume sometimes since, and it always reminds me of her.'

I look at the miniature orange trees in the lamplight, vivid against the white metallic framework of the orangery and the blue-black sky through the glass, and of course I think of Italy. 'What do you do, Andrea?' I ask. 'What do you do, I mean, during the day in London? Do you have a job?'

'No, I don't need to. My husband works in the City. The boys – we have two, they're fourteen and sixteen – are at school in Kent. So I run the house, and I do some voluntary work. At the moment, I'm helping organize a mother and toddlers' club in Stoke Newington. There are lots of single parents there, lots of problems.'

'You don't ever wish you had a . . . a career?' I ask this question as much for my own benefit as for Andrea's.

'I wish lots of things. But long ago I learnt such wishes don't come true.' Andrea leans back in her chair and runs her fingers like an excited little mouse through the light brown curls of her hair. 'I expect my mother told you my husband and I are having problems.'

'No.'

'Well, we are.' Andrea smiles to herself. 'Sometimes I think that's my proper vocation – to have problems but never to solve them. The only constructive thing I've done recently is to go and see an analyst. He's really making me think about myself. It's painful. You get used to the pain, though. You even get dependent on it. I became aware of that recently, when he went away for a month. He went to Italy to write a book. Of course he left me the telephone number of a colleague in case of need, but it wasn't the same.'

I stare at Andrea. Everything falls into place. Instead of seeing Andrea, I see myself in that chair. A descendant of the Kargar family, inheritor of these quirky genes that send young men off into rainforests and young women into dead-end marriages. Also the person who has an indisputable connection with Isaac Simons. As Mr Simons himself had said on the promontory, Andrea and I could be regarded as the same woman – tied to the same biological pool by fates of war and the British Museum; borne along by parallel tides of boredom and discomfort; seeking answers where there are none, paradises in place of realities.

But all I say to Andrea is, 'Isaac Simons. I met him in Italy. I was at the same place. Isn't that extraordinary?'

15

My mother came back from that weekend in a really hyped-up state. I only asked her about the food and the peacocks. Apparently, they ate quails. There was honey for tea, still. The peacocks put in a brief appearance in between their other local engagements.

It was deliberate on my part, not asking the other questions. Like, 'What really happened to the old man, then?' Or, 'What is my grandfather's sister really like? Does she have gold teeth?' I've always been quite glad, actually, I don't have that much of a family. That way you aren't presented with so many reminders of how you could turn out if you aren't careful.

Anyway, I knew she'd tell me. She was fairly bursting with information. She turned the television news on and then she turned it off again. She began, very matter of factly, 'He died in Africa, in 1970. They think it was AIDS.'

'I wouldn't worry about it, Mother,' I said, 'It's a good thing you didn't see an awful lot of him, isn't it? If you'd met him for tea in Fortnum and Mason's once a year, he might have passed you AIDS in a teacup.'

'Becky! Don't be so dreadful. It's serious!'

'Was, Mother,' I said, 'was. It isn't any more. So he got AIDS, and it knocked him out at the age of what?'

'Sixty-seven.'

'That's not bad. Not bad at all, for an anthropologist, I would say.'

'What do you know about anthropologists, Becky?'

'Not a lot.' But we did touch on Malinowski recently in my sociology class. How the natives told Malinowski a pack of lies about their cultural beliefs. So off he goes and writes this tome about these people who don't know where babies come from, and they do, all the time. I enjoyed that. 'Anyway Mother,' I said, 'I expect he had a good life. He did what he wanted, he got away from his family. He enjoyed some mortal pleasures. Presumably. So I wouldn't get too upset about it, really I wouldn't.'

'I'm not upset, Becky. I'm strangely relieved. Now I know that both my parents are dead I feel relieved. I know the dates of their deaths, the exact dates. I've got their birth and death certificates.'

'Well, I'm glad you find that helpful, Mother,' I said. 'I wouldn't myself. Not particularly.'

'You're too young to understand, Becky,' she said, predictably.

I began to object, as one must on these occasions, but she wouldn't let me get a word in. 'You *are* too young, Becky. Think. Try to imagine: the dates of everyone's deaths are fixed. They're fixed, *now*. But you don't know. Put yourself in the position of having that knowledge. I died, Becky, *I* died on, let's say. . . .'

'And my old man, when did he die?'

'Not your old man, Rebecca, your father.'

'Whom I have to see tomorrow. In Fortnum and Mason's.'

'Do you really? Good God.'

'Would you like to see him, too, Mother?'

'I don't think so Becky. It's too long ago.'

For which read it hurts too much still. When she said that, I thought, perhaps I will show her Granny's diary after all. There may be things in it she ought to know, such as how my grandparents got together in the first place, and what Granny really felt about her.

I gave it to her before I set off for Fortnum's, being anxious to get all the history over with in one afternoon. 'Here you are, Mother,' I said, 'Granny gave this to me, I've read it. Now I think it's your turn. I've checked it out for you, made sure there isn't anything too terrible in it. You might have one or two little shocks, but I think on the whole you deserve the truth now.'

16

So I read my father's papers and my mother's diary: not both at the same time, but alternate snatches of each.

I'm surprised, and at first insulted, that Mother gave her diary to Rebecca and not to me. When I have time to think this through, I recognize the old feeling of exclusion. Then I think I'm able to get beyond this feeling, to the fact that Mother had probably only wanted to ensure the continuity of knowledge from one generation to another. She wanted her granddaughter to have guaranteed access to the past. Her only mistake, perhaps, was to assume that I, her daughter, knew enough about it. She ought to have known that living through something isn't the same as retaining any sensible mental record of it. Time and again this fact impresses itself on me. That memories can be wrong, though as important in their wrongness as their rightness; that different people can have totally different versions of the same event. Nonetheless, I tremble as I open Mother's diary. But the writing, a good italic script, in a faded black ink, bears me along with it, endearing in its familiarity if nothing else.

The diary begins in 1945 and the last entry's in 1985. Some entries are markers of mundane events, others are accounts that put scaffolding around some of the crumbling structures in my head.

October 1945

It's been raining solidly for two weeks. Mrs Wilkins, next door, fell down and broke her hip yesterday. I'm going to see her this evening in hospital, with Isobel. To take her some clean nighties and cheer her up. How dreadful to be old! Yet I'm middle-aged already – I do resent the thought. A respectable forty-seven-year-old woman living a straightforward life in my little house in Highgate, shopping, cooking, mothering. All the rest has faded. My successes – modest, but they *were* successes – are part of another age. The other day while turning out the drawers in my bedroom, I found a bunch of theatre programmes from the 1930s. I was Cordelia in *King Lear* in Coventry in 1931. There's even a photograph of me in the programme, all dreamy eyed and sleek haired. I'll keep them for Izzy, she might be interested to see them one day.

She started school last week. It's quite a tough school, taking in children from the whole neighbourhood. Some of them are very disturbed – they were evacuated during the war and one has the impression they don't know who their mothers are any longer. That must have been a dreadful experience – being put on a train with a ticket round your neck, bound for an unknown destination with strangers. I hope someone writes the social history of the evacuation some day, there must be a lot to say.

I never could have put Izzy on a train. Though of course I was lucky, I didn't need to, we could hide with the Morrises in Yorkshire. I don't miss it, I'm not really the country type. I've had enough of sheep as living companions.

Izzy's such a serious little girl, I'm worried she could have problems at school. I took her into the school the day she started and I said to her, now, Isobel, you do understand, you're going to stay here without me, don't you? I'll come and fetch you at lunchtime today. But when you get used to it, you can stay to lunch as well! She was holding my hand very tightly, as though her life depended on it, and then she let go as though I'd ordered her to release her hand, and she sprang away from me, and said, 'Yes, Mummy.' She looked pale, so I knew she was anxious, but I thought the best thing was just to leave her there and go. The woman who takes her class, Miss Boyles, seems very capable.

It's strange without her here during the day. I pace up and down looking for things to do. I'm up to date with my correspondence now, I've mended the cushions in the sitting room, I've had my hair done – what luxury, without a little girl around! I suppose I could start some of my own work again. Not acting – there would be no one to take care of Isobel when I'm not here. Acting's no career for a single mother. Perhaps I could do some freelance illustrating. There's that book of short stories I've got at the back of a drawer somewhere.

Robert's coming on Monday, I'm looking forward to that, he'll be here for a whole month. We're going to leave Isobel with Mrs Harrison and go off on a trip for a few days. We thought we'd hire a car and drive to Wales. The Black Mountains. Robert says he wants to go somewhere rugged, he's had enough of civilization.

I'm worried about Robert. He's doing too much. He works too hard – of course he says he's doing that so he can avoid Delia. But I think he'd be doing it anyway. Well, the least I can do is to give him some time off, some relaxation. I must try not to ask too many questions this time. If I don't ask questions, I don't have to deal with the answers.

I do love him. Why can't he leave Delia and live with me and Izzy!

I know the answer, of course. If I'm honest, I think that perhaps Robert will never make the break with Delia. One reason is he's not sure I really want him here all the time. Sometimes I think I do: but then I know I don't. I'm quite a solitary person, I've got used to being on my own, running my own life. I like to be able to organize things the way I want them, I don't want to have breakfast when someone else wants, I like to be able to go into my sitting room and see the chair as *I* left it, with the depression in the middle where *I* sat, the book where *I* put it down.

It's nearly time to fetch Isobel. She's staying to lunch now. I always go early so I'm waiting outside the playground when she comes out. I like to feel I'm doing my best for her.

December 1945

Robert left last Monday. The trip to the Black Mountains was wonderful, one of the best times we've had together. I found this proper country hotel: we even had a four-poster bed. We walked several hours each day, though the weather was extremely cold.

But we had some rows. As usual. The worst one was when we came back here. Robert has been lying to me about Delia. He'd told me they no longer share a room, then it came out that that's not true, he was lying, he was only saying it to pacify me, because he knows how upset I get at the thought of the two of them together night after night, while I . . . . I told him I can't have a relationship with a man who deceives me. He said he couldn't have a relationship with me anyway, I was much too selfish. All I could think about was myself. It doesn't work, the two of us, etc., etc. I threw a vase of flowers at him (not the nice Wedgwood one he bought me, but the one Evan's mother gave us when we married). R. left the house, banging the front door like a cannon. He crept home eventually, he always does. We made love – such splendid love.

I told him I don't mind the rows if they produce such reconciliations. Anyway, I need a man I can fight with. Tony was like that in the old days, I remember once on tour in Leeds, Tony and I had a dreadful fight just before the curtain went up and the director, a fussy old woman, said he'd have to fire us if we went on behaving like that. But I did well that night – I was Juliet. My performance was lost on the Leedites but Tony appreciated it.

So now Robert's back home in Brandywine Street, in Washington, and I'm here alone with Isobel. It'll be Christmas soon. A war-free Christmas at last. No blackout, but I suppose some of the rationing will go on for a long time. At least we can get soap without it now, I found a bar of Imperial Leather in Harrods last week. My Christmas present to myself! Robert wasn't impressed by the new availability of soap – they haven't had to endure such deprivations in Washington. He was much more impressed by the business of the United Nations being set up in October. 'It's the beginning of a new phase of history', he said, 'the end of war, a new political spirit walks the earth.' He's too much of a romantic. It won't be like that. The human memory is short. I tell him so, and he puts his hands on my shoulders and says with fiery eyes, 'Molly, we *have* to believe things can change. That people can learn from their mistakes.' I wish *he* would. Will I see Robert at Christmas? No, of course I won't, he'll be locked up with Delia, having a happy family Christmas. I don't suppose Izzy's father will send her anything, either. I haven't got the faintest idea where he is. I'm not surprised I'm cynical about men, I ask myself why I bother sometimes. The only sign of Evan these days is this money that appears in my bank account each month. It doesn't come from him, it comes from his mother, busy fulfilling her son's moral obligation to this awful woman who trapped him into marriage and parenthood. I can't stand Evan's mother, she's never smiled at me in her life. She disapproved of me from the start. It amuses me to think of it now, but I never said anything about the pregnancy, every time I saw her I was just a little fatter. At some point she must have worked out when poor little Izzy was conceived. She would have been horrified to know how the evil deed took place. It was an absolutely impulsive thing, I've never done anything like it before or since. I'd just been to my agent, no luck, nothing. I wandered around for a bit, and then I saw the B. M. and thought why not go in? Just for an hour. It might take your mind off things. So there I was in front of the Egyptian mummies, and Evan was there too with his notebook, and we got into conversation, and then we went off and had a drunken lunch and there was a tremendous attraction between us and we sort of just fell into this hotel. Of course I didn't have my Dutch cap with me, you don't normally take that kind of equipment on trips round London, do you?

I'm sure things like that were happening all the time, then. You looked at someone, and you thought, I'd like to go to bed with him, and then you thought, no, that's not the kind of thought to have, but all these little moral voices in your head got swept away by the simple overpowering thought that there might never be another time like this. Hitler had invaded Poland a few weeks before. The Government had just moved about one and a half million people out of the cities, expecting immediate bombing. Now we know the boffins had done their sums wrong, but then we were panicking, we thought we could all be dead tomorrow. So why not give in to these impulses? We talk about 'giving in', about 'The Fall'. Sex is a synonym for original sin, but there's really nothing else as *positive* human beings can do. I honestly believe the sexual drive is so strong that man had to dream up religion to deal with it. He had to invent God as some kind of voyeur: it's never just the two of you doing it or thinking about doing it, or trying not to do it. Of course I didn't know it at the time, but Izzy was conceived the day Freud died. I'm not claiming any particular meaning for this, I'm just amused by the temporal link between the two events.

As a matter of fact, I think it's the best affirmation of life there is, conjugation. I like that word. I looked it up the other day. It says 'temporary cytoplasmic union with exchange of nuclear material that is the usual sexual process in ciliated protozoans'. Now, we're not protozoans (though we do have a few cilia here and there), but the sexual process makes us pretend we are: we're just two cells trying to make it together. It comes from the Latin *'conjungare'*, 'to join or unite in marriage'. That's what the dictionary says, but I think God's had his prurient hand in that as well. There are other ways of uniting, aside from marriage.

When Evan and I left that hotel we said goodbye and thank you, and I remember thinking I haven't had the right kind of language training for such an encounter. We exchanged addresses, of course. There was some possibility that we would see each other again.

I got a job with a touring company in the south of England the next week, and I didn't really think much about my afternoon with Evan Kargar. We were doing a James Barrie season in places like Bournemouth and Lewes. We didn't try *Peter Pan*, not having the right technical equipment for flying people. We did *Dear Brutus*, *The Admirable Crichton* and *The Twelve Pound Look* instead. Matthew Church was Mr Lob, the sprite in *Dear Brutus*, who liberates everyone by allowing them all those experiences they believe circumstances have prevented them from having in real life. Matthew was a great actor. He was killed in 1943 crossing the street when a bomb fell – he didn't believe in shelters, or gas masks or any such preventative actions. But my favourite was *The Twelve Pound Look*.

It's about these two men and their wives who are friends. One of the wives gets restless; she manages to save £12 out of the housekeeping money, and she buys herself a typewriter so she can make some more money for herself. In the last scene her husband is saying to the other one, 'Watch out for the Twelve Pound look!'

I wasn't at home, so I didn't even know if Evan was trying to contact me. And then we moved to Lewes, and I started throwing up in the evenings. Not in the mornings, the evenings. I thought it was the food. Some of the landladies we stayed with had odd ideas of nutrition. It clicked of course, eventually: no period either. I raged around for a bit, here I was at forty-one, I'd always been terribly careful to avoid pregnancy before, I didn't see myself as a mother at all – I didn't mind *acting* mothers from time to time, but this was different.

When I came back to London I was on the top of a bus going down Tottenham Court Road one morning on my way to lunch at the Arts Club, when I looked out of the window and I saw a woman walking along with a little girl. I looked down at them and I thought how nice it must be to have that sort of connection with someone else, and then I thought, there you are Molly, that's your answer, have the child. And in a few years you can be walking down Tottenham Court Road hand-in-hand with something like that, something that really belongs to you. It didn't occur to me to think about Evan when I decided to have the child. It was my decision, I was taking it on my own behalf, as it were. But I did later on think well, I ought to tell him. He did have something to do with it, after all. So I got out the card he'd given me and I rang his number. 'Evan,' I said, 'remember me? This is Molly Brandon speaking.' There was a silence, I knew he was routing around in his memory. 'Oh, Molly!' he exclaimed somewhat falsely after a bit, 'how nice to hear from you!'

'I'll come straight to the point,' I said, 'As a result of our afternoon in the Hotel Russell, I'm pregnant. I've decided to have the child. I don't intend you to be involved. But as it is yours as well, I did think I should tell you.'

'Bloody hell!' I could hear a voice in the background, perhaps he had another woman there? 'I need to think about this,' he said. 'I'll call you back. Or, better, can we meet?' The voice in the background started doing something with itself, going up and down all over the place. 'Okay,' I said. 'The B. M. tearoom, four o'clock tomorrow.' I thought we should revisit the scene of the crime, we could even go and look at the mummies again.

I wonder why I'm writing all this now? I know why, it's because I ought to tell little Izzy about her real father. I know she thinks Robert's her father. He'd like to be of course, he's always saying he wishes he'd had a little girl like her, but that's a different matter.

I don't know what I thought the meeting would be like – a ritual, I suppose. You know, 'if you ever need anything', 'I'm really sorry', etc. But he carried this tray of tea and muffins to the table – the B. M. did a good line in muffins then – and plonked it down and sat down himself and his face sort of screwed itself up and before I'd had time to get into my muffin, there was this man I hardly knew saying, 'I think we ought to get married.'

'What for?' was all I could say – not a very romantic response – 'Because you want to do the right thing?' He didn't answer. 'Don't bother about that, Evan. I'm perfectly capable of taking care of myself. I'm not a child. I'll be forty-two when it's born. Lots of single women are having babies now. Polite society might not like it, but politeness gets pushed out of the door when there's war around.'

I think he was shocked, but he didn't say so. Instead he said, 'I'd like to marry you, Molly. I like you, you're an interesting woman. Beyond that, I've been thinking for some time that I'd like to settle down.'

No mention of the child, you note. Or of love. 'I'll think about it,' I said.

Well, I did think about it and I decided I ought to be practical and accept his offer. I didn't know how I was going to finance this motherhood thing, I'd just assumed something would turn up. If I'd had parents to go back to I might not have done that, but my mother died of polio in 1920 and my father followed her with something that was probably lung cancer in 1930. In any case, even if they'd been alive, they wouldn't have been able to help me. My father ran a sewing machine shop, my mum 'did' for people – there's not much money in either of those occupations. No, I realized it'd be sensible to marry Evan Kargar. I knew his background had money, even if he didn't.

So that's the story I've got to tell Izzy one day. It won't be easy. I suppose she won't think a lot of me for doing what I did. Maybe I'll just leave that part out. Isobel never knew her father. He went off to Africa when she was three months old. The marriage didn't work out. Well, I didn't really expect it to. But I didn't think Evan would be quite so dreadful to live with as he was. We didn't fit together at all. He wanted to sit around reading books about savage customs and I wanted to go out and perform some – I wanted to enjoy life, when I wasn't having to look after Isobel. He wouldn't do a thing for her, that was the other thing. And when I said I was going back to work – my old company wanted me back, they were going to start the season with Shaw's *Major Barbara*, one of my favourites – we had the most frightful row, he said no wife of his would work, I said in that case he'd better get himself another one.

The next day he said, 'Okay, Molly, I'm off. I don't know when I'll be back. You're quite right, I'm no good at family life. It's not my mission. I don't enjoy being urban man and writing my monographs in libraries, either. I need to be out there in the middle of it, having the experience.' So off he went.

Sometimes I think, men are always leaving me. Perhaps I do something to drive them away.

(There's a long gap at this point. The writing resumes briefly in 1948 and then again, more solidly, in 1950.)

April 1948

The crocuses and daffodils are out in the garden. I didn't plant them, so it's some kind of miracle, the way they come up year after year. This year they're early, we've had an unusually mild spring. Everyone's been bursting out of their houses and looking for sunspots, patches of yellow where they can sit and forget about the awfulness of the winter. They've just nationalized the electricity industry. Will it help? I'm not sure I'm in favour of this Labour Government. And the newspaper says we've all become part of something called the World Health Organization which has been set up 'with the aim of attaining the highest possible level of health for all people'. Apparently, we're about to get a National Health Service, too. We'll all be able to get free dentures and spectacles. Mrs Wilkins will like that, she's wearing someone else's at the moment.

Izzy will be eight next month. Eight years! I should say they've been difficult – years of struggle and deprivation, but I can't honestly say that. I don't deny that the cheque from old Lady Kargar hasn't helped, it has. I simply haven't had to worry about the bills, or the house, which is mine apparently so long as Isobel is in it too. That's a bit of a mean trick, isn't it: you support the mother while she's bringing up the child, but then you cast her off like an old rag when the child's old enough to go. Would things have been different if Isobel hadn't been the

Kargars' only grandchild at the time? That miserable Elizabeth has just pushed out a new female for the clan to spoil. Andrea Sylvia Penelope Kargar Whittington, I think they gave her a lot of names to make up for the absence of hair and beauty. I expect Lady K. is miffed the child isn't a boy. Well, there'd be no use looking to me for a son to carry on the line even if Evan *were* around – I haven't had a period for two years. I miss that. It's strange, you complain about having 'the curse' for thirty or forty years, and then, when you're curseless, you curse that too. It's one of rather a lot of things I wish I'd talked to my own mother about. I'd like to know how she felt. But she didn't talk easily. I used to think it was because she was always too tired, but that wasn't the only reason. She wasn't a communicator, she and my father interacted in a morse code of grunts and silences, I was just a comma in the middle of it all.

It's the absence of cyclical change I notice most, the feeling of building up to something, and then the eruption of the blood and with it the tension going in your breasts, your stomach and all the places that blow up like bicycle tyres every month, they deflate overnight and you're back to square one. Full of energy until the next time. I feel sorry for men, their bodies are always the same. Perhaps that's why they need to have all these theories about the penis. It's the only bit of them that ever changes, so they have to make a big thing about it.

I do sometimes wonder where Evan is: I suppose he's sitting in a jungle in Africa. Or maybe the natives got him finally. Isobel asks about him from time to time. The story about your father being a famous anthropologist is beginning to wear a bit thin. She went to the library the other day and looked up Kargar in the catalogue. She came back and told me, 'But there's nothing there! There's a Tom Kargar who wrote a book about waterskiing. Maybe that library's not big enough to have my father's books?' Her faith in him is very touching.

I had a party here a couple of weeks ago. An April Fools' Day party. I told everyone they had to come as fools. But since that's what we all are anyway, no fancy dress is required!

I had a hundred people in this little house. R. was here, he made a champagne punch – champagne and orange juice and fruit – grapes, strawberries, redcurrants. God knows where he got them from at this time of the year. But he's quite a scavenger – he prides himself on always being able to locate the exotic.

I invited practically everyone I know. All my theatre friends – even Tony. He looked thin, terribly tired around the eyes where it tells. He told me I've aged much better than him. It's true. But then I haven't been rampaging all over the place staying up till the early hours of the morning, travelling, eating hideous food, pursuing unhealthy habits. I remember Tony best in Shaw's *Getting Married*. We were only a pair of young things at the time in a Manchester rep, but resources were limited, so we sometimes had to play parts that didn't quite suit us. Actually, Shaw describes Lesbia as 'a tall, handsome, slender lady in her prime: that is, between 36 and 55'. A good definition. Tony was the General, who'd been in love with Lesbia for years, but she wouldn't marry him. Tony wanted to marry me. In the play Lesbia says, 'You are a sentimental noodle: you don't see women as they really are. You don't see me as I really am . . . I'm a regular old maid. I'm very particular about my belongings. I like to have my own house, and to have it to myself. I have a very keen sense of beauty and fitness and cleanliness and order. I am proud of my independence and jealous for it. I have a sufficiently well-stocked mind to be very good company for myself. . . .' And the General interrupts her, 'But love . . . .' Lesbia replies: 'Oh, love? Have you no imagination? Do you think I have never been in love with wonderful men? Heroes! Archangels! Princes! Sages! Even fascinating rascals! And had the strangest adventures with them? Do you know what it is to look at a mere real man after that!'

A woman after my own heart, Lesbia. She wouldn't marry because she would only do so to have children, but if she had children she couldn't do with having a husband as well to bother with all the time. Tony didn't like that. And look how we ended up – him gallivanting round the world with a wife at home, and me caged up with a little girl but no husband!

It doesn't come easily to me, motherhood, I knew it wouldn't. Oh, I love Izzy of course, she's a dear little thing. But she makes me mad with her tempers. Was I like that? I suspect I was. And what did Mother do? I think she went on polishing the linoleum, so I could see my unhappy infant face in its slippery surface. Most of the time, Izzy's very sensible, adult almost, but then she gets these explosions, all these feelings fall out of her like lava. The only problem is I'm the mountain, I'm the villages, I'm the people, I'm the one who gets buried in it. I don't know what to do with her sometimes. I lock her in her room. She screams and shouts and stamps. I have to lock her away from me because if I didn't I'd lash out at her. There's something so absolutely dreadful about Isobel in a rage. I look at her and she feels like a bit of me that got detached and walked off and set up an entirely separate state of its own. Like a rebellious colonist, but then it finds out it's left its twin behind, it can't manage without this other person. It would be easier for me, and perhaps for her, if there was a man around. I could be all softness and light and cuddliness and he could do the disciplining, I could wait for him to come home at night and threaten Isobel with that. Again, I wonder if that was what happened in my own childhood. I have a strong memory of my father's physical presence. He was a dark bulk of a man, smelling of newsprint and cheap cigars, like a hard chocolate you couldn't get your teeth into, that has a soft centre locked up in it somewhere.

It's hard being both father and mother. I won't let R. do the fathering, though at times he verges on it. One day when he'd been out, he came back and I'd shut Izzy in her room for something, I can't remember what – some misdemeanour or other – and he said, 'What's that noise?' I said, 'That's my daughter trying to kick the door down.' And he frowned and said, 'Molly, I don't think you should do that to the child. It can't be good for her. Doesn't it make the whole thing worse? I hate to think of her in there screaming like that. Why don't you let her out. Talk to her?'

'Robert,' I said, 'she's *my* daughter. You must let me treat her as I think fit. I will not have you telling me what to do.' Which I wouldn't.

When Izzy was a baby I read these books which said it isn't bad for babies to cry, they need to learn that they can't get their own way by making a fuss about it. The earlier they learn that, the better. So I'd feed her – I didn't feed her myself, I wanted to keep my breasts the way they are – and change her and put her down and if she cried, well, that was it. She had to cry. I was only doing what the books said. Isn't that being a good mother?

I would have thought so. I didn't like to look at her when she was crying, anyway. I found that frightening, revolting almost.

These tantrums of hers started early, when she was about one and a half. She'd want something and I'd say no, and I'd be watching her face to see how she'd react, and there'd be a pause as though she were considering what to do about it all, and then off she'd go. Anywhere, shops, restaurants, parks, it didn't matter to her. But the rest of the time she was – still is – an absolute charmer, delightful to be with. I think sometimes about that woman walking down Tottenham Court Road with the little girl. How did she manage? Women must have secrets they could pass on. But you've got to be willing to take in secrets as well as let them out.

Is Izzy insecure? I don't know. What could I have done about it? I've given her all I've got. I know I'm not a perfect mother, but then neither was mine and neither will Izzy be when it's her turn, I don't suppose.

To get back to my April Fools' party: that was a really nice day. I know why, as well. All those people from my past were there – most of the old crowd from before the war when I was a struggling London actress not averse to a bit of nightclubbing from time to time, right back to the beginning in the Manchester days, even Monckton, the scenery designer, still wearing pink jeans – not the same ones, he says of course they're easier to buy now. R. was behaving himself, he was a good host, affectionate towards me, people could see he loved me, that we loved each other. At midnight, when no one had to be a fool any more, someone – Elaine I think – raised her glass and said, 'To Molly', and everyone held their glasses up and shouted 'To Molly', and R. put his arm around me and it was all glowing, sparkling, happiness. . . .

October 1950
I've just re-read the last entry. How optimistic it sounds. I could say life has let me down. Or maybe it's the other way round.

It all started when Delia gave Robert an ultimatum in May. Either her or me, she said, and that she should have said it long ago. Which is true. One of us should have put our foot down. Why wasn't it me?

In June I took Izzy to the States. The three of us toured New

England and then R. had a meeting in San Francisco so off we went to San Francisco. It was a marvellous month. Every time I caught myself thinking we're a family, I said no, it can't be true, and this isn't what you want anyway, but the feeling persisted. We went to a vineyard near San Francisco one day, a glorious golden day, to a place full of redwoods, and we bought some of their light white wine and sat under the trees and Izzy was wearing a yellow frock and was picking wild flowers to press — oh it was a lovely time.

He didn't tell me about Delia's ultimatum until we got to the airport and he was about to put us on the plane home. We left Izzy guarding the luggage and went off for a goodbye drink and he bought me a cognac — he knows I need some Dutch courage for flying — and he handed it to me and said, 'Molly, my dear, I've got something to tell you, it's going to be hard — it's hard for me to say it, and it'll be hard for you to hear it.'

And it was. 'What can I do?' he said, 'I must stay. For the children's sake' — which I never believed. 'And for Delia's.'

I cried all the way home on the plane. Izzy was wonderful. 'Don't cry, Mummy,' she kept saying, 'you'll see Robert again soon.' I couldn't tell her I wouldn't. That I'd probably never see him again.

When we got home, it was the end of July and school was over for the year. I couldn't bear to have her with me, I wanted to be alone, so I sent her off to stay with a schoolfriend, and then I came back to the empty house and sat down in the living room and thought, what should I do next?

I'd read a review of this book that had come out recently, called *Modern Woman: the Lost Sex*, and the newspaper was lying there on the corner of the coffee table. That's what I am, lost, I thought. Lost. And all because of a man, which the authors of *Modern Woman* would have approved of, but I didn't.

It just seemed as though my life were over. I couldn't think about Izzy, I couldn't recall her presence, I couldn't see her face, I couldn't hear her voice say 'Mummy'. All I could think of was that Robert had chosen Delia, not me — that I would never hear his voice on the telephone again. He used to shout, 'Molly, it's me!' and my heart would lift and he'd talk as though we'd never been apart at all. I'd never hear him coming in the door again. We'd never lie together again. He'd never say, gently, as he used to, 'Do you want me to touch you, Molly? Would you like me to touch you?' He was a wonderful lover. He didn't look like it, because he's a big coarse man, but in bed he was the lithest, most skilful lover imaginable. We used to come together every time. I'm sure that's what the people who wrote that book recommend. But I didn't do it because I wanted to please Robert, or because it was some sort of inevitable female response to his own rhythms – we did it because we were together, and we couldn't help it. Just near the end, when he could tell I was ready, I'd watch his face and he'd time the last few strokes, and I would know exactly how long each would be and then he would throw his head back and cry like an animal, but only for a moment. The marvellous thing about Robert was the affection afterwards, he'd kiss me all over as if I were the greatest gift anyone on this earth could ever have, and I'd feel so treasured and so warm, and then eventually, when he came out of me and lay beside me, he had this little thing he did of laying his penis on my leg and pulling the foreskin right back, lying it there 'to dry it off' as he'd say, smiling. And I would look down and see its little head resting there and think of what we had been doing – it was so erotic and so domestic, both at once.

Oh Robert. You see I couldn't bear it, I still can't. I mourn his loss every day. I don't want to live without him.

After I'd sent Izzy away I knew what I had to do. I wrote a letter to Elaine Morris, and said if anything happened to me please would she and her husband take Izzy in, bring her up as one of their own. They had three boys and a girl, the girl a few years older than Izzy. I felt they would make a good job of looking after her. I hadn't made a will, but I took a piece of paper and I wrote, 'I leave all my property and possessions to Elaine Morris of 108 Rosemount Road, Islington, in trust for my daughter, Isobel Miranda Kargar,' and signed it and put that in the envelope too. The Morrises should have any money I had if they were to take care of Izzy. It wasn't a legal document, but I hoped it would do.

And then I went upstairs and took my pills out of the bathroom cupboard. I've had them since that bout of tiredness the doctor said was depression, years ago. There were twenty of them. I went to my bedroom with a glass of water and swallowed them all. I lay down on top of the bed neatly with my letter to Elaine Morris propped up beside me. I cried a little as I fell asleep. I felt so sorry for myself, I had to annihilate everything – I didn't want to die, so much as go to sleep for a long long time, for all the time that the pain of losing Robert would endure, so that when I woke up it would all be gone and I'd be able to feel happy again.

A hundred years would have done, like the Sleeping Beauty. But as it turned out I only got a few days, because Mrs Harrison, my cleaning lady, came in that evening to get the house ready for Izzy and me coming home. I'd given her the wrong date. It really was an accident, I had no idea she'd find me.

I woke up in hospital feeling not at all happy. I was all wired up to some sort of machine that beeped every second or so. They said it was my heart. I watched it with some amazement when I wasn't feeling so sleepy, but it didn't like me watching it, it went all kind of wild, missing or doubling up on beats, so I thought it would probably get on with the job better if left to its own devices.

I was in intensive care for a week. They'd had to pump my stomach out. I'd had convulsions as well, apparently. As soon as I realized where I was and had any strength at all, I started getting out of bed. But this horrible male nurse came over and said, 'You can't do that, Mrs Kargar, you'll unhitch the monitor.' I said, 'I don't care about the bloody monitor,' and I ripped it off anyway and threw it at him. He strapped me down then, to the bed, so I couldn't move at all. Apparently the drugs I'd taken make you abusive. I really couldn't trust myself to say the right thing to anyone for quite a long time.

Elaine came to see me. Mrs Harrison had sent her the letter with a note explaining what had happened. She'd also fetched Isobel from her friend's house. Now Elaine had her. I was glad of that. I said, 'I'm sorry, Elaine, to have caused you all this trouble.'

'You're a fool, Molly,' she said, 'that was a very stupid thing you did. How could you think Isobel would be better off without you?' I didn't think, I didn't, but there was nothing else to be done. Simply nothing else. Elaine came to see me every day. One day she brought Isobel. I remember her hair needed washing. She was ten. She was wearing her yellow frock, the one she'd had on that day in California. I wept to see it.

So that's the story, the whole sad story. It helps to write it down.

I'm feeling a little better now, I keep going. It was difficult for Isobel, though. She kept wanting to know what had happened, what had gone wrong. I told her R. wouldn't be coming here again, that was why I'd been crying on the plane. She understood that. But about the suicide, no, she didn't see that. How could she? She begged me to talk to her, and I remember saying very clearly, surprising myself, 'I can't have a relationship with you, Isobel, because I can't have a relationship with myself.' I suppose it was true. One loses one's self-respect. You have to. You have to lose it in order to do it, but then you can't get it back afterwards because you failed again, didn't you?

Somebody told Robert what I'd done. He sent me some white flowers. I threw them away. I burnt everything to do with him – all his letters, presents, photographs, every kind of memento. I burnt nine years of my life. It gave me some satisfaction, that. I knew I would regret it, though. Even as I did it, I knew there would come a day when I would be able to think about the time Robert and I had together with affection, without wanting to deny or forget it, or punish him or myself for it.

June 1953

The Coronation. Izzy and I watched it on Mrs Wilkins' television next door. The whole street was there. Her son bought the set for her. He's made a lot of money out of elevators. Izzy really got excited about it. They gave them books at school with the whole ceremony in them, she's been dressing up with her friends and acting the part of the Queen for weeks, waltzing round the garden with an old curtain round her shoulders making people promise perpetual obedience to her.

Myself, I could take or leave the Coronation. But I suppose pageantry is one of the few things England does well. I have to admit to being a little moved by the procession down Horse Guards' Parade, and by watching how well that poor young woman coped with the crown – it must weigh a ton. It was obvious she was nervous. You must have to have a good bladder to be a Royal.

Tony came to see me last week. He's decided to leave Rosemary. He's sad about it, but he says they're destroying each other. He's planning to go to New Zealand to start a theatre company there. Would I like to go with him? How can I, Tony? I said. Isobel's thirteen, it wouldn't be fair to uproot her now. Why not, he said. It might be just what she needs, a bit of culture shock at the start of her adolescence.

I thought about it. But I think my acting days are over. I enjoy the memories – the camaraderie, the exhaustion, the thrill of a good performance, the odd extraordinary moment when you feel you've got them with you, everything hangs on you.

It's in this connection, oddly enough, that I now increasingly think of Robert. R. and I had a script. We played it out with meticulous attention to detail – I can see now how it was all ordained, all written down in advance. The end was inevitable from the beginning. We loved each other because of, not in spite of, the difficulties. The Atlantic ocean kept us together not apart. The separation was responsible for the intensity.

What wisdom! The plain fact is, however, that my life now, by comparison with what it was, is dull. I shall have to do something about that.

I've been reading Katherine Mansfield. She said once, 'Risk – risk anything. Care no more for the opinion of others, for those voices. Do the hardest thing on earth for you to do. Act for yourself. Face the truth.' I wonder whether that's the reason people go into acting, so they don't have to face the truth about themselves.

December 1953

I've decided what to do. I'm going to sell this house and put the money into something bigger, so I can rent out rooms in it. That should give me something to do.

The other thing that's happened is that David Morris has hired me as an illustrator for a new series of children's books. He remembers my work from the old days, I told him I've had quite a break from it, but he's fond of me, I think, and he's willing to give it a try. So life is looking up!

This Christmas will be the last one in this little house. I want to make it a nice one for Izzy, she's had a pretty miserable time recently. We'll get a big tree and some proper lights. I'll let Izzy do it all. I've invited the Morrises for Christmas lunch. I'm going to buy Izzy a whole new wardrobe for Christmas. She's not interested in clothes, she'd wear anything, but at thirteen she ought to be. I shall get her a satin dress for Christmas Day, and parties, and her first nylon stockings, and some smart jackets and skirts. Maybe a little make-up. I can't wait to see the transformation.

April 1954

Work in the new house is nearly finished. It's been a horrible few months. Izzy and I have a sort of flat at the top – a room each, a sitting room, kitchen and bathroom. Then there'll be five or six rooms to let out, with a communal kitchen and a couple of other bathrooms. I've already got a queue of prospective guests. The most interesting is a writer called Neil Kanter. He's in his early forties, and he writes really original stuff – plays about extraordinary happenings no one can make sense of, a sort of British version of the theatre of the absurd. I saw one just after Christmas – it had a brief run in London, the critics didn't like it much – but who are they to judge? A beetle comes out of the woodwork claiming to be Jesus. So what do people do faced with this outrageous claim? The main male character, the antihero – who up until this point has been shown as brave and wonderful and wholly admirable – looks at the Jesus-beetle and calls the pest control department. His wife, who was pretty silly anyway, runs off screaming. Their son, an argumentative young man, sits down and has a dialogue with the beetle about the meaning of existence. 'I can tell you all about the meaning of life' says the beetle, 'living in the woodwork gives me a very good vantage point from which to study human beings. I see them from the feet upwards, you understand. You can tell a lot from people's feet. Their inclination in relation to the ground, the spring in the step, or its absence. Whether the feet turn outwards or inwards. How clean the shoes are, their probable cost, whether they are giving the wearer callouses. You don't need to see people's faces, people have learnt all sorts of disguises and guards for their faces. There are visors that come down all the time. But not for feet, my son, not for feet.'

Izzy didn't like her Christmas present. She said she'd rather have had a new doll. I don't understand that girl. She's got fifteen of them anyway. Why doesn't she want to grow up? *I* couldn't wait to. She had one of her tantrums after Christmas lunch. I told her, I'm not putting up with this any more. She called me some terrible names in front of the Morrises. Elaine says I shouldn't worry about her. She says what Izzy's doing is normal. Well, it may be normal but I don't have to like it, do I?

August 1954

I'm so happy. When did I last say that? It's no good pretending I enjoy life without a man. I can survive now better than I could, but I miss the companionship – intellectual, emotional *and* physical.

Neil is ten years younger than me, but it doesn't seem to matter. He says he doesn't care how old I am: I'm the woman for him. I tell him I'm a mother figure. He says we're all mother and father figures to each other, so what the hell? He's very unconventional, that's what I like about him. You can't have serious conversations with him at all about such issues – he sidesteps things, talks around them, takes unusual angles on them. He's writing a novel now. It's called *Fog*. He won't let me read it yet, he says you can't see anything in it for the first hundred pages. It all becomes clear later.

Neil and I go out a lot, four or five nights a week. It's much easier with Izzy now. First of all, she's fourteen. Secondly, there are all these other people in the house, she's not alone in the evenings. I should have done this years ago.

Izzy's taken to glowering all the time. She glowers in the mornings at me, she glowers when she comes home from school, I suppose she glowers at school too. And most of all she glowers at Neil.

The first time Neil and I really talked, it was in the kitchen, everyone else was out, we'd had two martini cocktails each, the conversation was really flowing, and then Izzy appeared in the doorway. She immediately knew what was going on. Neil had just put his hand on mine and said, 'I'd like to make love to you, Molly.' And there was Izzy in the doorway like a damned policeman. I'm afraid I said rather sharply, 'Do you want anything, Isobel?' She said nothing, just turned away, glowering presumably.

I tried to talk to her about it later. 'What's the matter, Isobel,' I asked her, 'why do you mind the fact that I have friends?'

'You don't have friends, Mother,' she said, 'you have *lovers*. I think it's disgusting at your age.'

'Why is it disgusting, Isobel?'

'It just is!'

I think she objects to the fact that I'm leading a life of my own. I really don't see why motherhood should condemn one to celibacy. Why should it be my daughter, of all people, who tells me how I ought to behave? I want her to be happy, don't I? I want the best for her. Why can't she want the same for me?

Oh Izzy, if only you understood! I'd like you to see that loving you and loving other people aren't in conflict with one another. It works the other way round, actually: the more love there is in my life, the more I'm able to give to you. What is it that disturbs you about it? Do you want me to yourself? Is that the primitive impulse we all have? To get inside the people we love, put ourselves like stakes in their hearts. A baby doesn't have to bother. It *is* there, joined to its mother, pulsing, contracting, dancing, breathing, eating, dreaming, *existing* together.

So I think I know what you mean, Izzy, I even felt it in relationship to my own mother, who was a dreadfully boring and repressed woman. But I still looked on her as some kind of paradise lost; I wanted to get into her soul, spread my roots forever there like some great oak tree. But she couldn't be bothered either. It was enough to have given birth to me. It is, you see. I learnt my lesson, now it's time for yours, Izzy. Leave me alone. Go and get on with your own life. If you want to berate me, to complain about me, then tell it all to someone else. This would be hard for you to understand, Izzy, but actually I don't want to hear what you think about me any more. I consider you lack the imagination to understand my life. I can't myself work out why: with me as a mother, you should have been doubly blessed. Perhaps it was old Kargar back there looking at the mummies that did it. I'm sorry, Isobel, I should have picked a better father for you. You can blame me for that if you like, but not for anything else. I'm fed up with being made to feel guilty for everything.

January 1955

My first children's book comes out next week. It's called *Rosemary and the Lavender Garden.* The text is a bit sickly, but my illustrations aren't at all bad, though I say it myself. I made Rosemary quite a satirical figure. Some of the Lavender Garden creatures are modelled on politicians. I wonder if anyone will notice?

The publishers had a party, it was quite like the old days. Neil came with me. I wanted to dedicate the book to him, but he wouldn't let me, he says people might think he's Rosemary. Some of his weird humour has rubbed off onto me. Actually, Rosemary and the Jesus-beetle have quite a lot in common.

I've started to write poetry too. I've only showed it to Neil so far. He says it's an art form he doesn't understand, but he'd defend absolutely my right to engage in it.

June 1956

Izzy's in the middle of her 'O' levels. She's taking seven — French, German, Latin, maths, English language, English literature, geography. She's a clever girl, she should do well.

I tried to talk to her about her future. But all she would say is that she wants to be left alone to get on with it. I could be sure of one thing, though, she wasn't going to make the same mess of her life as I had! I started to come back at her on this, but she interrupted me, she said the most extraordinary thing. She said, 'Do you know, Mother, I've never been able to believe that any of your so-called suffering is real.'

'But, Izzy,' I said, 'I've been depressed on and off for years, I've been taking pills since you were a few years old, I even tried to kill myself a few years ago, how can you say I haven't suffered?'

'Your suffering is a way of controlling people,' she said. 'You make them feel sorry for you, so they'll do what you want. But you don't make *me* feel sorry for you, Mother. Oh no. I see through all that. I don't want to have anything to do with it.'

I was speechless. I stick to what I said before — none of this has anything to do with me.

July 1963

Well, I went and I behaved, and she ought to be pleased with me. Gerald Lennox is a devious piece of work, it's apparent to everyone except Isobel. I suppose she wants to have babies. She probably will, too, she seems incapable of giving any serious thought to reproduction – or its avoidance. Gerald's parents were quite repulsive. Mrs Lennox the elder – I have difficulty thinking of my Izzy as Mrs Lennox – shook my hand as though I had some dreadful disease. I suppose Gerald had told her all kinds of stories about me. I was tempted to take Piers along to the wedding, but Izzy begged me not to. '*Please*, Mother, it'll only create problems. How would you introduce him anyway?' 'Simple,' I said, 'This is my friend Piers Cassidy, the composer.' 'He'd be out of place, Mother,' she said. 'Can't you see that?' Fortunately he didn't want to come anyway: the Birmingham Symphony Orchestra's rehearsing his *Urban Rhapsody* and he's very agitated about it, feels he needs to be there.

I tried to detach myself from the proceedings and see it as a spectacle that has nothing to do with me. But all I could see as she came down the aisle in her heavy cream gown was Izzy in the garden in 1953 pretending to be the Queen. It won't last. They went to Norfolk for their honeymoon. Gerald's a writer, apparently. Well, I won't read any of his books.

Piers and I are thinking of going to live in France. I could sell the house. I'm tired of having lodgers, anyway, I'm sixty-five now, five years past women's retiring age (why it should be different for men and women I've never understood). Izzy doesn't need me any longer. We could buy a stone house in Provence and wander through the lavender fields. Piers has got some money, so that'll be all right. I suppose I ought to worry about my old age, but I won't. Either I won't have one or something will turn up: that's my philosophy of life. It's not Isobel's, she wants to plan everything out of existence I sometimes think.

(There's another long gap here. But I know Mother went to live in France with Piers, that Piers had eventually tired of her and fled to Paris, and Mother took up with Maurice Rambeau, a historian, and married him without telling anybody, in May 1968 when, as she said, the student revolution had suddenly made her believe in a future again. These were the years when Mother and I had had little contact, the absence of meetings confirming the gap between us.)

September 1973

Maurice and I came back from the Dordogne on Saturday. It was a tiring journey, and we were sad to leave.

When we got back here, the flat was a frightful mess, of course. Owen, Maurice's young cousin, who'd been using it, had succeeded in breaking the stereo, and the fridge was leaking water all over the floor. I ranted and raved. Maurice said, calm down Molly, let's go to bed, Mrs Alton'll be in in the morning, I'll get the stereo repaired. You're only in a state because you didn't want to come back to London.

He was right. But I'm beginning to feel my age. I find these little practical things much more difficult than I used to.

And the next day Izzy turns up with Rebecca in her arms. She just stands there on the doorstep, holding the baby. Izzy's wearing the most dreadful old pair of trousers, the baby's got uncombed hair and a dirty face. They have a suitcase with them. 'May we come and stay, Mother?' asks Izzy. 'Just for a few days. It'll only be for a few days, I promise. Gerald's gone, you see.'

'Gone?' Passed away? Died? I didn't know what she meant. She looked like a little girl with a doll, sent home from school for misbehaviour.

It seems Gerald had tired of Izzy and had fallen in love with someone else. I could see why, of course: my Izzy isn't the world's most seductive woman. She'd not spoken about it at all, but I had the distinct feeling she didn't like sex any more than she had at the beginning. Oh, she loved Gerald, she was devoted to him, but that was exactly the problem; she'd become a doormat. He wiped his feet on her and went out the front door looking for adventure. Not of course unlike her own father. But I don't think adventure was what Evan wanted, he had enough of that with me. I never let him take anything for granted. No, what Evan was after was escape from responsibility. From the moralities of his childhood. He was a total misfit. Marrying me was his last try at conformity, and it didn't work.

Gerald, on the other hand, always seemed to me an eminently conforming figure, in that sense men have of wanting to have their cake and eat it too. He wanted a wife and a family as a foundation for everything else. A base for his excursions. It wouldn't surprise me if he didn't go off and do the same thing again with this new woman.

I took the baby, and told Izzy to go and have a bath, put on some clean clothes. I advised Maurice to stay out of the way for a bit. He had some errands to run, and he said he'd go and arrange for someone to pick up the stereo. I asked him to get us some lunch at the delicatessen. The baby and I sat on the sofa and looked at each other. She has these big dark, sad eyes. Izzy hadn't brought her any toys, so I picked up a magazine, *Vogue* or some such, and we looked at the pictures in that. She got quite animated. Then she got onto my knee and hugged me tightly. Put her thumb in her mouth, soon she was asleep. Izzy came into the room looking a lot better. 'It's not the end of the world, darling,' I said, 'it happened to me, so I know. You'll recover. It might even have been a good thing.' I wanted to tell her I didn't mind seeing the end of Gerald, but she wouldn't have appreciated that.

'But Mother,' she protested, 'I'm not like you. I'm not independent. I don't *want* to be on my own. You did.'

Did I? 'No, I know,' I said, 'but the first thing you must do is to accept what's happened.'

'How can I get him back? There must be ways.'

'Don't demean yourself, Izzy. Don't think about the past. Think about the future.' She sat and cried. I wanted to hug her, but I was holding Becky, I couldn't comfort both of them at the same time. I often feel critical of Izzy. I know I'm not patient with her, but I do have such feeling for her underneath. I didn't know how to express it, I don't know how to, but that doesn't mean it isn't there.

(Gerald hadn't come back: I did recover, but not because Mother had said I would. Maurice died in 1976 and Mother was terribly upset. She didn't write about it in her diary much, apart from a few remarks about the fact that she couldn't believe he'd gone. And then she'd had news of Robert's death too, from his much-loathed wife Delia, and that had rubbed salt into the wound — or wounds caused by men's constant departures from her life, including the old one made by Robert all those years ago. The last entry in the diary is in 1985, and the writing's very uncertain; Mother was 87 then. But the sentiments are as clear as ever.)

Snow coating the window panes. I've turned the gas fire right up, but I worry about the money. There's no one to help me if I run out, Isobel can't. Had a letter from Rosemary, Tony's wife. Why do all the women soldier on? All about her grandchildren; Sadie from the village read it to me. I need some new glasses. I haven't been out for a year, opticians don't do home visits. What are we old people supposed to do? I hate it, I absolutely hate it. It's time to go, it's been time for me to go for ages. What have I got? Only Isobel, who helps me out of duty, and one grandchild I never see. Don't even know what she looks like these days. Isobel keeps her away from me. Thinks I might contaminate her or something. Christ, what a life! Rang Dr Willard. Came to see me, I said I think I've got cancer. 'Where do you think you've got it, Molly?' Anywhere, I said, I don't care. Can't swallow, it hurts. Pains everywhere. Haven't had a bath for three weeks. Can't be bloody bothered! Listened to my heart, poked around a bit, said, 'No such luck, Molly. You're as strong as anything. I'll send the district nurse in.' I'm not thanking him; she's like a schoolmistress, plonked me in the bathtub and scrubbed me all over. I'm not having that again. Why don't I die? I asked Dr Willard that. 'I don't know, Molly,' he said, 'I'm only a doctor, I can't answer questions like that.' Well, you're a bloody fool then, I said, it's the only important question left. He looked embarrassed, said he had to go. Nobody listens to what I say any more. I'm just a cross old lady. I wish they'd remember me as I was, not as I am. Funny, I've been thinking of Mother recently, before she was ill, she was a beautiful woman but she had a sad life, it seems to be the fate of all of us. I remember her smile, the way she had of putting her head on one side when you'd asked her a question or said something she needed to think about. 'Not now, Molly,' she'd say when I was little, 'don't be so impatient, you must learn to wait for things. Patience is its own reward.' Which it isn't.

17

The diary fills in some things I ought to have known, others that I've guessed, some I've never been able to remember. Through its pages, I do begin to see Mother not simply as an awkward person, who deliberately set out to make life difficult for everyone around her, but rather as someone who was fighting the tide of the time, who'd been born at the wrong moment historically, and who wanted to do things and in ways that offended convention. Her artistic life as an actress had in itself been deviant, her attitude to men made even more problematic the gap between who she was and who she was allowed to be. I feel I'd like to have a new dialogue with her now, one which is able to breach all these divisions; between reaction and counter-reaction, between the identification and disconnection and falling apart of mother–daughter relations. But Mr Simons' words come back to me: 'There is nothing to be done about this.' Some conversations are impossible during life. Death, a form of liberation, introduces the paradox of silence. When we may talk, we can't; when we can, we mayn't. The old syntax of Peter's question on the park bench. We can't live without our bonds to one another, but society at the same time presents us with this limitation: that we both cannot and may not do what we want.

The nature of love becomes more clear to me. All my life I've seen a mother as possessing the capacity for unconditional love, and this is wrong. There's no such thing as unconditional love. All love has its own terms and conditions: all love exists in time, not outside it, is therefore limited. My mother loved me in her way, according to her own background and personality. She had no patience for a child, in a way she gave in to violence in all her relationships and so also in that with me, her daughter;

she hated all social constraints and stereotypes of motherhood and anything remotely resembling wifehood. But she loved me despite all this. I was loved. What I experienced as a childhood deprivation was not Mother's fault, anymore than the complaints my own daughter makes against me should, on their own, be taken as the truth about me.

My father's letters, on the other hand, over the twenty years from 1940 on, give little evidence of his true character, interests and ways of living, being written either to his mother or his sister in such a manner that they wouldn't learn too many uncomfortable truths. He set himself up in this village on Fernando Po, the island off the West African coast which had once been a Spanish colony, and in his letters home he describes some of the bureaucratic and domestic complications of life as an anthropologist. How he'd fought to acquire a paraffin fridge so he could have cold beer – and he showed the natives ice, which they'd never seen, and they insisted it had something to do with the sun, as it burnt them when they touched it. In another letter he writes of filling in a tax form because his residence permit has run out. The form asks, 'Number of children? Any still living?' – a sad reminder, says Evan Kargar, of the high infant death rates. It makes him think of me, his own living child, but in passing only.

There are few references either to myself or to Mother. Once he says, in a letter to his mother, 'I know you're taking care of Molly and the child financially. I'm glad I can count on you, for, as you know, I can't count on myself. Molly knew that, that's one of the reasons I had to leave. I'm penniless here, which is right for me. I always found economics distasteful, I much prefer a place where responsibility takes the form of exchange: an eye for an eye, a tooth for a tooth. I run a kind of clinic here, handing out antibiotics and antimalaria shots – the natives treat everything with three herbs, and faith only cures sometimes. I gave the rainmaker (a person of great local importance) advice about an eye infection last week, and yesterday, as the infection had cleared up (I recommended a saline bathing of the eye thrice daily) his eldest son brought me a batch of wood.'

Some months later, there's another reference. 'As I write this, a little girl, about five, is playing on the earth outside my hut. She makes me think of Isobel: I hope she's well and growing up well. Do *not* send me a photograph. I've chosen to cut myself off from all that, and I don't want to be made to think that might have been the wrong decision.'

I find this hard, but not as hard as I might have done without the experience of my own situation, of Gerald leaving and insisting on these ritual connections with Becky, such as the one Becky described to me the other day. She made it sound very amusing – but does she care, I wonder? Of course she must. But so long as one holds onto this view of men as marginal to family life, no great harm's been done. Either by my own father's retreat to a hut in West Africa or by Rebecca's to a newspaper office in Detroit.

Leafing through this material and coming to these conclusions makes me think about my pregnancy, if it was one. I can find in my heart guilt, self-recrimination, grief, anger, sadness. If I let myself, I can feel such things, be affected, suffer. But it's a choice I have: there's a choice to make.

Maybe I shall choose not to be affected this time. Not the way the women in the Villa Cellini were; not in the manner of Caroline Goldman, a shadow of any possible self, cartwheeling along in her husband's pompous orbit, nor in that of the adoring, and deceived, Susie Moore, nor according to the rules of the statuesque Carla Dichter's various liaisons, neither as Martha Kraus spoke of witchcraft in order to snatch her own perspective back from the stigma of madness. They each have something to say to me about what *not* to do. It seems to me that women always have something unique to say to each other, but sadly it is frequently put in this form: do *not* do, do *not* say, do *not* believe, do *not* dream this. Mother's diary, for instance, was full of what I had done wrong, with scarcely a mention of what I might have done right. A few positive remarks would be welcome for a change. Possibly the only woman I've met recently who impresses me as having got it right is Gina Lucca. Gina has something close to her which she loves and cares for, and it isn't anything as fickle as the sentiments of another human being.

18

In the village above the lake, Gina Lucca takes her flashlight, as dawn is just beginning to break. She walks up the terraces, past the clipped yews and holly bushes, and flashes her light at the big trees to wake the birds a little before their natural time. She enjoys playing this trick; the birds rise screeching, with a great flapping of their wings and then, when she takes the light away again, they settle down for a few further minutes of respectful silence. Respectful of nature, of its own particular intervals and occurrences.

Up she walks on a ground hardened by snowfalls and several weeks of frost. Now, at the end of February, there are signs of life again, a feeling of a new season about to appear round the edge of the mountains. She passes the place where Carla Dichter fell to her death. She and Tomaso knew of an earlier incident round about here also, although they had not spoken of it at the time. About twenty years ago, a gardener carrying a basket of roots and leaves on his back, had overbalanced and fallen four hundred feet to the rocks. For two days they'd searched, and then the head gardener had sensibly taken a boat out and rowed round the whole of the promontory until he'd seen a foot sticking out between two rocks. That death had clearly been accidental. As Gina believes Carla Dichter's was. One might think that something should be done to prevent such disasters, but they had put rails round all the edges of the paths where it was possible to put them, and that was all they could do.

Gina Lucca's a believer in fate. She's a believer in this house, too, and especially in its manner of looking out over the promontory, the town, the lake's two arms, of peering both forwards into the future and backwards into the past. Very little of the life of the house is lived in the present. There's too much work to be done looking ahead and behind.

Now the sky is pink and white, and the water below is full of blossom. She climbs further, between two steep mossy walls, until she comes to the tunnel where Mrs Lennox had collapsed. That had been a queer incident. Gina had been afraid it would lead to public accusations of violence. There are places on this promontory which *are* violent. But the people who receive the message are lucky: Gina is sure of this. It's their privilege to be allowed back into the past.

She reaches the top, the old castle, spread with its apron of green. Here, for hundreds of years people had stood and argued and eaten and slept and committed acts of love and violence. And now they come in an attempt to create something for themselves. Views of their own, some kind of retreat, a chance to 'do' the sights – she hates these the most. They spoil the place for her, she feels they should go to some ordinary little hotel which will furnish them efficiently with details of daily excursions.

It's interesting that no one who comes to the Villa Cellini ever comes back. Oh, they write warm enthusiastic letters, she and Tomaso get many, many Christmas cards. They all say the same thing; they'll be back one day. But none of them ever keep their word. Gina knows why. The experience is too strong for them. Sometimes negative, sometimes positive, sometimes destructive, sometimes creative, but never nothing. No one ever goes home and says, yes, I had a nice holiday. They all speak of the Villa Cellini in terms that cause their eyes to darken and the blood to flow more jerkily in their veins.

Now the sun is high enough to throw a tinsel path across the lake, a line broken only by an even band of mist which crosses it horizontally from one lakeshore to another. The different substances, the light, the mist, implode but do not affect one another. In a while the mist will be gone and the light higher, seeping into the rocky bays where villages crouch against the watchful panorama of the Alps.

Four thousand, six hundred million years of geological time, thinks Gina. From clouds and gas to stone and rock: from fire to ice and water. The sun and the moon and the earth and all the planets of the solar system splitting off from one another in a moment.

And, beyond that, non-geological time: the probable life of the galaxy itself: eleven thousand million years at least. People need to put a figure on it – she'd always found that odd. For to measure is only that: to measure. To count is to count. To live is to live, to die, to die. One may do all of these things without picking up any wisdom on the way.

And human life: a mere fifty thousand years or so. Within this, only some five thousand years of recorded history. Agriculture and cities: civilization. The ability to communicate from past to future. Gina has always considered that this is what civilization is: communication across time zones. And it is what people do not understand, what they learnt when they come here, to this place. People fear displacement from past to future, from present to past, what cannot be counted or measured and is beyond the terminology and techniques of science. But she knows they have no real reason to be afraid. For this is the very power of being human: what the dinosaurs did not have, what the lizards and the hedgehogs and cats of all colours cannot know, what the sun and the moon and the stars, with their endless amazing light will never possess – for all the wonder and enchantment they are able to give us. For it is in the end only up to us to understand the world and time: to live in time, at the same time as understanding what time does to us.

19

I got there late on purpose. It's really draggy being early for things, especially in places like Fortnum's – not that I've ever been there before. Last time it was the White House hotel at the top of Great Portland Street. But it isn't much fun trying to make yourself look conspicuous in Fortnum's restaurant so your ex-father's got a chance of recognizing you.

I saw *them* straight away. They seemed to be having an argument. They had their heads kind of lowered at each other like bulls across the table. 'Hallo, *Father*.' I put the accent on Father deliberately, so that the youth would know he was mine, originally. Father Lennox rose to his feet and kissed me. I noticed he'd shaved recently. He had a little less hair on top of his head than he'd had two years before, and he looked somewhat more generally creased, but otherwise things were the same.

'This is Charlie, your half brother,' was all he could think of saying by way of introduction to the youth. Who handed out a paw to me as, presumably, he'd been instructed to do. Being observant, I noticed that he had a crewcut and wore a Calvin Klein shirt. If he'd stood up, I might have been able to spot the presence or absence of designer jeans.

'Would you care for some tea, Becky?'

Since when does deciding to drink a cup of tea constitute caring for it? My father was getting too American for words.

'I wouldn't mind some, Father,' I said, offhandedly.

'Tea. Tea and toast? Tea and English muffins?'

'Crumpets,' I said. 'How are you, Father?' I'd decided I'd try to manage this conversation, so it didn't get into places I didn't want it to go.

'We're fine,' he replied.

I didn't ask about you plural, Father. I asked about you singular. But I suppose you mean you and the woman, Carol whatsit, you made off with back when I was three. 'That's good,' I said.

'And you?'

'I'm fine too.'

We looked at each other. I observed the table was moving rhythmically. I looked down and could see Charlie's left leg twitching at incredible speed. I put my hand on it to stop it. It was as though I'd lit the fuse on a bomb. His leg leapt instantly away from my hand.

'Does he always do that?' I asked my father.

'Do what?'

'Have this nervous twitch?'

'I hadn't noticed, to be honest.'

'I don't know what young men are coming to these days,' I remarked, trying to be funny, but neither of them laughed.

I ate my crumpets and made a few inquiries of Charlie; his attitudes to life, the reasons for his demeanour, the general condition of his affections, that sort of thing. It didn't go down well. For his part, my father seemed to have a technical interest in my progress: was I likely to pass my examinations, which university, etc. He took a few skirmishes into the area of friends, including those of Charlie's gender.

'A boyfriend, no,' I told him. 'Boyfriends, yes.' I was glad Charlie was there then, as it stopped us getting into more delicate issues.

Then he wanted to know how my mother was. I decided not to tell him she had just had a miscarriage and was absolutely flourishing, as I wasn't sure he'd be able to deal with this information, and I didn't much fancy a family freak-out in Fortnum's.

'She's fine, too,' I said. Today everyone's fine. Today's the day the teddy bears have their picnic. 'She's just had a holiday in Italy. You know the old lady died, don't you?'

'Which old lady?'

'Hers. Molly. My maternal grandmother.'

'I thought she died years ago. I was sure. . . .'

'Look, Father, I can promise you she only just passed away.' I thought, being American now, he might appreciate this nice old-fashioned type of term.

Charlie pretended to choke on his crumpet.

'What else, Becky?'

'What else about what?'

'You. Your life in England now.'

'Well, oh well . . .' I was rendered fairly speechless. This man who people have told you is your father arrives from another planet biennially and requests an instant summary of all intervening events, developments, etc., so he doesn't need to make the effort to keep in touch personally! I wasn't sure this was on. 'If you want a progress report, you have to notify me ahead of time, Father.'

'Oh Becky,' he laughed, 'You're turning into quite a young lady, aren't you?'

'Woman, Father.'

'Whatever, whatever!' He took out an ironed blue handkerchief (had whatsit ironed it along with Charlie's designer jeans?) and mopped his brow with it. I, too, thought it was getting hot in there.

'Okay, Father. Here's a quick rundown. I, having been a bit, shall we say difficult, for some years, have finally given up being difficult in a generational type of way. The difficulty is now confined to my personality alone. I am thinking of becoming a moral philosopher. To atone for my former sins. If that doesn't work out, I might try my hand at plumbing. Something structural, down to earth. I am a person who likes challenges, you see. Furthermore, aside from studying, I am not on drugs of any kind, except toothpaste. I understand the peppermint oil in that is carcinogenic. I smoke the occasional cigarette because I enjoy the feeling of something long and thin between my fingers.'

Charlie had developed a further attack of coughing. Little bits of angel cake were flying out of the corners of his mouth.

'As for Mother,' I continued, 'well, she's decided to change her life a little, too. She's given up her job and is planning to go back to school.' I knew this was what the Americans called it, though it produced this ridiculous cartoon picture of my mother in short white socks and pigtails.

'Jesus!'

'Yes, Mother is doing quite well. Of course, the money helps. The money the old lady left. We haven't exactly had a surfeit of money the past few years, Father.' I wasn't above inducing a little guilt in him. While Charlie on my right had been enjoying private health insurance and electronic nose-pickers, we in Shepherd's Bush had been forced to economize by turning the lights out at night.

My father's hand was now behaving as though it were on its way to his pocket. I'd seen this response before. I waited, expectantly, Charlie boy was watching too. I was handed two £50 notes. I put them in my purse without looking at them too closely to see if they were real. That sort of terminated it. Apparently Charlie and my father were off to the theatre. To see *Les Misérables*. I told them I hoped very much they were able to enjoy the show.

20

A letter comes from Gerald.

> Dear Isobel,
>
> I'm glad to hear from Rebecca that you are well and keen to embark on some new life plans. Rebecca seems a most mature young woman these days. We had a pleasant talk. She probably told you I am over here with Charlie, our eldest. I thought it was time he saw a little of his father's country.
>
> Rebecca mentioned that you have had a problem with money. I am truly sorry about this. Well, Isobel, I'm glad to say that I've been able to make some money out of investments over the last few years, and I'd be happy to let you have some of the proceeds. I enclose a cheque: I hope it will help you with whatever you want to do in the future. I shall, of course, make separate provision for the costs of Rebecca's university education and be in touch with her about that when I return to the States.
>
> With my very best regards,
> Gerald.

The cheque is for £3000. The account is entitled 'Mr and Mrs Gerald A. S. Lennox'. I tear the cheque into pieces and, not content with this, I take the pieces into the kitchen and burn them. I don't want Gerald's money. I would have liked some of it before, but not now, it's too late. I shan't even write and explain; he'll notice eventually, I suppose, that the cheque hasn't been cashed, and if he ever asks about it I'll tell him, but just now I do have other things on my mind.

The last week of February: minus one outside, black snow packed on the margins of the pavements and only in some of London's highest places can any whiteness still be seen. Here and there, on the peaks of Hampstead Heath, or in Richmond Park, occasional angles of white flash a crystalline brightness at the sky in a manner reminiscent of the Central Italian Alps.

I pack my mementoes away tightly into an old suitcase. I take Mother's diary and put it on the desk in Becky's room amidst the scribbled notes and half-finished essays. Blake's *The Sentiments of Shakespeare* watches me, with its brightly coloured cover. The lights are on, though Becky left at five for her evening class. I turn two of them off, but leave the third on to welcome her home.

I drag the suitcase upstairs and put it on top of the cupboard in my bedroom. Then I have a bath, wash my hair, and, wrapping myself in a towel, go back downstairs to the shelf in the sitting room where I keep the telephone books. I take 'S–Z' off the pile and sit down under a standard lamp where I'll be able to see the small print easily. 'Simons, Isaac, 24 Shepreth St, NW3.' That's it. I memorize the phone number – a habit acquired in my years of labouring for Mr Jefferson – and pick up the phone. After I've dialled it, the number rings several times; I begin to think no one is home. Then a low answer, his voice, 'Isaac Simons.'

'Hallo, Isaac. This is Isobel Lennox speaking.'

'Isobel! How are you?'

'Very well. Isaac, you must be surprised to hear from me. . . .'

'Not especially, as a matter of fact.'

'I wondered if you might be free for a drink this evening?'

'This evening? I have my last patient in an hour. I won't be through till seven.'

'I have some things I should like to talk to you about.'

'Yes?'

'After seven would be fine. Where should we meet?' I'm not used to fixing evening meetings in central London, and I can't think of a place to suggest.

'How about the cocktail bar of the Hotel Triton? There are two bars,' he cautions. 'The cocktail bar is on the left as you go in. Would seven-thirty be all right? That should give me enough time.'

'I'll see you there.'

He's already there when I arrive, comfortably settled into a leather-buttoned sofa. He stands up and shakes my hand, rather formally. I sit down opposite him on another such sofa. The bar's relatively empty. The waiter brings me a campari and soda. I sip it, before starting on what I have to say: 'I met your girlfriend the other day, Andrea Collins. She may have told you she's actually a relation of mine.'

'Yes, she did mention meeting you. But I don't see her any more. In either a professional or a personal capacity.'

'Oh?'

He puts his glass down on the table and scoops a handful of peanuts from a small glass dish. 'It wasn't any good for either of us. She was using me, I was using her. I knew that when I came back from the Villa Cellini.'

'She seemed quite an unhappy person.'

'She is.'

'She needs to get rid of that husband and get herself something decent to do. A job,' I venture.

He nods, picks up his glass again, tucks one hand characteristically in the angle of the arm that holds it. 'I dare say you're right. But who am I to tell her? I think she has to find that out for herself. And you, Isobel. What did you find out when you were in Italy?'

'Oh, a lot of things. To accept my mother's death. And her life – which is more difficult. That my daughter isn't such a burden, after all. But I can be quite a burden to myself at times.' I shake my head as I say this. 'Perhaps also that I'm capable of mothering others more easily than myself.'

'None of that surprises me.'

'But remember,' I tell him, 'that I didn't obtain this understanding from years and years of psychoanalysis, or from you.'

He doesn't react directly to this. Instead he says, 'The Japanese have a proverb, that two people looking at the same view communicate through that view. It might have been the place that did it.'

'Would you like another drink?' This is me asking him, not vice versa.

'Why not?'

When I've got the second campari in my hand I frame a further question, or rather a statement. 'I want to know what happened in the tunnel, Isaac.'

'Yes, I thought you might ask me that. That's the real purpose of this meeting, isn't it? Well, it's better now than it would have been then. You seem full of psychic health now, Isobel.'

'I'm okay.'

'What happened in the tunnel is that we made love, Isobel.'

'Love? I understood that something violent had happened.'

'Yes, I know.'

'You attacked me, didn't you – or someone did: I had bruises all down my lefthand side.'

'The bruises were an unfortunate side-effect of the inevitable and necessary act.'

'Why can't you talk in language other people can understand! What's wrong with plain English?'

'We weren't in plain England when it happened, Isobel. We were in an extraordinary place. Because of the place, its history, we were bound to do certain things, come to certain realizations. One of yours was to do with mothering. As you yourself said. But reproduction, the having and bringing up of children, is initiated, normally, by the sexual act. Therefore the recreation of the sexual act was needed to create your own understanding.'

'I find that very hard to believe.'

'So are many things.'

'We didn't make love,' I protest – for we didn't.

'I don't expect you to remember everything, Isobel. But I can promise you there was absolutely no violence in the act itself. Did you ever have any evidence of that?'

I remember the late bleeding. Too late, I now think, to be only a period. 'On the contrary. I conceived. Probably. You made me pregnant, I think.'

He looks at me intently for a moment or two. 'There you are, then. It is as I said: the act of making love was designed to make you understand you're a fit mother after all. You, and your mother, and your daughter. Congratulations, Isobel!' He leans forward and takes my hand.

'Oh, I'm not having a child,' I say hastily, I don't want him to get the wrong idea. 'It aborted, you see.' The language of Harley Street.

'I'm sure that was the right thing to happen.'

'It was.'

'I read a book in Italy,' says Isaac Simons, changing the subject to some degree. 'It was a book I just chanced on in the library, I wasn't looking for it. Not at all. It was a book about the devil by a woman called Ruth Anshen. It had some very memorable passages in it. Appropriate, really, to the situations we've been discussing. I think I can remember one of them.'

'Go on.'

'"The devil owes everything to woman. It was Eve who started the process of history, which was all the devil wanted or needed. One would expect the devil to show himself grateful by granting to women the decisive role in human history. But no such thing happened. The devil has an excellent memory, but gratitude is not one of his virtues." You see, Isobel Lennox, the devil remembers. Only angels forget. Good women are hard to find. Be thankful, Isobel, you've turned out to be a good woman after all!'

21

'Where on earth have you been, Mother?'

She wasn't home when I got back from my evening class. She hadn't even left a note; there wasn't any supper. I was quite worried about her. I knew she'd been reading all this old stuff of her father's, and the diary the old lady had given me. I noticed it was back on my desk. Also that she hadn't turned *all* the lights off this time. One doesn't expect inconsistency from one's mother. I understand they say that in the childrearing manuals: whatever you do, be consistent. If you feed them smarties at breakfast, do it every day. Anyway, she came in around ten-thirty.

Her face was wet and shiny: there were snowflakes on her shoulders and her shoes. 'It's snowing again.' She took off her coat and draped it over the banister rail. 'I went out to meet a friend for a drink.'

'You might have left me a note!'

She looked at me and giggled. 'Don't sound so severe, Becky!'

I thought she might be pissed. 'How many drinks have you had, Mother?'

'Only a couple.' She moved herself past me into the kitchen like a minor tornado. 'I'm starving, have you eaten?'

I admitted I hadn't.

She was digging around in the freezer like a demented dog in a rubbish bin. 'Prawns, we could have some prawns. And rice. How about that, Becky? Isn't there some tomato juice? Make me a bloody Mary, will you? Would you like one?'

Ye Gods. I fixed the bloody Marys; she must have dragged the vodka back with her on Alitalia. We sat and ate our peculiar meal. She had some mango chutney with hers.

'You're not pregnant again, are you, Mother?' She giggled again. Or was still giggling, I wasn't sure which.

'No, no I'm fine. Just hungry.'

'Who *did* you go to meet, Mother?'

'I don't ask *you* those sorts of questions, Rebecca, why should *you* ask me?'

The old mother mode, the use of the proper name creeping back, how reassuring. 'Okay, Mother, I give up.'

'Look!' she said, pointing with her fork at the window. Neither of us had bothered to draw the curtains: snow was falling fast and thick, snowflakes were hurling themselves against the glass like lemmings.

'Let's go for a walk. I want to go for a walk in the snow, Becky.'

I wasn't sure I could take this. 'Is that wise, Mother? You've already been out in it once. So have I. We might catch a chill. We wouldn't like that, would we?'

'You might not. I don't much care. You only live once. It might never snow like this again. Come on, Becky.'

So like a pair of nutty polar bears we muffled ourselves up in coats and boots and scarves and trooped off into the local snowstorm. She wouldn't even take an umbrella. *I* remembered the key.

We walked down the road to Ravenscourt Park. She pulled me out into the middle of the park. You can be sure I was awfully glad none of my friends were around to see this performance. We stood there being snowed on. A train passed on the bridge, it rattled its way across like a rusty glow worm. 'Think of all those people in there, nice and warm, Mother!'

I hoped no one could see us. Maybe we looked entirely like snowmen by now. Snowwomen.

'What are we doing here, Mother?' I asked after a bit, since I wasn't myself completely sure.

She didn't answer, but took her gloves off and held her hands out to receive the snowflakes. She seemed a little upset that she couldn't hold the snowflakes for long, the warmth of her skin turned them rapidly to slush. I touched her hand. 'You're nuts, Mother. Aren't you?' I smiled at her in the snowy blackness. 'But you're not bad really. I mean, I'm a little concerned at this change of personality you seem to have developed, but if it makes you happy, then it's fine by me.'

'Happiness, Becky. You know, I always thought if you did the right thing, you'd be happy. If you did what's expected of you then you'd feel good. But it doesn't work like that. I've discovered it doesn't work like that. I spent years of my life being a dutiful daughter, putting up with my mother, not telling her what I really thought about anything, and devoting myself to you, worrying about you, taking care of Mr Jefferson's correspondence and his waiting room, paying the bills on time, but it didn't make me happy. Do you know what, it didn't even stop me feeling guilty. Which is what I'd assumed it was designed to do.'

'I could have told you all that, Mother,' I said. 'Why didn't you ask me?'

'Oh Becky! There are things mothers can't ask daughters, just as there are things daughters won't talk to mothers about.'

'Why do you think that is, Mother?'

'I don't know. It's a pity, though, that we can't be friends.' She appeared to be studying the stars, now. There were a few up there desperately twinkling away behind the snowclouds.

'The stars won't tell you anything.' I thought of explaining to her some of the different theories of personality development we've been doing in psychology. How, in order to get a sense of itself as a person, a baby has to work out how it's different from its mother, etc., etc. Whose arm belongs to who, is that my temper I feel flaring up or yours? If you tickle my feet that would be a great help. We could then have moved onto adolescent conflict – is there any in Samoa – not to mention the 'empty nest' syndrome and the psychological problems of meno-pausal ladies. But I wasn't sure she was in a mood to listen. And my feet had become, as it were, fairly cold. Frozen. In fact, you could say I was having problems differentiating their personality from the snow's.

'Friends.' I picked up on her last word instead. 'Is that what you want us to be?'

She looked a little surprised at the question. Then pleased. 'Yes, why not?'

'No,' I said. 'No, I don't think so. I don't think that's what I want, Mother. I have a slight feeling I'd like to go on thinking of you as my mother. Yes, definitely. It's definitely the case that in order to mature emotionally I still need a mother. No,' I correct myself, 'not *a* mother. *My* mother. You.'

She put her arms around me, we were two cold wet snow-people hugging each other. Very undignified. 'You see,' I said into her collar, being considerably constrained by her embrace, 'I would feel quite lost if you weren't here to complain about me. I need you to say I'm a lazy, selfish, inconsiderate, uneconomical shit from time to time. In order to realize I'm not. It's kind of friendly, in a way. I'll go on doing the same for you, if you like. And, by the way, Mother, I think you ought to let me go now, I'm finding it sort of difficult to breathe.'

'Oh God.' She was crying. The items coming out of her eyes were definitely not snowflakes. I got hold of her arm and marched her firmly home. 'It's all right, Mother,' I said, 'everything's all right.'

We got back and started melting into the rugs in the hall. My feet were pleased to be home, I can tell you. 'Thank you for coming out with me, Rebecca,' she said, 'and for what you said. Tomorrow I'm going to start getting myself registered for this Open University course. You'll go away to university, and I'll stay at home for the same purpose. I've got it all worked out. When the money from Mother's house comes through, I'll pay off the mortgage on this place. I'll invest the rest, so you can have the income to live off. Then I should only need a part time job. I'll get something local. Some secretarial job, or whatever. No problem. We'll be all right, Becky, as you said. We'll have a good time. And then, after a while, you'll go off and come back with a daughter of your own. And then the whole thing will start up all over again! That's life, Becky. One thing after another. Repetition, renewal. The same pattern, but it shifts slightly. That's the great thing about it: we all make a difference to the pattern. So it's never totally predictable. None of us quite knows what's going to happen next.'

I listened to this little speech while disrobing myself out of the snowperson image. I didn't like to respond to the bit about going off and coming back with a daughter of my own, she made it sound as though I'd poke around under some bush and find one. It wasn't the time to point out that, as I've said before, procreation isn't part of my lifeplan. I'd break the news about that gently. I'd choose the moment. She herself said we all change the pattern.

I got to my room around midnight. I sat down at my desk and lit an incense stick. I watched the brown dust collect around the bottom of the stick on the red leather surface of the desk (it's some kind of family heirloom, it landed up in my room only because my mother couldn't stand the sight of it), and I thought about her bustling round me clicking her tongue disapprovingly. I heard myself say, 'It's my mess, Mother, I'll clear it up when I'm ready. It's not doing any harm, it's only a bit of dust after all'.